KT-158-992

A GIFT OF TIME

After the death of her daughter and her husband's desertion, Beth feels as though everything has been taken from her. But her life changes drastically when she moves to a smaller house on a new development. Firstly, suspecting that her new home is haunted, she uncovers a disturbing story. She feels the only way to exorcise this ghost is to write about it . . . Then there is Dr Tom Masterson, who has moved nearby with his two daughters and an invalid wife. Beth and Tom grow closer each day and Tom reveals that his marriage is in name only. But Beth is not going to find a relationship with him easy . . .

Books by Barbara Murphy
Published by The House of Ulverscroft:

JANEY'S WAR
FIVEPENNY LANES
A RESTLESS PEACE

SPECIAL MESSAGE TO READERS

This book is published under the auspices of

THE ULVERSCROFT FOUNDATION

(registered charity No. 264873 UK)

Established in 1972 to provide funds for research, diagnosis and treatment of eye diseases. Examples of contributions made are: —

A Children's Assessment Unit at
Moorfield's Hospital, London.

•

Twin operating theatres at the
Western Ophthalmic Hospital, London.

•

A Chair of Ophthalmology at the
Royal Australian College of Ophthalmologists.

•

The Ulverscroft Children's Eye Unit at the
Great Ormond Street Hospital For Sick Children,
London.

You can help further the work of the Foundation by making a donation or leaving a legacy. Every contribution, no matter how small, is received with gratitude. Please write for details to:

**THE ULVERSCROFT FOUNDATION,
The Green, Bradgate Road, Anstey,
Leicester LE7 7FU, England.
Telephone: (0116) 236 4325**

**In Australia write to:
THE ULVERSCROFT FOUNDATION,
c/o The Royal Australian College of
Ophthalmologists,
27, Commonwealth Street, Sydney,
N.S.W. 2010.**

Barbara Murphy was Music Director to a concert party and then went into advertising before she switched to publishing, as a secretary to the editor of Home Notes and Modern Woman magazines, and moved to Hampshire with her husband and two children. A keen member of a local music and drama group, Barbara has also written three other novels, *Janey's War*, *A Restless Peace* and *Fivepenny Lanes*.

BARBARA MURPHY

A GIFT
OF TIME

WARWICKSHIRE
COUNTY LIBRARY.

CONTROL No.

Complete and Unabridged

ULVERSCROFT
Leicester

First published in Great Britain in 2001 by
Inner Circle, an imprint of
Judy Piatkus (Publishers) Limited
London

First Large Print Edition
published 2003
by arrangement with
Judy Piatkus (Publishers) Limited
London

The moral right of the author has been asserted

Copyright © 2001 by Barbara Murphy
All rights reserved

British Library CIP Data

Murphy, Barbara
  A gift of time.—Large print ed.—
  Ulverscroft large print series: general fiction
  1. Life change events—Fiction
  2. Love stories 3. Large type books
  I. Title
  823.9′14 [F]

  ISBN 0–7089–4781–6

Published by
F. A. Thorpe (Publishing)
Anstey, Leicestershire

Set by Words & Graphics Ltd.
Anstey, Leicestershire
Printed and bound in Great Britain by
T. J. International Ltd., Padstow, Cornwall

This book is printed on acid-free paper

For Andrew and Joanna
Lisa, Kerry and Steven

because they bring such joy
to their grandmother

Acknowledgements

Writers always need help from others in specific areas. I received such help from the following, and would like to thank them:

County Records Office
Mr A D Burke, Southampton City Athletics Club
Chris Benning, athlete
Cherie Thomas
Julia Allen
Gary & Becky Coultas
Mark Moss
Hythe Historians

And I tread a regular path to Hythe Library.

Before the beginning of years
　There came to the making of man
Time, with a gift of tears;
　Grief, with a glass that ran;
Pleasure, with pain for leaven;
　Summer, with flowers that fell;
Remembrance fallen from heaven,
　And madness risen from hell;
Strength without hands to smite;
　Love that endures for a breath;
Night, the shadow of light,
　And life, the shadow of death.

　　　　(From *The Chorus*, by
　　　Algernon Charles Swinburne)

1

'Why did they die? Find out why. I'm not talking about TV soaps, but real life. It may have happened on your own doorstep.'

The words jolted Beth into awareness. She raised her head from the featureless doodles.

'Forget the news bulletins. Forget the Budget. Forget the weather. You can't change them.' The lecturer's voice fired with enthusiasm. 'I know, you can't change history, either,' he went on, 'but I can promise you one thing. If you try to find out the truth, it will take your mind off all those things in your life you wish you *could* change, but can't.'

Driving home, Beth pondered on his words. There were so many things in her life she wished she *could* change. The empty house awaiting her was the only change that might be possible. A dark house, with dark memories. Fumbling with her key, she wondered whether she should buy a security light, or one with a time switch — but did it really matter? The only things she valued had already been taken from her. The rest were mere chattels. They were welcome to them.

1

On the landing, she stood with her mug of hot chocolate, counting doors. Too many doors for one person. She should sell the house — but not yet. It was too soon.

Her head willed her to go straight to bed, but her feet led her towards the room that held the darkest memory of all.

She knew it was foolish, masochistic, but she couldn't keep away. Each time was like the first time. Silence, where there should have been gentle breathing. Teddy bears staring sightlessly from the shadows. Pink-edged cards grouped around a brightly coloured wooden clown. Each time her mind relived the horror, her body frozen with disbelief.

Making a supreme effort, she backed towards the door, the muscles in her arm trembling slightly with rigidity. As the scalding liquid splashed on to her hand, her reflex action jarred against the shelf and the clown rocked, as though he, too, remembered that single scream. Swiftly, she closed the door behind her.

Sleepless hours later, she carried the mug into the bathroom. The idea seduced her as she watched the remaining rivulets of cold brown liquid trickling towards the drain. It would be so simple. Would it hurt? Probably not. It hadn't hurt when she cut her finger on a broken glass, only when it was healing.

Bryn had never liked electric shavers. There might be a spare packet of razor blades. The left-hand shelves in the cabinet were empty. As empty as his bedside cabinet and fitted wardrobe. The bastard had taken everything.

She reached for her bottle of sleeping tablets, knowing it was almost empty. The doctor had only prescribed a few, and Ali counted them every day. They meant well, the two people who persisted in trying to help, but if only they'd leave her alone. Why shouldn't she be allowed to drift into oblivion and not wake up? She didn't want counselling, any more than she had wanted to be persuaded to go to the meeting. They couldn't bring back Bryn, or Katie. And the memories weren't fading with time.

Just as the drugged sleep took over, a different memory drifted into Beth's mind. A white-haired historian, asking a question that had remained unanswered for almost three hundred years. 'Why did they die?'

★   ★   ★

The chirrups intruded. It was too early for the dawn chorus. Whoever thought the countryside was peaceful had never lived on the edge of a forest. Beth buried her head

3

deeper under the duvet, but the chirruping went on, and on, and on . . . the blasted bird was in the house — here in the room! Opening one eye with great difficulty, she followed the sound to her bedside table. No bird. Only the telephone.

Her fumbling hand found the receiver. 'Whoever it is, go away. I'm asleep.' She tried to slam down the receiver, but only succeeded in dropping it. A familiar voice floated into her sleepiness as the telephone swung lazily to and fro.

'Beth, it's Ali . . . Beth! Where the hell are you?' Ali's voice was sharp enough to intrude.

Beth's hand groped around in mid-air until she caught the telephone. 'Why are you phoning me in the middle of the night?' she mumbled.

'It's the middle of the day!' Ali's voice changed to one of slight panic. 'Open your eyes, Beth! Don't go back to sleep.'

Beth's bleary eyes looked towards the window, but the drapes were so heavy it was impossible to know whether it was light or dark outside. The digital clock teetered dangerously on the edge of the bedside table. It couldn't possibly be eleven-thirty.

Ali's voice was still urgent. 'Did you take a sleeping pill?'

'No, I took two.'

After a pause, Ali quietly said, 'You promised you wouldn't.'

'Don't nag.'

'That's what best friends are for. Are you awake? Properly awake, I mean, and listening.'

Beth struggled against the tide of sleep. 'Why?'

'I want to ask you something, and I don't want excuses.'

'If it's another one of your meetings, I'm not going.'

'It's about going back to work — and don't you dare hang up, or I'll come straight round there.'

After a long pause, Beth murmured, 'It's too soon, Ali. Prestwicks have been very patient, but I can't . . . not yet.'

'Not your old job. Temping. There's a bug going around and I can't find enough good secretaries to meet the demand.'

'I'm not sure that I'm ready yet.'

'You're as ready as you'll ever be. And you need the money.'

Beth couldn't argue that point. Bryn had given her the house, complete with hefty mortgage, but nothing else, apart from an allowance for Katie — and that had ended when . . .

Ali was still talking. 'I've just had an urgent

phone call from Sarah Biddlecombe. She wants a temp for next week.'

'Who?'

'You must remember Sarah. She was head girl in our fourth year.'

Still struggling to think clearly, Beth conjured up a vague vision of a redhead in a gym slip. 'What does she want a temp for?' she asked.

'Sarah's just taken over the estate agents that sold you 'The Cherries'. Said she'd like to see you again and could use your legal know-how on the conveyancing side.'

'You didn't tell her . . . ?'

'Yes. You can't pretend it didn't happen.' After a pause, Ali went on. 'Sarah would like to put the house back on the market for you.'

Wide awake now, Beth sat up, clutching the telephone. Abruptly, she said, 'I haven't decided to sell.'

'You'll have to. 'The Cherries' is far too big and expensive to keep going on your own. Temping will help your cash-flow short-term, but it won't pay all the bills.'

'I know, but . . . '

'Listen, Beth. If you want to survive this, you've got two options. One is to take that low-life to court and claim maintenance.'

'You know how I feel about that. I couldn't face a long, acrimonious legal war over my ability to work and his ability to pay. I don't even want to read the divorce papers.'

'Then sell the house, buy something smaller and put some money in your piggy bank.'

'It won't be easy. The property round here is pretty static.'

'Sarah says it's on the move at last, and she has a client looking for an upmarket property in the New Forest.' Ali's voice softened. 'Don't worry, things will work out. Just take one step at a time.'

She was right, of course. But that first step struck Beth as a greater giant than Neil Armstrong's first leap on to the moon. 'I'll think about it,' she said.

'I need to know today.'

'I'll phone you — one way or the other.'

'Good. Now go and make yourself some strong black coffee, and have a shower.'

'Don't you ever get tired of bossing people about?'

'If you would only get back into the land of the living, I wouldn't need to boss you about.' Ali's voice softened. 'Come on, love, you know I'm right.'

The infuriating thing was that Ali usually was right. It was that edge of knowing what should be done that had made her the 'Business Woman of the Year'. Beth had always admired, but never envied, her friend's qualities. She had always been content to follow, rather than lead. But now she found herself rebelling against Ali's good advice. 'I said I'll think about it,' she said, tetchily. 'Let's leave it at that.'

'OK.' Ali might be bossy, but she'd always know when to back off. Beth wasn't surprised when the subject was quickly changed. 'What did you think of last night's speaker?' Ali asked.

'I'm afraid I wasn't really in the mood. But . . . ' Fragments of the lecturer's words came into Beth's mind. 'He said something about four people who died at Calshot Castle a long time ago. Do you remember what happened?'

'Sorry. Must have been when I was making coffee. I can give you his telephone number if you want?'

'It doesn't matter. Just something that caught my attention.'

Resisting the temptation to crawl back under the duvet, Beth followed instructions. The shower and black coffee did little to clear her mind, and the last thing she wanted was to make any hasty decision about her future. At the moment she had no faith in her judgement. Look how wrong she had been about Bryn. But sooner or later she was going to have to face up to the fact that her life would never be the same again. Perhaps a breath of air would help clear the cobwebs from her head.

As she drove slowly out of Badgers' Copse and into Roebuck Way, Beth was reminded of the evocative words, 'A host of golden daffodils'. They had awakened early this year, crowding banks, circling trees, lining paths. An elderly gentleman snipped withered heads so they should not spoil his formal display. In another garden, a young mother gently removed her toddler from the temptation of an earthenware trough packed with nodding blooms. They did not glance at Beth's car. They all lived in a 'Forest Glade Luxury Home', but they were strangers. And watching the child was like turning a knife in her heart. All the time she was pregnant Beth had planned their brand-new garden with children in mind. Lawns to play on, no ponds until they were bigger and lots of shrubs for games of hide-and-seek. Bryn hadn't been interested, but had told her to go ahead and order a climbing-frame and swing if she wanted. Now, gulping back the tears, she turned the car towards the beach.

The sun warmed her skin, but not her bones. Head down, she trudged along the shingle, half-aware of the black and white sheepdog quartering the beach ahead. Rufus had loved such a romp. But he had been taken by his master, along with the razor blades.

Ali was right. She should sell the house. But would it bring much of a smile to her bank manager's face? Bryn had insisted on taking out a higher mortgage than she advised, and the market was falling even before they moved in. Was it really eighteen months ago?

Everything was perfect then. Too perfect. Bryn had been over the moon when they offered him the partnership. 'I'll be handling some pretty big investments,' he said. 'Quite a feather in my cap. Your Mr Prestwick will have to ask my advice on his trust funds.'

'He'll be very pleased for us.'

'And I may have to entertain clients from time to time. So we'll need to move to a better neighbourhood.'

Cocooned in candy-floss blossom, 'The Cherries' was the house of their dreams. With a dramatically romantic gesture, Bryn had swept her up into his arms and carried her over the threshold.

'The removal men will think we're newly-weds,' Beth had laughed.

'Good. I want to forget the last ten years of pinching and scraping, and slogging at exams.' He'd set her down and gazed around the spacious hall, still smelling of new paint. 'I've made it,' he murmured. 'And this is only the beginning.'

That night, after the champagne and excitement, Beth forgot to take the pill. That night, Katie was conceived.

She forced her thoughts back to the present, to the future. *If* she sold the house, and it was a big *if*, what then? Return to Southampton? She'd never really cared for city life, but Bryn had insisted it was more economical, just as he had insisted that they couldn't both work for the same firm, adding that it was easier for a secretary to change jobs than an accountant. Ten years ago, it had never occurred to her to argue with this charismatic, ambitious young man she adored. So the firm where she had worked since she had left college had given them a Wedgewood bone china dinner service as a wedding present, and a glowing reference for Beth to the senior partner in one of the oldest legal firms in Southampton.

For ten years, they questioned every penny they spent. Their colleagues had wonderful holidays in the Seychelles, Florida, India, but Bryn and Beth never looked at the glossy brochures. Time for that when they had saved enough money for the deposit on a dream house. Their tiny studio flat might be sorely lacking in character as well as space, but it was within walking distance of Bryn's office and only a short bus journey to Prestwicks.

Her mood sinking lower and lower, Beth walked the full length of the spit, past the row of beach huts, past the activities centre, towards a round, squat tower. Perfectly sited for the defence of the realm, it commanded a superb view over the Solent on one side, Southampton Water on the other. The notice said, 'Welcome to Calshot Castle', but the door was closed.

An empty crisp packet skittered across the car park, reflecting the bleakness of her heart. In a few weeks the beaches would be teeming with life, but now they were deserted, apart from a solitary angler and an elderly couple watching a windsurfer bravely challenge the currents. A hydrofoil and small ferry journeyed, hare and tortoise fashion, towards the Isle of Wight. On the horizon a supertanker loomed into view, heading for anchorage.

Briefly Beth wondered why they had never walked this far before, but they had always driven back into the forest. She had grown up in Ashurst and knew every pathway to the other side of Lyndhurst. Rufus loved to have a good run around the clearings.

Ali had suggested she move back to

Ashurst, but most of her schoolfriends were married, with families, or had moved away. Those she had kept in touch with hadn't particularly taken to Bryn, so the friendships had petered out, apart from Ali. Beth couldn't face the gossip, the pity, the awkwardness.

If only Mum was still alive, she thought. Her mother would know exactly what Beth should do. She could always find a way out of any predicament. The breast cancer that had taken her mother from her had also stolen Beth's best friend and confidence. For a while, she and her father had clung together, but he didn't get on too well with Bryn, either, and the cottage held as many sad memories for him as 'The Cherries' now held for Beth. So he finally decided to make his home with his brother in British Columbia. Beth had an open invitation to join them, but the upheaval of moving to Canada was even more daunting.

She was no nearer to a decision than when she had taken the car out of the garage and, if anything, even more depressed. Hearing the sound of a heavy engine, Beth glanced across the car park. An army vehicle drove slowly alongside the vast hangar that had once housed flying-boats, turned at the corner and reversed towards the furthermost door. Idly, she watched two soldiers unloading, then turned back to the castle. An odd array of red-brick buildings seemed to cling to the inside of the ancient walls, and a modern walkway with metal handrail crossed to the gatehouse. The few remaining cannons had threatened invaders long before a radar scanner searched the skies from the nearby coastguard's tower. Viewed through a tiny recessed window, an electric kettle further symbolished the spanning of centuries.

Slowly circling the moat, she found herself drawn towards the far beach. The jump down wasn't too steep, and she scuffed through the stones, to the edge of the water. There wasn't a soul in sight and, suddenly, the loneliness overwhelmed her, and she allowed the tears to flow, unchecked. This was the only decision she needed to make. All she had to do was keep walking. No more pain. No more tears. No more questions. It would soon be over. Once and for all. Nobody else need be involved. With luck and the double tides, her body would be washed out to sea. Eternal blackness. Peace at last.

She glanced behind her, making sure there was nobody around who might be tempted to rescue her. No, she was out of sight of the soldiers, the elderly couple and the angler. Even the windsurfer must have stayed on the other side of the spit.

About to turn back to the sea, Beth hesitated. Was that a movement, at one of the windows set in the keep? Hell! It could be someone watching. A chill ran through her body. Not just the cold of the sea lapping at her ankles, but all over, as though she were leaning against a damp stone wall.

Disturbed, Beth looked out to sea, through eyes blurred with tears. A moment ago, it had been calm, almost inviting. Now, with an angry froth topping the waves, it was anything but a tempting refuge.

That was when she heard the voice, calling to her through the wind. 'Come back, Beth.' It was little more than a fierce whisper. She could not even tell the direction it came from.

She glanced over her shoulder at the castle. Even that had changed, the stone appearing cold and forbidding. Fiercely rubbing her eyes with her knuckles, Beth searched for the window that had first caught her attention. Yes, there it was. A vague movement, as faint as a cobweb, fluttered against the dark shadow. Could there be someone? Someone who knew her name?

Again the tiny voice. 'Beth, don't do it. Please — I beg you,' it breathed. Surely it could not have carried from that distance? And the beach was empty.

As an icy wave attacked her knees, Beth whimpered and backed away from the tidal onslaught. Then she began to run. Faster and faster she sprinted along the beach, the wind whipping her hair into her eyes. Suddenly, she was hurtled to the ground, crying aloud with pain.

2

'There's nothing to be afraid of, my dear. We're only trying to help you.'

Beth opened her eyes. Bending over her was the elderly man she had noticed watching the windsurfer. Confused, she whispered, 'Pardon?'

'You said, 'Please don't do it, I beg you.''

'Did I?'

'You're probably shocked. I'm not surprised, after a fall like that. You were going at such a speed, I thought you were going to jump it, like a hurdle, but you crashed straight into it.'

The breakwater rose about two feet from the beach. Standing on the edge of the path, the man's companion called out, 'Afraid I can't get down. Help her, Charles, do.'

Taking his hand, Beth tried to stand, but again cried out in pain.

He shouted back to the woman, 'Bring the car closer, May. I don't think she can walk far.' Then he turned to Beth. 'Do you want us to take you straight to the hospital? Or would you rather call the doctor in at home?'

'If you could just take me to where my

car's parked, please.'

'Are you sure you're able to drive? Changing gear will be agony.'

'The car is automatic.' Beth rotated her foot. 'Nothing broken. Just a knock on the knee. More pain than damage, I think.'

Eventually, between hoisting and hobbling, Beth sat in the back of their car, the sheepdog panting beside her. Her mind in a turmoil, she tried to politely answer their questions.

The woman could not understand why Beth had not seen the breakwater.

'I think it was because the wind had blown my hair into my eyes.' Beth knew it sounded rather lame, but she did not want to tell the kindly couple that her eyes had also been blinded by tears.

'But you were running so fast, dear. It's a wonder you didn't break your leg. Watch out for the ramp, Charles!' she warned.

Her husband was already braking, but he just murmured, 'Yes, dear.'

The ramp safely negotiated, the woman returned to her anxiety over Beth. 'Are you sure you don't want us to take you to the hospital?' she asked. 'I do feel you should have that leg X-rayed, and we don't mind waiting, do we, Charles?'

'Not at all,' he said, glancing at Beth in the driving mirror. 'Best to be on the safe side, my dear, and it's not that far to Southampton.'

'Honestly, I'll be fine.' Beth tried to keep the edge out of her voice. They wouldn't know that the last place she wanted to be was the General Hospital, and she couldn't tell them why. All she wanted was to be alone, sort out her troubled thoughts. 'Anyway, there's my car.'

'Isn't there someone who could pick it up for you?' he asked.

'No. No one at all. I'll be fine,' Beth repeated, noticing the glance between her Samaritans. Thankfully, they had reached her car. Once they had helped her into the driving seat, and been thanked, Beth put the car into the drive mode. Better to grasp the nettle straight away. The sooner she was home, the sooner she could take another tablet. She wasn't sure how many she had taken already, but she didn't care. Just now she really needed the medication.

There had been many times recently when she had feared she was heading for a nervous breakdown. Curled up in the foetal position, she would stare at the wall for hours. Once she had read that patients with mental illness could suffer from hallucinations. But never before had she imagined voices. Unless . . . she pulled on the handbrake as the car halted in her drive. Unless . . . she had not imagined the voice.

★ ★ ★

Soaking in a hot bath, Beth tried to reason it out. There had to be a logical explanation. Mr Prestwick had often commented on her uncluttered, logical mind. In fact, he had urged Beth to train as a legal executive. She would have liked that, but Bryn persuaded her that it would be difficult for two of them to be engrossed in intensive study and exams at the same time and, as she wanted to have a child eventually, rather pointless.

Mr Prestwick always insisted that, first and foremost, you needed to study the facts. But what were the facts? A sharp weather deterioration, and a mysterious voice. The weather could be explained easily enough. Sudden squalls often put small boats at risk and confounded the meteorologists. That left the voice. Auto suggestion?

Beth struggled to put her logical, uncluttered mind into action. Although she had contemplated suicide every day since Katie had died, today was the first time she had seriously tried to take that final step.

Perhaps it was merely a subconscious effort to survive. A deeply rooted feeling that life might be worth living after all, even though she felt she had nothing to live for. She'd seen programmes on television about people pulled back from the brink of death by something supernatural — but her experience had been different. She might have accepted her mother appearing in a vision, or speaking to her. But the voice of a stranger, calling her back from a watery grave? It didn't make sense.

So what logical conclusion could she make? A side effect from too many anti-depressants and sleeping tablets? The rambling imagination of a woman who has, within the space of a few months, given birth to a handicapped child, followed by the desertion of her husband and death of the infant? Whatever, she still had the empty house and empty heart. Nothing had changed — except that the overwhelming urge to die had gone.

Perhaps she should use the experience as a turning point? Struggle back into the real world, and forget about strange images from the distant past. What was that saying? Take one day at a time.

She phoned Ali. 'I'm still not sure, but I'll see what Sarah has to say about the house.'

'And the job?'

Beth hesitated. She didn't want to think

that far ahead, neither did she want an argument with Ali. Her knee hurt too much. She compromised by murmuring, 'Maybe.'

'Hmm. I know that tone. Still, I suppose it's better than nothing. I'll phone you back.'

The appointment was for nine-thirty the following morning, but by then Beth's knee had ballooned and coloured violently. She could barely put her leg to the ground, let alone drive.

Foraging through the bureau, Beth found the correspondence from when they'd purchased the house. Yes, there was the telephone number of the estate agent. After all these years, it was strange, talking to the head girl again.

'Don't worry,' Sarah said. 'I'll come to you. I know the road.'

'But . . . '

'I need to take details. To send to Mr Grainger.'

Sarah had changed little. Her hair was still glorious, her figure trim, even after childbirth. Beth left her to measure the rooms while she hopped around the kitchen.

'Mr Grainger is being transferred to Fawley from Brussels,' Sarah explained, as they sipped their coffee. 'So he'd like to view as soon as possible, if that's all right with you.

He flies over to the refinery at least once a week.'

'Sarah, I haven't really decided . . . '

'Is your husband still paying the mortgage?'

Sarah's voice was gentle, but it brought home to Beth the truth of her financial situation.

'No,' she answered. Then she took a deep breath, and a positive step. 'Go ahead and make an appointment.'

Sarah nodded. 'But first, I'll take you to the General.'

'No!' Beth almost shouted, then lowered her voice. 'I'm sorry, but I can't go to the General. It's where I took Katie.'

'Do you want to talk about it?'

'There isn't much to tell.' Beth sighed. 'One night, I went into the nursery, and she was blue — and cold. So terribly cold.'

'Oh, Beth. I'm so sorry.' They didn't speak for a moment, then Sarah said, 'I used to have nightmares about it, wondering what I would do if it happened to me.'

'I just screamed, once. Then I drove her to the hospital. There wasn't anything they could do, of course.'

'In a way, I suppose it was for the best, as she was so severely handicapped. But it doesn't really help, does it?' Sarah had always been perceptive.

'No. I didn't want Katie to die. But I didn't want her to live the way she was. She could never have lived a normal life.'

'Did they ever tell you the cause? German measles, or anything like that?'

'I think it was genetic. On Bryn's side. Apparently there had been an aunt with the same disease. She had lived for five years, but they put her in a home.'

'And you didn't know?'

'Not until I phoned the Lewises after she was born. They called it the family curse.'

'Why didn't he tell you?'

'I think he was ashamed. And we'd agreed not to start a family until he was a full partner. He probably thought he could put it off until it was too late. But one night I forgot to take the pill, and . . . '

'You'd have thought his mother would have warned you.'

'She never forgave me for marrying her son. Said he was too good to marry a gypsy. None of them came to the wedding.'

Sarah looked startled. 'I didn't know you were a gypsy, although — yes, you've got that lovely dark colouring.'

'I'm not. Well, not really. My grandmother married a New Forest gypsy, and I made the mistake of telling Bryn's mother, trying to make conversation on the one and only occasion I met the family. Old Jake Smith was quite a colourful character, and it had never occurred to me to be ashamed of him.'

'What were they like, apart from bigoted?'

'Dreadful. They live halfway up a mountain, miles from anywhere, and when they spoke to Bryn in Welsh, I knew they were talking about me. Even the sheep were hostile.'

'Has he gone back to Wales?'

'God, no.' Beth couldn't keep the bitterness from her voice. 'Bryn's fine plans didn't include a Welsh-speaking family any more than they included a handicapped child, or a wife who had outlasted her usefulness.'

'I can't understand how any man can be that cruel.'

'Bryn never saw things in terms of cruelty, or kindness. He stated what he wanted, and that was that. Only this time I didn't meekly fall in with his demands.'

'What did he want you to do?'

'Put Katie in a residential home, like his aunt, and never refer to her again.' Beth recalled his face when he gave her the ultimatum. 'When I brought her home from the hospital, he'd gone. And pinned on that notice board I found a cheque that barely covered the current outstanding bills, and a detailed inventory of the assets he considered

I was entitled to. Oh, and there was a neatly written little postscript advising me of the date and time the removal people would arrive to collect his share. He didn't even answer my letter when I wrote to tell him that Katie had died.'

'Ali said he was an arsehole.'

It was ages since Beth had laughed. Then she became serious again. 'I don't know what I would have done without her.'

'I remembered Ali as a jolly hockey stick type, always in some scrape with the prefects,' Sarah mused. 'Who would have thought she'd turn out to be the girl in a suit, with a business of her own?'

'And a good Samaritan.'

'And a good Samaritan,' Sarah echoed. 'Come on, let's get that knee to the medical centre. If you need an X-ray, I'll take you over to Lymington Hospital.'

⋆　⋆　⋆

The X-rays didn't reveal any broken bones and, after Beth's knee was imprisoned in an elastic bandage, she was told not to put any weight on it for a few days. The irony of the situation struck Beth as she hobbled from Sarah's car to her front door. Having decided to try to get back into the real

26

world, now she was housebound.

'You really need to rest that knee completely,' Sarah commented, as she made a pot of tea. 'Do you have any neighbours who would help out with shopping and so on?'

Beth shook her head. 'They're out at work each side, and I've never said more than 'Good morning' to them. Don't worry, I'll manage.'

As Sarah opened the fridge, Beth realised that there was just about enough milk left for their tea, and very little else. Not even the makings of a sandwich.

'Well,' Sarah said, 'I hope you've got more than this in your freezer, or you'll die of starvation.' She gulped down her tea. 'Tell you what, I've got to dash back to the office now, but I'll pop back later with some supplies.'

The supplies would have fed an army for a week and a bemused Beth watched, as Sarah quietly stowed away the shopping, plunged fresh pasta into boiling water, microwaved a creamy sauce with a tantalising aroma and opened a bottle of Jacob's Creek. Suddenly, Beth began to giggle.

'What?' Sarah looked up in surprise.

'I'm sorry. It's just that . . . ' Beth had been thinking that, only a few hours ago, she had fully intended to walk into the sea and not turn back. And now she was anticipating with pleasure a meal and a glass of wine. For a brief moment, she was tempted to tell Sarah about the incident on the beach, but she couldn't. This was the first time she had felt comfortable with another person for months, and she didn't want to spoil it. It was probably all in her imagination, anyway.

'What?' Sarah repeated.

'Oh, I don't know — it just reminded me of our school-days.'

'You're surely not comparing school dinners to this gourmet concoction?'

'No. It's just you. You haven't changed. Ali was the bossy one who got things done, but with a great deal of noise. Whereas you just got on with it calmly and efficiently. No wonder you were head girl.' She sipped her wine thoughtfully. 'I'm very grateful to you, you know.'

Sarah smiled. 'There is a catch, I'm afraid.'

'Oh, yes. The bill for the groceries. Don't let me forget to give you a cheque.'

'No, there's no hurry for that. I want to ask you a favour, actually.'

Curious, Beth waited.

'Ali told you I'm desperate for some help, didn't she?'

'Yes, but I won't be able to drive for a few days.'

'I know, but do you think you could do some typing for me, here? I've got some surveyor's reports which are really urgent.'

'Well, I'd be glad to, but Bryn took the PC when he left.'

'Was there anything he didn't take?'

Beth thought for a moment. 'My husband was a very good accountant. His idea of splitting everything fifty-fifty was that he should take the lawnmower, and I should have the garden shears.'

When Sarah had finished spluttering into her wine, she said, 'If I bring you a lap-top tomorrow morning, could you type the reports?'

Beth could hardly refuse. Half an hour later, nitty gritty details explained, and dishes back in their cupboards, Sarah said, 'I really must go. Promised Jamie I'd read him a bit more of Winnie the Pooh before he goes to sleep. By the way, Damon sends his best.'

'Damon?'

'My husband. Didn't Ali tell you? I married Damon Martin. He was in my year. Do you remember him?'

Suddenly, Beth was back in the school library, playing a stupid game with the old gang of girls, who were trying to guess which of the prefects would be most likely to marry a millionaire. Sarah Biddlecombe had been the one with the most votes and they were all giggling hysterically when the door opened and Damon Martin stood there, looking as though he wished the ground would open up and swallow him.

'Oh, God,' Ali had stage-whispered, loudly enough for him to hear, 'it's Dopey Damon. Wonder what he wants. Can't possibly be a book.'

Damon had blushed scarlet and wandered aimlessly between the rows of books, until Sarah came in, quickly summed up the situation and helped her classmate find the book he was looking for.

As though reading her mind, Sarah went on, 'Ali used to tease him something rotten because he couldn't read very well. Of course, in those days we didn't realise it was dyslexia.' She chuckled, without bitterness. 'Poor Ali. She was so embarrassed when he turned up to mend her dishwasher. I don't think she ever thought that he would also finish up with a flourishing business of his own.'

'That's great.' Beth was genuinely pleased. 'It couldn't have been easy for him, and we didn't help much.'

'True. But Damon never bears a grudge. You'll have to come over to dinner when you're mobile again.'

'I'd like that.'

After Sarah had left, Beth poured herself another glass of wine and stretched out on the settee, thinking over the events of the day. Should she have confided in Sarah about her strange experience? Probably not. After all, tomorrow she would be working again, like it or not. And it was unlikely that it would ever happen again.

3

Mr Grainger was so taken with Beth's house, he phoned his wife in Brussels and suggested she take the next available flight to Southampton. Mrs Grainger went into raptures over the locality, the kitchen, the spaciousness and the garden — but it would depend on accessibility of schools. One child would soon be starting school, one was already at an infants' school and one at the junior level. Then a good nursery school would be required later for the baby expected in August. Between them, Sarah and Beth put the Graingers in touch with the necessary head teachers, and waited. Beth wasn't sure whether she wanted a positive answer or not and, when it came, she still didn't know whether her tears were of joy or sadness.

'A little of each, I expect,' Sarah commented, as she handed Beth the box of tissues.

'I know I've got to accept the inevitable, but I didn't expect it to happen quite so quickly,' Beth sniffed.

'Don't knock it. Some houses have been on my books for yonks.'

'You're right, of course. And this house should be filled with children. The only thing is, the Graingers want to move in as soon as possible, and I haven't a clue where I'm going to live.'

Sarah passed her a file. 'Take a look at that.'

The artist's impressions of the proposed 'Seascape' development were good enough to attract any would-be buyers. Some were of the same quality and price range as 'The Cherries', but Beth's attention was taken by drawings of a small terrace of two-bedroomed, Georgian-style houses.

'Those are within your price limit, and phase one will be completed soon.' Sarah studied Beth thoughtfully for a moment, then went on, 'And there's something else. The developers need someone to run the sales office and keep an eye on the showhouse. Interested?'

Slowly, Beth nodded. The development was only a couple of miles away, and now she was able to drive again, it was worth considering, even if she didn't take one of the houses. That sort of temporary job might well suit while she was looking for something more permanent. For there was no doubt she would have to increase her income. The bank statement in the morning post had made that fact only too clear.

Sarah looked at her watch. 'Tempus fugit and all that jazz,' she said. 'Have you managed to finish those last reports?' Briefly scanning through the pages, she nodded. 'These look fine, as usual. You'll never be out of a job for long.' As she shrugged into her coat, she said, 'Why don't you take a look at the site? It's all a bit messy at the moment, but it'll give you some idea of the location. Keep the file to remind yourself of the finished product.' She picked up her car keys. 'Would you like to come over for a meal on Friday? Good. I'll find out more about the job by then — and you can say 'Hallo' to Damon and Jamie.'

★ ★ ★

Beth drove out to the site the next morning. A little rain splattered as she gingerly made her way along duckboards, between JCBs and piles of bricks, trying to visualise the neat squares and drives on the architect's drawings, enhanced by mature shrubs and trees. It had been the same when they had chosen 'The Cherries'. But then there had been two of them to ask questions and discuss features, although Bryn had made the final choice. Now, she was the one who would have the last word, and it was a very new experience.

★ ★ ★

Sarah's cottage was thatched and rambling, and cried out to be photographed. When Beth asked if an artist had ever painted it, Sarah chuckled and said they often had local art classes camping out on the lawn. There was a particularly nice watercolour of 'Hawthorns' hanging in the hall, alongside an aerial photograph, which showed the extent of the garden, and Beth was studying it when Damon appeared.

'Hi.' His smile was welcoming as he held out his hand.

For a moment, Beth was too surprised to speak. She'd remembered a rather gauche, painfully shy boy with a slight stammer, and was confronted with a gorgeous hunk of thirty-something who wasn't at all put out that one of the girls who used to tease him unmercifully was now a guest in his house.

As though reading her mind, he said, 'It's been a long time since schooldays. And it's very good to see you again.'

'Thank you.' Now it was Beth who was at a loss for words. 'I was just admiring . . . ' She nodded towards the painting.

'It's one of the few that do the cottage justice. The guy didn't want to sell, but I managed to twist his arm, just a little.'

Could this pleasant, assured man really be the Damon Martin who'd been the target for Ali's acid humor? Beth wondered.

'Before I offer you a drink, Beth, would you mind having a quick word with Jamie? Afraid I promised him you would.' Halfway up the stairs, Damon stopped and turned to Beth. 'I've just remembered what Ali told me. It's not too painful for you, is it?'

'No.' Beth smiled. 'I'd love to see Jamie, but thank you for the thought.'

Jamie had inherited his mother's copper-coloured curls and his father's engaging smile. 'Have you ever seen a dinosaur?' was the first question he asked.

'Afraid not, Jamie. Have you?'

'Of course.' The boy scrambled under the duvet and reappeared with a lurid green, cross-eyed creature at least two feet long. 'This is Fluff. He's my best friend.'

'Did you call him Fluff because he wishes he was pretty, like the rabbits and bears?' Beth nodded towards the pile of fluffy toys on the chair.

The red curls shook vigorously. 'He doesn't know he's ugly, but he is naughty sometimes.'

'Oh, what does he do?'

'Sometimes he makes rude noises, so I have to say 'pardon' whenever he fluffs.'

Lips twitching, and not looking at Beth, Damon kissed his son's cheek. 'Sleepy time, Jamie. Say goodnight to Beth.'

Also avoiding eye contact with Damon, Beth struggled to keep a straight face, and tucked Fluff back under the duvet. She was quite unprepared for the feeling of two chubby arms reaching up and twining round her neck.

'Did you really go to school with Mummy and Daddy?'

'Yes.'

'That was a long time ago, wasn't it?'

'A very long time ago.'

'Grandma says they didn't have computers in her school, and they had to sit in rows.'

'That's true.'

Sleepy blue eyes stared back, thoughtfully. 'Were you good friends with Mummy and Daddy at school?'

Beth hesitated, then softly said, 'Not at school, Jamie — but I think we are now.' She kissed the child's cheek, marvelling at the softness of his skin.

As Damon switched off the light and stood to one side to allow Beth to go through the door, he said, 'I'm glad you've come back into Sarah's life.'

Surprised, Beth glanced back at him.

'You were always the nicest one of that crowd,' he went on. 'Ali's great fun, but she can be a little too . . . cynical at times.'

'She's been a good friend to me.'

'I know. Sarah told me.' He closed Jamie's door behind him, and slipped his arm around Beth's shoulders. 'I hope you meant what you said in there — about us being good friends.'

'Of course. Sarah has been another very good friend.'

He nodded. 'Pure gold, is Sarah.' For a moment his expression became wistful. 'I remember only too well what it feels like to be lonely, so I do understand what you must be going through.'

'Well, I'm beginning to see a light at the end of the tunnel at last.'

'Good.' He ushered her towards the staircase. 'Now I'd better get you that drink and take over in the kitchen. It's my turn tonight. Hope you like Thai food.'

'To be honest, I've never had it, but I'm sure I shall enjoy it.'

Bryn had hated what he called 'trendy' or 'spicy' foods and never set foot in the kitchen if he could help it, but Damon was obviously quite comfortable with his Rick Stein cookbook, leaving his wife and their guest to soak up the evening sun on the terrace, only

38

interrupting to top up their glasses.

'This is absolute bliss,' Beth murmured, as she pushed a straw through the decorative fruit bobbing on top of the Pimms. 'Did you train Damon, or did he come as a package?'

Sarah's laugh tinkled as pleasantly as the ice bouncing off the side of her glass. 'He'd lived alone for some years before we met up again,' she explained, 'and was determined that he wasn't going to live out of tins and junk food. A bit of a health freak in a way — not that I'm complaining.'

'Does he always cook when you entertain?'

'Only when he wants to try out a new recipe.'

'Are you adventurous, too?'

'Sometimes, but I haven't Damon's patience to fiddle with all the little bits and pieces. Italian is my speciality. Pasta is so easy — and quick.' Sarah glanced at her watch. 'Have some more nibbles. We'll be lucky if we eat before nine o'clock — but it will be worth waiting for.'

After a few minutes of discussion on the merits or otherwise of different styles of cookery gurus, Beth asked, 'Is Jamie at school yet?'

'He goes to a private nursery school every morning, but will be starting at the infants' school in September.'

'How do you manage when he's not at school?'

'Oh, Lorraine has been with us since he was a few weeks old. Really don't know what I'd do without her. And Jamie adores her. She's visiting her folks for the weekend, or you'd have met her.'

Bryn had discussed having a live-in nanny when Beth became pregnant. She hadn't been too keen on the idea of returning to work but, as it happened, it hadn't become an issue between them — poor little Katie had become the thorn in Bryn's side.

Suddenly, Beth realised that Sarah was talking. 'I'm sorry,' she said. 'What did you say?'

'I just wondered whether you'd had a chance to look at the site yet?'

Nodding, Beth said, 'It's difficult to imagine the end product, but it's certainly a nice location, and not too far from the beach.' Idly watching a bee wriggling around the lilac tree, she went on, 'You shouldn't have any difficulty in selling them.'

'I'm taking deposits already, so I think they'll go quite quickly, even in today's market.' Sarah went back into the house and reappeared with a large site plan, which she spread on the table before her. Five of the houses were marked with a name, including one of the cheaper range. 'Would you like me to pencil your name in on one of the others?' she asked. 'There are only four in the 'Seahorse' terrace. I'm not trying to be pushy, Beth, but I honestly don't think you'll find anything more suitable within your range.'

Decision time. Beth had studied the house details and there was no point in delaying any longer, not with the Graingers anxious to move into 'The Cherries'. She pointed to the end of terrace on the site plan. 'Put me down for that one. It looks more secluded.'

'It is, and the garden's bigger.' Sarah wrote Beth's name in the little square, then pushed a typed sheet of paper across the table. 'This is the information about the temporary job in the showhouse. It will mean working weekends and some evenings, of course, but I might be able to help out on the odd occasion.'

Beth scanned the page. The hours didn't bother her. She wouldn't be going anywhere — and the money wasn't bad. Also, she'd be able to watch her own house being built, step by step.

'When would you want me to start?' she asked.

'Monday if possible.'

'But the showhouse isn't ready yet.'

41

'You could work in my office first — familiarise yourself with the various details, liaise with the people who have already shown interest, and take any new potential clients out to the site.'

Slowly, Beth nodded. It was sooner than she'd anticipated, but there was really no reason to delay, apart from her own reluctance to get back into the real world.

'Great!' Sarah grinned. 'And the first thing you can do on Monday is to draw up your contract.' She raised her glass. 'Here's to us.'

'I hope I'm included in that.' Damon appeared in the door, a tea towel draped over his shoulder. 'Beth, your glass is empty. Let me get you another.'

'Oh, no.' Beth laughed as she covered her glass with her hand. 'Don't forget I'm driving.'

'Nonsense. You can always stay the night — can't she, Sarah?'

'Of course.'

Faintly embarrassed, Beth demurred. 'It's very kind of you, but I must go home.' She tried to make a joke of the suggestion. 'I forgot to bring my toothbrush.'

'Oh, we can always rustle up a spare toothbrush and nightie, can't we, Sarah?'

Sarah hesitated, then seemed to sense Beth's feelings. 'Perhaps another time,

Damon,' she said, then laughed, 'and for goodness sake, when are we going to eat? Our stomachs are rumbling like thunder.'

The meal was certainly worth the wait and, as Beth drove home, she reflected that her future didn't seem quite so dismal as it had a week or so ago. She had a new job to fill her days — and nights — and new friends, or at least a renewal of old friendships. This could be the turning point — the beginning of a new way of life. Perhaps she would be able to sleep more soundly in her new house, without the fear that she was losing her senses.

4

It was amazing how houses could grow in two weeks, Beth thought, as she turned her car into the entrance of the 'Seascape' site. The showhouse was in the last stages of being plastered, and the suntanned young men deftly mortaring another row of bricks into place lifted her own house from a drawing to reality. She was becoming quite fond of it already.

Turning to the couple standing uncertainly behind her, she pointed to a row of conifers at the edge of the site. 'The 'Sea Breeze' houses will be built over there. The footings are in already. Mind how you step.'

The young couple held hands and gazed at the outlines of rooms as though already placing their furniture here — or maybe there.

'They look rather small,' Mr Ryecroft commented.

'Yes, I know.' Beth smiled. 'That's just what I said when I saw my own house at that stage. It's a bit of an optical illusion, really.' She turned to a page on the brochure. 'The lounge-diner is eighteen by twelve — and there's plenty of room for a breakfast bar in the kitchen.'

'It's really the bedroom sizes I'm thinking of,' Mrs Ryecroft said, shyly. 'You see — we're expecting a baby at Christmas, and we'd like to have our family fairly close together, so we don't want poky bedrooms.'

'Congratulations.' The second future happy event Beth had heard of that day — but she forced herself to smile as she went on, 'I think you'll find the bedrooms are quite evenly sized. The designers have recognised at last that the days of the third bedroom being a cupboard are long gone. Two point four children may be a statistic, but even a point four child takes up as much room as its parents — or so I am told.'

'You don't have children, then?'

'No.' In an attempt to change the subject, Beth turned the pages of the brochure. 'Of course, the rooms of the detached houses are larger.' She pointed to an attractive sketch of a 'Sea Anchor' house.

The Ryecrofts stared at the page longingly. 'Afraid they're out of our range,' the young man sighed. 'Even these three-bedroomed semis are a bit high, but there's no point in taking a two-bedroomed place and looking around for something bigger in a couple of years. This has got to last us for a bit, so can you tell us exactly what the repayments would be?'

After a few minutes tapping away at her calculator, Beth had given the Ryecrofts all the information they required. They seemed fairly positive, but needed to talk about it, privately.

'Tell you what,' Mr Ryecroft suggested. 'Could you take us along to Calshot Castle? Sandra's Mum asked us to pick up a leaflet about English Heritage, and if you could give us enough time to have a walk along the beach, we can make up our minds today.'

The last place Beth wanted to visit was Calshot Castle, but she really didn't have much choice, not if she was going to clinch the sale for Sarah. She waited by the car while the Ryecrofts picked up their literature, then watched as they climbed down on to the shingle and scrunched along the beach, wishing she had suggested that they follow her in their own car instead of offering to drive them from the office to the site.

The promised heatwave was materialising at last, and Beth looked around for some shade. The only place that offered any respite from the blazing sun was the castle. Beth scanned the windows. No shadowy figure, no voices — and the sea could not have been more benign, filled with yachts of all sizes scudding hither and thither along the sparkling waves. It was almost high tide — the breakwaters covered and the moat full. Behind her, dozens of twin-hulled craft waited patiently while their covers were removed and they were trundled down the slipway by owners lucky enough to have time off mid-week. Nothing at all to send a chill down the spine.

Let's lay that figment of my imagination to rest once and for all, Beth thought, as she passed through the open door, into welcome shade provided by the gatehouse. In a small room to her left, the custodian raised her eyes from her book and took Beth's money with a pleasant smile.

'Would you like a guidebook?' she asked.

About to shake her head, Beth changed her mind. After all, other clients of Sarah's might want to know about the local tourist attractions. Heat fired from the cobbles of the open courtyard, so she quickly scurried through a doorway into part of the living area, where a photographic exhibition told of the exploits of those connected with the flying-boats, and the Schneider trophy. She hadn't realised that T.E. Lawrence, when he wasn't fighting in Arabia, had worked at Calshot. An old photograph of a funeral cortège caught her eye, and she read the memo giving permission for workers at the nearby refinery to have thirty minutes' leave, with pay if they were ex-servicemen, to attend the funeral of Fl. Lt. Kinkaid. Beth had never heard of him, but there were hundreds of men walking behind the coffin in the photograph, so he must have been well loved. Interested, she read on. He had been one of the most highly decorated aces of the First World War, but in 1928 his plane had dived into the sea off Calshot when he attempted the world speed record.

Saddened by the tale, Beth crossed the courtyard to the keep and climbed the stone stairs to the first floor, where the octagonal room was sparsely furnished with nine iron beds, a large plain table with benches and an iron stove. Barrack-room life in the earlier part of the century must have been bare and spare, Beth thought, then listened, wondering where the rattle was coming from, but it was only a loose-fitting sash window nudged into life by the wind. Shaking her head, Beth smiled. No ghosts here.

More stone steps led upwards, and Beth decided to continue up to the roof. The stiff breeze cooled the heat of the sun on her head as she circled the roof, enthralled by the spectacular views across to the Isle of Wight in one direction, up Southampton Water and across to Hamble in another, the colourful row of beach huts completing the picture. The Ryecrofts were slowly walking along the beach away from the castle, heads together in deep conversation, so Beth knew she had time to linger and watch the car ferry edge its way past the spit and across to Cowes, the yachts keeping a respectful distance.

As she gazed over the tranquil scene, her thoughts went back to earlier that morning when Sarah had arrived, unusually for her, a little late. Beth had known by the expression on her face that she was pregnant again. She was delighted for her friend, but couldn't help a little pang of envy, which had stabbed again when the Ryecrofts told of their expected child. Things usually happen in threes, she mused, wondering who the third would be. Not Beth, that was for sure.

For no particular reason, she thought of the flier who had gambled with his life, and lost. The photograph of his funeral procession had touched a chord in her heart and she tried to imagine how his family had coped with the irony of his death. He had already proved he was a hero, why did he also need to prove he was the fastest? Gazing across the sparkling Solent, which had almost become her own watery grave, Beth pondered on the frailty of life, and wondered whether a whispering voice had tried to warn him, before it was too late.

Trying to shake off the black mood that threatened to engulf her, Beth decided to go back down, but paused on the second floor of the keep, where an exhibition showed the history of the castle from the time when King Henry VIII decided it should be built.

Part of Beth wanted to continue down to the sunny courtyard, but curiosity overcame her better judgement and she was drawn into the room. Following around the circular display in the centre of the room, she stopped at a huge drawing of the castle in 1733. A voice behind her startled Beth. 'Did you go right up to the top?' It was the custodian.

'Yes.'

'Quite a view, isn't it?'

Beth was still staring at the drawing. 'It looks quite different now, doesn't it?'

The woman followed Beth's gaze. 'Personally, I think it looked much more like a castle when it had the castellated keep and drawbridge. It had been more or less like that for about two hundred years.'

'When was it changed?'

'One of the governors probably started the ball rolling later in the eighteenth century. Wanted more rooms added on to the gatehouse.'

'But why do away with the castellations? Surely they would have given better protection from the enemy?'

'You'd think so, wouldn't you. But somebody or other decided that a continuous parapet would be safer.' The custodian smiled. 'Probably someone who'd never fired a musket in their life.'

Beth smiled back. 'Nothing changes much, does it?'

The custodian crossed to the window. 'Seems odd to think that the beach was once full of cockle shells, heaped up around the castle like a wall.' Suddenly, she imitated a cockney accent. 'Not many people know that,' she said, then chuckled. 'Just one of those useless bits of information I read in a very old letter.'

'I wonder what it was like for the families?' Beth mused. 'Living in a garrison like this.'

'Very isolated and cold, I would imagine. Those fires wouldn't win the fight against stone walls and savage winters.' The custodian turned, her nose wrinkled in distaste. 'And it would have been incredibly smelly.'

'Yes, I suppose it would.'

'Think about it. Young families crowded in with soldiers too old or ill for active service, many of them wounded in battle.'

'So this place would have been like the

Chelsea Pensioners' home.'

'Something like that. They called them 'Invalid Companies'. With poor sanitation, not much in the way of nutritious food and inadequate medical attention, disease would have been rife.'

'Do you have records of the people who lived here?'

'Sadly, no. Lots of folklore, of course, but not much documented.' The custodian sighed. 'If only these walls could speak. What tales they would tell.' She walked towards the door. 'You're the only visitor at the moment, so I'll shut up shop for half an hour when you're through. No need to rush, I only want to get something for my lunch.' She smiled ruefully. 'Left my sandwiches at home.'

'So did I.' Beth laughed. 'I won't be long.'

After she had finished reading the display boards, Beth slowly made her way down the uneven steps, remembering the words of the local historian. Four people had died here in mysterious circumstances. Why did they die? The walls knew, but they silently kept their secrets.

Pausing by the entrance to the barrack room, she noticed a slight movement. It must be the custodian, so she might as well tell her she was leaving — there was nothing more to be seen.

As she entered the room, a wave of nausea overcame Beth and she slumped on to one of the benches. The room was empty, but slightly fuzzy, and seemed to be spinning. What a fool she had been to skip breakfast. Her blood sugar levels must be seriously low. Resting her elbows on the table, she held her head in her hands, breathing deeply.

Even with her eyes closed, she felt the room moving, like the deck of a ship. Pictures flashed through her mind, images of this room centuries ago, teeming with unwashed bodies, some dying, some dead. She could almost smell the stench of putrid flesh.

'Disease would have been rife. Old soldiers. Ill. Wounded.' The words of the custodian chanted over and over, whispering inside her head.

Now another voice. 'That's what it were like, Beth.' A younger voice.

Eyes tightly shut, Beth whispered, 'Who are you?'

'Eliza. Same name as you.'

'No, I'm Beth. No one has ever called me Eliza.' Then she remembered that she had been christened Elizabeth, after her grandmother. But her mother had read *Little Women* while she was pregnant, and was smitten with the character of Beth March. So the new baby soon became . . . She might have been Eliza. Or Liz. Common enough abbreviations. Grandmother had been called Eliza.

Beth opened her eyes. The room was still empty. No custodian. No younger person. But it was still fuzzy, and still moving. Perhaps the sun had affected her. Yet she felt so cold.

Now she imagined she could hear a low wailing. And still the voice whispered to her.

'It were dreadful, Beth. You've no idea how dreadful. I thought I was going mad.'

The way she felt at the moment, Beth had a very good idea of what it might feel like to go mad. 'Where is your voice coming from?' she cried. Then she realised what must have happened. The custodian had managed a good imitation of Michael Caine. A Wessex accent wouldn't present any problems. Perhaps they were trying out some remote voices, like virtual reality, to impress the tourists.

Anger replaced Beth's fear. 'How dare you try a trick like this without warning,' she shouted. 'And how do you know my name?'

'It ain't no trick,' the voice persisted. 'I just wants you to know the truth, that's all.'

'The truth? What truth?'

'About what happened here. Go on. You know you wants to find out.'

'No, I don't. Leave me alone.' Beth knew she had to get out of that room. She struggled to her feet. Her mouth dry, she staggered towards the doorway, trying to shut out the voice in her head. Screaming hoarsely, Beth flung herself through the opening.

Her next recollection was of the custodian bending over her, looking anxious.

'Oh, dear. Are you badly hurt?' she asked.

Beth touched her forehead. There was blood on her fingers.

'I'm afraid you were quite hysterical. You must have slipped and banged your head. I'd better phone for an ambulance. That's a nasty cut you have there.'

'No — thank you. I'm all right.' Beth tried to clear the woolliness from her mind. 'What did I say?'

'You were asking for help. Did something frighten you?'

'Yes . . . I thought I heard . . . are you using sound effects? Voices? To give atmosphere?'

'Now that's a good idea. We need to do something to compete with the other tourist attractions.'

'But there's nothing like that happening at the moment?'

'No. Just the display, I'm afraid.'

Cautiously, Beth asked, 'Is the castle haunted?'

'Not that I've heard of. If it was, we might have more visitors.'

'If something dreadful happened here, you would know about it, wouldn't you?'

The custodian touched Beth's face. 'Looks like you've got a touch of the sun to me. Perhaps you stayed up on the roof too long. Even with the breeze, it can still be quite risky.'

A man's voice called from the courtyard, 'Mrs Lewis? Are you up there?'

The Ryecrofts. She'd completely forgotten about them.

Weakly, she called back. 'Yes. I won't be a moment.'

'Let me explain to your friends, my dear. Perhaps they can take you home?'

Before Beth could protest further, the custodian had hurried downstairs, and returned with Mr Ryecroft. 'The young lady really ought to see a doctor,' she advised, as he examined the cut on Beth's head.

'What on earth happened?' he asked, as he helped Beth to her feet. 'I heard you screaming from outside.'

There was no way she could even attempt to explain. He had enough problems of his own. Beth shook her head. 'I — I thought I saw a rat. It must have been my imagination. I'm so sorry I startled you. Is your wife OK?'

He laughed. 'She's having a nice little snooze in your car. Didn't even hear you.' He held out his hand. 'Let me have your keys. I've driven an automatic before.'

Beth was relieved. The cut continued to bleed through the tissues — and the plaster Mr Ryecroft administered from her first-aid box.

'There. Hopefully that will hold until we get you back to the office, although I think you might need a couple of stitches.' He glanced in the direction of his wife, who was carefully looking in the opposite direction. 'By the way, Mrs Lewis. You can tell your boss that you've made a sale. We've decided that the semi will be big enough — at least to start with.'

'That's good.' Beth lay back against the headrest and closed her eyes. Sarah would be curious about the injury, and Beth would dearly have liked to tell her what had really happened. She needed someone to confide in. But Sarah was preoccupied, and Ali was setting up a training course in Bournemouth.

Once again, Beth felt that total loneliness that a person can only feel when there is no one in the world they can turn to for help.

5

'Not again!' Sarah stared at the bloodstained dressing. 'I don't remember you as being particularly accident-prone at school. It must be something about that place.'

'The steps are very uneven. I suppose my knee let me down.'

'Come on, I'll take you to Hythe Hospital. At this time of day there should be someone who can stitch that cut. Jane can draw up the agreement for the Ryecrofts.'

'I'm sorry, Sarah. I feel I've let you down.'

'Rubbish! Nobody gets a wallop like that on purpose. And you clinched the sale, so there's no need to look so troubled.'

Leaving the signed documents with her secretary, Sarah gave Beth a wadge of tissues to help stem the blood, and bundled her into her own car. 'What I can't understand,' she said as she fastened her seatbelt, 'is why you were so hysterical over a rat. You didn't seem particularly bothered when we found one near the site.'

'Oh, well — I thought this one was going to run over my foot. But it was probably all in my imagination, anyway.'

Sarah glanced sideways, looking as though she wasn't sure whether she believed Beth. Then she said, 'Hmmm. Perhaps it's the atmosphere of the place, and all the old stories.'

'What stories?'

'You know — the sort of stories that sprout from ancient buildings. Look at the history of All Saints Church at Fawley. There was smuggling galore in these parts in days of yore, not to mention the goings-on around Beaulieu with the dissolution of the monasteries.'

Beth mulled over this for a while, then asked, 'Where would you find out? About the stories, I mean.'

Sarah pursed her lips in concentration before she answered, 'I suppose local historians are your best bet. They've got some good groups in Fawley and Hythe.'

Local historians. The man who had spoken to Ali's writers' circle. He would know.

After Beth had been stitched up, literally, and her cuts and bruises cleaned and attended to, Sarah drove her home and insisted she take the rest of the day off.

'I'll pick you up in the morning.'

'But it's out of your way.'

'Not that much. Don't worry if I'm a bit late. I'll probably still be offloading my breakfast down the loo.'

'I'm glad I wasn't too afflicted with morning sickness. It must be awful.'

'It's worse with this one than when I was pregnant with Jamie. Still, it's usually only for a few weeks. I'll survive.'

After Sarah had left, Beth thought about her words, 'I'll survive.' That's what life was all about, surviving from one crisis to another. Certainly Ali had helped Beth to survive her grief, and Sarah had helped her to survive tackling a new career. But there was no one who could help her survive the trauma of hearing a strange voice talking to her. Calling her name. Should she make an appointment to see Dr Nichols?

Then she recalled reading somewhere that imagined voices in the head could be a symptom of schizophrenia. God, no! She couldn't face the questions, the tests, the wondering. It had to be imagination. The giddiness must have been brought on by lack of food, the disorientation by heatstroke.

For a long time, she sat thinking about the events of the day, then remembered the guidebook. It was true what the voice, imaginary or otherwise, had said. Her curiosity was well and truly aroused. She really needed to speak to the local historian, but Ali was in Bournemouth until the end of the week, and Beth couldn't even get to the library before tomorrow. The best thing she could do was to write down everything she remembered and then check the details later. Perhaps she might even tell Ali about the experience when she came back. They could talk over a meal at Beth's house on Friday evening. She left a message on her answering machine.

⋆   ⋆   ⋆

Ali had experiences of her own to talk about. In fact, she bubbled for so long, Beth had to keep reminding herself to ask her friend about the historian, in case it was forgotten in all the excitement. For Ali had fallen in love.

'He's one of the managers on the training course, and absolutely drop dead gorgeous. Oh, Beth! I've never felt like this before.'

'You were pretty keen on the ski instructor, and the architect, not to mention the . . . '

'For goodness sake, Beth. There's no comparison.' For a brief moment, Ali frowned, then her happiness broke through the irritation and she grinned. 'OK, so I've had a few . . . relationships. But not once have I instantly known that this is the man I want to spend the rest of my life with.'

It was certainly true that there had been

casual romances in Ali's life, and a handsome naval officer had actually proposed, but been promptly turned down. Ali had sworn that she liked her independence too much to make a commitment for life to one person. Beth studied her friend's face. Never before had she glowed with that look — of love.

Gently, Beth asked, 'And does this gorgeous hunk feel the same way about you?'

'Oh, yes,' Ali breathed. 'That's the wonderful thing about it. It was love at first sight for both of us. I know it sounds dreadfully corny, but please don't laugh. I couldn't bear it.'

'Wouldn't dream of it.' Beth hugged her friend. 'So . . . when do I get to meet him?'

A slight shadow crossed Ali's face. 'I'm not sure,' she sighed. 'His firm is based up north so he has to spend some time at HQ, but he's trying to persuade them to set up a regional office in the south, so he'll come down as often as he can.'

'I see.' Beth felt a slight unease.

'It's not what you think,' Ali protested.

'How do you know what I was thinking?'

'I can tell from the look on your face, and Gavin hasn't got a wife and kids waiting for him in Cheshire. As a matter of fact, he's divorced, and he's been planning to move down here for some time. He likes sailing.'

'Good. That's something you have in common.'

'Amongst other things.' Ali's jaw jutted just a little defiantly. 'In fact, we've discussed buying a boat together.'

'To live on?'

'Course not, idiot. Perhaps a Westerly, or something like that. We could cruise around the Isle of Wight or the Channel Islands at weekends. Maybe even the Mediterranean for holidays.'

'Sounds good. Shall we hear wedding bells, or are you just going to be 'an item'?'

'All in good time, Beth. All in good time.' Ali gazed dreamily out of the window. 'Just for now, he'll stay with me when he's in the area, but we'll look for something bigger later on.'

'Well, I'm sure Sarah will be able to come up with a few properties.'

'Oh, yes. I'd forgotten Sarah. Tell you what, as soon as Gavin comes down south again, we'll all go out to dinner together.'

'That should be fun. By the way, Sarah has some news as well, but I'll let her tell you herself.'

'She's not pregnant again?'

'Oh dear. Did I make it that obvious? Just don't tell her that I let it slip.'

Ali was thoughtful for a moment, and Beth

thought she was about to say more, but she changed the subject completely.

'So what have you been up to while I've been away, Beth?' she asked. 'And how did you get that egg on your forehead?'

This really wasn't the time to take Ali into her confidence, Beth thought, so she just said that she'd tripped on the steps at Calshot Castle, then asked whether Ali had the telephone number of the historian.

'What on earth do you want to phone him for?' Ali asked. 'That talk was weeks ago.'

'Nothing really. Just something that the custodian of the castle mentioned. It made me curious, and she said a local historian probably knew more about it.'

'It's at home somewhere. I'll phone you tomorrow. Now, when will you be moving in to your new house?'

'Not just yet, but I shall be working in the showhouse from Monday.'

'You'd better keep away from the castle, then. Your body is running out of luck.'

It's not my body I'm worried about, Beth thought. It's my mind.

* * *

True to her word, Ali phoned Beth the next morning. Mr Brooke lived locally and he invited Beth round for coffee. Like many people who lectured on their hobbies, he was keenly enthusiastic about local history, and delighted that Beth remembered his talk to the writers' circle.

'So what are you writing, my dear?' he asked, after his wife had left the coffee tray and returned to her bedding plants. 'An historical novel?'

More likely an hysterical novel, if it was based on my experiences, Beth thought wryly, pausing before she answered. Agreeing that she was writing something would be an acceptable reason for calling him, but she didn't want to be pressured into joining his society, for the purposes of research.

'Actually,' she said, 'I am not writing anything. It's just that I'm working on the new 'Seascape' development, and potential buyers ask all sorts of questions about the area where they might be living. As I'm fairly new to the area myself, I thought you might be able to point me in the right direction.'

'You mean the historical background?'

'Yes . . . particularly of Calshot Castle. I believe you mentioned it in your talk? Something about four mysterious deaths.'

'Ah, yes. I remember.' Thoughtfully, he sipped his coffee. 'I have always been fascinated by old records, gravestones and so on. My work involved research into technology that would be used in the future, and for some contradictory reason, I love delving into the past as a hobby.' Mr Brooke put his coffee cup back on to the tray and smiled at Beth over the top of his half-moon spectacles. 'After I retired, I had more time to spend browsing through parish records, and that particular item intrigued me, so I decided to use it for the writers. Bear with me a moment, and I'll fetch the notes from my study.'

While he was rustling through papers in the next room, Beth glanced around the comfortable sitting room, with its chintz-covered armchairs and visible signs of many years of family life. On the piano, three wedding photographs and a variety of school photographs fought for space among the piles of music, and a small occasional table housed a collection of glass paperweights. The bookshelves were crammed with books on every subject imaginable; most of them must have overflowed from the study, Beth was sure. There were also some rather fine watercolour paintings, many of local views, and her attention was taken by a superb firescreen of a peacock in full feather.

'Lovely, isn't it?' Mr Brooke had returned with an armful of books, and followed her gaze. 'Molly is very clever with her needle.'

'I thought it was a painting.'

'Most people do. She's a pretty good pianist as well.'

'Obviously a lady of many talents. I envy her.' For a moment, Beth watched Mrs Brooke carry another tray of marigolds from the greenhouse. 'Is she an artist, too?' She nodded towards a painting of a forest clearing.

'No, that's our daughter's work. Once the children have gone to school, she trots off with her easel to find another view. Sometimes Molly goes with her and photographs something to design for her embroidery. They're very close.'

That was the sort of family life Beth had envisaged. Growing old together with Bryn, and children and grandchildren. But no use dwelling on the impossible.

'They're very good paintings,' she said, trying to keep the catch out of her voice.

'She exhibits at the local art festivals. Sold three last time,' he said, with obvious pride. Then he put the books down on the coffee table and opened a buff file. 'These are the notes I made for the talk.' He ran a finger down the page. 'Yes, here it is. The year was 1709, and between May 10th and 20th, four deaths at Calshot Castle had been registered.'

'Do you have the names?'

He read out the list, 'Master Gunner Thomas Pitman. His daughter Mary. Another Mary, Mary Seal. And Elizabeth, wife of Francis Stoyl, a soldier.'

Elizabeth. Could she be Eliza? Could she be trying to talk to Beth? Almost three hundred years later?

'No other details, I'm afraid,' Mr Brooke went on. 'Not even the cause of death.'

'Could it have been an epidemic? Something like smallpox?'

'Possible, I suppose. I've no doubt it existed in this area. Why do you ask?'

'I just wondered if that might have been the cause.' It was becoming more and more difficult to speak, but Beth had to ask. 'People are always fascinated by hauntings. Have you heard any tales?'

Still turning pages, he smiled. 'Personally, I think ghostly sightings are invented by hotel landlords and the tourist industry. But no, I've no recollection — oh, wait a minute. When I was a tiddler, there was a very old lady who told me a story about a poor little kitchen maid who swore a ghost had tried to talk to her.'

'Do you know what the ghost was like?'

'Oh, dear. Now you are asking.' Mr Brooke's brow furrowed as he delved back into his memory. 'Like a gypsy, I think she said, but old Mrs Wheeler's tales were always embellished. Besides, she said the poor girl was a bit gormless, and she finished up in an institution, so I wouldn't hold too much store by the tale.' He closed the file and looked at Beth. 'Are you all right, my dear?' he asked. 'You look quite flushed.'

Desperately trying to find a normal voice, Beth said, 'It's the heat, I expect. Could I have a glass of water, please?'

The water was refreshing, and cooling, but it did little to soothe Beth's troubled thoughts.

'I mustn't take up any more of your time,' she said, handing him back the empty glass.

'Not at all. I just wish I could have been of more help.'

'There is something that might help. Can you tell me where I can find the records?'

'You could go to Winchester.' Mr Brooke hesitated, then searched the pile of books. 'Or — would you like to borrow this?' He handed her a small booklet, well thumbed. 'It was written in 1920 by Mary Gould, whose husband was the rector of All Saints at the time.'

Beth read the title page: *Three Hundred Years in a New Forest Parish. Being a Short History of Fawley, compiled from the Church and Parish Records and Local Traditions.*

'This is most kind of you,' she said. 'I'll take great care of it.'

'Please do. It's the only copy I have, and I believe it is out of print.'

There were less than thirty pages in the little book. 'I'll photocopy it, and return this to you immediately,' she promised, hoping that this might give her the enlightenment she was seeking.

6

According to forest law, anyone able to put up a hut capable of sheltering himself, and to boil a kettle on a fireplace in it undisturbed by the authorities, had a right to the plot so enclosed; and the ground on which the Hardley Cottages stand is all said to have been acquired in this way, and doubtless much other as well.

That was one variation of boundary disputes new to Beth, but that particular law had been relevant in the fourteenth century. She hoped it wouldn't still hold good today, or she could find a family of new age travellers staking out a tepee and making herbal tea in her back garden. She read on, fascinated by accounts where payment for beer was frequently noted. Foxhunters did not surprise her, nor bell-ringers on Gunpowder Treason Day. But a midwife claiming ale money for a delivery? And then an entry for the poor child's funeral? Beth shuddered.

Suddenly, her attention was taken by an entry on February 6th, 1725, that *Charles Iviney, of Hieth, taken by pirates and carried captive by force, entered upon a brave resolution to destroy ye captain of ye pirates, which he attacked, and redeemed himself and his companions, but died at home of the smallpox.* Hieth must have been the old spelling of Hythe — only five miles from Calshot.

On the next page Beth found gory details of a murder and suicide in 1781, and a note had been recorded that no grass would grow on the murderer's grave. Another murder, this time at Calshot Castle! The entry was dated December 15th, 1785, and the victim's name was John Kental, matross (sailor). That was all.

Some of the doctor's bills made interesting reading, considering the low wages patients must have been earning. One charged a hefty eight shillings for a woman to bring leeches and ten shillings per head for inoculation, but it was considered to be less expensive than the large parish bills for a family 'set aside for the smallpox'. No NHS in those days, and no particular mention of an outbreak at Calshot, but it was within the Fawley parish.

The rest of the book contained inventories of goods and chattels from bygone days, and some sad, illiterate letters of application for parish relief. Among the extracts from the registers, Beth read accounts of women whose husbands were in slavery to the Turks, seamen taken prisoner by the Dutch, more beer money for *conveying gypsies out of ye parish*, and payments made to French prisoners in 1704 and 1705. Would they have been imprisoned in the castle, Beth wondered? Probably.

Finally, a list of rectors of Fawley from 1273 until 1915, including one who was ejected during the Civil War. Mary and Elizabeth were consistently popular names throughout the book, but no mention was made of a Stoyl, Pitman or Seal. Disappointed, Beth leaned back in her chair and wondered when she would have an opportunity to research further in Winchester.

★   ★   ★

The following Monday, Beth sat at her new desk in the showhouse, scanning the list of appointments for the day. Thanks to a feature in the property supplement of a local paper, interest in the 'Seascape' development had snowballed, and she would certainly be too busy to ask for time off for a while, at least until Sarah was feeling well enough to cover Beth's absence. The sickness that dogged her pregnancy showed no signs of easing and there were days, like today, when she looked so ill that Beth and Jane sent her straight home to rest, dividing the day's appointments between them.

Although she was concerned about her friend, it suited Beth to be busy and, for the first time since Katie had died, she found herself humming a little tune as she reorganised her schedule. While she waited for the first potential house-buyers to arrive, she dialled Ali's office number.

'When is lover boy coming down?' she asked as soon as she heard the distinctive throaty, 'Quality Temps. How may I help you?'

Alison chuckled. 'This weekend. And don't you sound all bright-eyed and bushy-tailed? Found a new lover boy of your own?'

Beth snorted. 'No, thank you. I've had enough of one lover boy to last me a lifetime.'

'Now don't spoil it by going all cynical and bitter on me. I just thought you sounded — better, that's all.'

'Sorry.' Beth reflected on Ali's words. 'Actually, I do feel much better, and you were right.'

'I'm always right. But how right in particular?'

'When you told me I needed a job.' Beth explained about Sarah's pregnancy problems and how the extra work-load was helping Beth to get back to normal.

'Great.' Ali's tone was warm. 'Fixed a moving date yet?'

'Should have been this week, but the plasterers have started work at last, so I'm keeping my fingers crossed that there won't be any more delays.'

'Hope you're right — but don't hold your breath.' Ali chuckled, then asked, 'Are you having a house-warming?'

'Hadn't really thought about it . . . yes, of course I will, when I'm properly settled in. Which reminds me — I really phoned to invite you and Gavin over on Saturday evening.'

'Lovely. One of your barbecues?'

'Sorry. Bryn took all the equipment with him.'

Ali muttered something unintelligible. Beth ignored the comment, which was probably very rude, and went on, 'Never mind, I'll rustle up a crust of bread and a glass of water.'

'Can't wait. Is Sarah coming?'

'I'll ask her, but she can't keep any food down at the moment, so I'm not sure that she'll come.'

'That's a shame. She sailed through her pregnancy with Jamie.' Alison paused for a moment, almost as though thinking out loud. 'Hope Damon doesn't come without her.'

Surprised, Beth asked, 'Why?'

'No reason, really.'

'You don't still think of him as Dopey Damon, do you? I thought he was quite charming.'

'Oh, yes. He's certainly charming.'

'Then what?'

'Nothing.' Ali's laugh was a little self-conscious. 'Forget I said it. What time on Saturday?'

'Eightish?' Beth would have liked to question Ali further, but noticed a car parking outside the showhouse. 'Must go, my first appointment has arrived. Look forward to meeting Gavin on Saturday.'

After the eager young couple had inspected one of the more expensive properties, and Beth had logged their name on the site plan, she wondered what Gavin would be like, then pondered on the rather strange remark about Sarah's husband. Although there had been no love lost between Ali and Damon at school, it wasn't really his fault, and he was obviously a devoted husband and father. Perhaps Ali felt she had been left with egg on her face now she knew he had dyslexia. Another car drawing up outside prevented any further speculation.

*　*　*

76

Sarah suggested that Beth take an extended lunch-hour on the Friday, as she had evening appointments throughout the week and all day Saturday, so wouldn't have much chance to shop for the dinner party. While she was about it, could she take some documents to Sarah's solicitor in Southampton? The last batch had been delayed in the post and these really were urgent.

After she had dropped off the papers, Beth's eye was caught by a stylish trouser suit in a store window. She had lost so much weight over the past year that most of her skirts were in danger of collapsing around her ankles, and even her jeans had to be belted. The suit was really more than she could afford, but the vibrant crimson suited her dark colouring perfectly, and Sarah had promised a decent bonus at the end of the month.

★ ★ ★

As she crossed the road, the civic centre clock struck the half-hour. Yes — if she was quick, she had enough time to pop into the city library.

The staff were helpful, but couldn't find anything on Calshot Castle, other than the guidebook, which she already had, and suggested she try the county records in Winchester.

A quick dash around the supermarket on the way back and Beth had everything she needed. The steaks were not cheap, but would be quick and easy, and she knew Ali loved steak. So did Sarah, usually, but whether or not she would be able to enjoy her meal remained to be seen. As Beth tucked them into the fridge in the showhouse, along with the salad and first strawberries of the season, the telephone rang. Her next appointment was cancelled, which meant she was free until late afternoon. Half an hour later, the filing was up to date and a draft contract typed, ready for Sarah's attention. As she opened her briefcase, she noticed the Calshot Castle guidebook. Suddenly, an idea occurred. Before she could dismiss the idea as being fool-hardy, she switched on the Ansafone, hung the 'Back soon' sign on the locked door, and drove towards the sea.

The custodian seemed surprised to see Beth. 'I hope you don't have another nasty tumble like last time,' she commented. 'You gave us quite a fright.'

'Didn't do me much good,' Beth laughed, as she handed over her money.

'Have you considered becoming a member of English Heritage?' The custodian reached for an application form. 'It would give you free entry to many beautiful places throughout the country. Have you ever been to Osborne House? Or Carisbrooke Castle?'

'No.' Beth hesitated. 'I might consider it later, but I just want a quick look around for now.' She felt obliged to elaborate just a little. 'Didn't see everything last time.'

'There's not much to see at the moment, that's why the entrance fee is low. But we are hoping that there will be more to attract tourists now that the county council is involved.' She pushed some leaflets towards Beth. 'Take those with you, anyway. You can browse through them at your leisure.'

'Thanks.' As Beth crossed the courtyard, she wondered for a brief moment about the wisdom of being there at all, then took a deep breath and began to climb the steps. Last time she had not been prepared. In fact, she had been quite nervous. Now, she felt calm, and ready for anything ... well, almost anything. She had already decided that, if the opportunity arose, she would talk to her friends tomorrow about her experiences. Although she realised she was throwing herself open to disbelief, even ridicule, she desperately needed to talk to someone rationally and sensibly about it. Perhaps it could be tossed around the dinner table in a light-hearted fashion. After all, many intelligent people believed in ghosts, spiritualism, near-death experiences and such like. So why should her friends think she was insane because something very strange and frightening had occurred to her? Perhaps Damon or Gavin might throw a new light on the experience.

If they quickly changed the subject, or appeared to fear she was relapsing into an unstable mental state, she would drop it.

Beth made up her mind that she would not run away if she heard the voice. If Eliza spoke to her, or appeared in any form, she would ask her what it was she wanted to tell Beth. And she would stand her ground, and listen. Maybe she was only an unhappy soul, who could not settle until she had told her story. Beth had heard tales of ghosts who could not rest in peace because their deaths had been sudden, or shocking. It could be that the poor distraught girl, if she had existed, meant no harm. What possible harm could come to Beth from anyone who had been dead for hundreds of years? For her mental state to be affected, she would have to be afraid — and she didn't feel afraid.

Even so, she paused at the door of the barrack room, feeling a little foolish, and thankful that there was no one else in the castle. What should she do? Go in and call Eliza? Don't be ridiculous, she told herself. You can't stand in the doorway and say, 'Here, ghostie,' as though you're calling a pet cat or dog.

Taking another deep breath, she walked through the door, trying to ignore the fact that her heart was beating just a little faster. Slowly, she walked around the perimeter, pausing by each window. Each view the same. Blue skies, a score or more dinghies racing each other around the buoys, a superstructured liner heading for the oceans of the world. No sense of fear.

Now what? She would have to go back soon. Feeling even more foolish, Beth returned to the middle of the room and whispered, 'Eliza? I'm here. Do you want to tell me your story?'

'I beg your pardon?'

Startled, Beth swung around. She hadn't heard the soft tread of the custodian on the stairs.

'Nothing,' she murmured. 'It was only — I was just talking to myself. Habit of mine, I'm afraid.'

The woman smiled. 'I do it all the time. They say it's the first sign.'

'Perhaps they are right.' Beth paused in the

doorway. 'Has anyone ever mentioned hearing voices in the castle? Peculiar acoustics or something?'

'Only once, and that was when I was chuntering away to myself downstairs, and my voice carried up here.' The custodian sighed. 'Better stagger on up, I suppose. Just had a phone call from someone who left their camera on the roof earlier. Hope it's still there.'

Well, Beth thought, that's that. Must have been just my imagination working in overdrive. Nice to know I'm not losing my mind. They would have to talk about something else at dinner tomorrow.

7

'Well? What do you think, Beth? Isn't he the most . . . ?' Ali's voice trailed off as she failed to find suitable words to describe the new love of her life.

Following her gaze out into the garden, Beth smiled. Being extremely tall, Gavin had to stoop to listen to Sarah and, with his unruly hair and hesitant manner, he struck Beth as more of a 'little boy lost' than 'drop dead gorgeous'. Remembering Ali's previous conquests, she had expected yet another dashing cavalier, but there was no doubt that Ali was totally besotted with him — and, it was true, opposites often attracted and forged powerful and long-lasting relationships. Perhaps he was exactly the type of man that Ali needed.

'Yes,' Beth agreed. 'He really is the most . . . '

They were still laughing when Damon came back into the kitchen. 'Would you like some help with the drinks, Beth?' he asked.

'Yes, please.' For a moment she felt guilty that she hadn't yet offered her guests a drink, but they had only arrived a few minutes ago.

'Sherry, gin and whisky over there with the mixers. White wine and beer in the fridge. Glasses in the dining room. Oh, and I've made a jug of fruit punch for the drivers and Sarah.'

'Handy for me, Sarah being on the wagon. Means she can drive. I'll just find out what Gavin wants.'

A tiny frown between her eyebrows, Ali watched as Damon went back into the garden. Then she murmured, 'I wondered how long it would be before he asked for a drink.'

'Does he have a problem?' asked Beth, wondering if this was what Ali had meant by her previous remark.

'He has been known to . . . ' Ali stopped as Damon came back into the room.

'Shandy for Gavin,' he said. 'White wine for you, Beth?'

Surprised, she nodded.

'Thought so. By the way, I like the outfit. That colour really suits you.'

'Thank you.'

He hummed a few bars of 'Lady in Red' as he poured the drinks, then said, 'I've been on at Sarah to buy herself some new clothes. Might cheer her up a bit. But she doesn't seem interested.'

'Maybe she'll be more in the mood when

she's not feeling sick all the time.'

'Buying clothes isn't the only thing she's not in the mood for.'

Beth glanced quickly round at Damon, but he was grinning.

'I think she's depressed about getting so fat. I call her my little Porky-Babe but, like the old Queen Vic, we are not amused.'

Ali snorted. 'Would you be amused, if you were in her shoes?' she asked. 'You ought to be thankful that you're not the pregnant one.'

For a moment there was silence, then Damon quietly said, 'You're right, of course. And I'm a clot.' He handed a glass to Ali with a bright smile. 'G and T with lemon and ice, if I remember rightly.'

'You remember rightly. Thank you.' Ali's smile was less bright than Damon's as she picked up a bowl of nibbles and carried it outside. And Beth wondered.

As the evening was warm and still, and the midges not yet too busy, Beth had decided that it would be rather nice to eat out on the patio. Although Bryn had taken the very expensive barbecue that Ali had bought them as a house-warming gift, he had left the table and chairs, probably because they were plastic. He had wanted to order top of the range garden furniture in teak, with matching hammock and canopy, so he could impress his clients, but Beth had gently pointed out that a fully equipped nursery should take priority, and they had already used up all their savings, plus hire purchase, on new furniture for the house. Anyway, she quite liked the green oval table and chairs she had purchased in a mid-winter sale. They were the only things she had ever chosen without Bryn's approval, she reflected, as she carried plates of smoked salmon and thinly sliced brown bread and butter out to her guests.

By the time they were reaching for the jug of cream to pour on plump, juicy strawberries, the conversation had covered every subject from politics to weather. Then Sarah, who had managed to eat a small amount of smoked salmon and sirloin steak without disappearing into the house, asked, 'What do you do exactly, Gavin?'

For a moment there was a pause, while all eyes turned to Gavin, who stared at the strawberry on his spoon, poised halfway to his mouth. 'Excuse me?' he questioned, looking up at Sarah, a tiny smile playing around his mouth.

She looked a little embarrassed. 'I'm sorry,' she said. 'That must have sounded dreadfully rude.'

'Not at all.' Gavin popped the strawberry into his mouth.

'It's just that I wondered if you were in human resources?'

Damon topped up their wine glasses. 'Now there's a title that has many connotations,' he said, his voice very slightly slurred. 'Why the hell can't they still call it personnel? Then we'd all know what we're talking about.'

After the murmur of laughter, Gavin asked, 'Why do you think I'm in human resources, Sarah?'

'Oh, I don't know. Because you were part of Ali's training course, I suppose.'

'Ah! Now I see.' Gavin reflected, then teased. 'So you put two and two together — and it added up to five.'

Sarah smiled. 'Does that mean you don't want to talk about it? Official secrets, and all that . . . ?'

Gavin's smile was equally full of warmth. 'Sorry, Sarah. I was only joking.' Carefully slicing another huge strawberry in two, he mysteriously said, 'Actually — I am an industrial espionage agent, and I was working under cover.'

Damon guffawed. 'As what?' he asked.

With a shy grin, as though not sure whether they would share his joke, Gavin said, 'As a Mafia godfather, Damon. What else?'

After the laughter faded, Ali changed the

subject. 'Did anyone see that programme on telly last night? About ghosts.'

Sarah shook her head. 'I daren't watch anything like that just before I go to bed,' she said, then turned to her husband. 'What did you think of it?' she asked.

'Not a lot. All they had to show for staying up all night in a so-called haunted house was a few weird noises on the tape that could have been caused by anything.'

'Such as?' Sarah asked.

'The wind. Or a faulty tape. It was the same with the photograph. They tried to convince us that the blur was a ghost. Looked more like a finger over the lens to me.'

Shaking her head, Ali murmured, 'Well, that poor couple who live there looked scared out of their wits. It was enough to make them put the house up for sale.'

'Come on, Ali. Anyone who believes in all that rubbish must be a bit pathetic, surely?'

Thoughtfully, Gavin entered the conversation. 'I seem to remember reading something recently about ghosts at a theatre in Winchester. Apparently, Michael Bentine once saw a woman in Victorian costume standing beside him when he was performing there.'

Sarah nodded. 'I read that. He was always interested in spiritualism, wasn't he?'

Damon spread out his hands. 'Then that explains it. If you believe in something, you'll find the evidence somehow.'

'But what about the dancer who fainted on stage during the First World War?'

'What about her?'

'Well, her boyfriend had just been killed, and she saw him standing by the spotlight — the one he used to operate before he went away.'

Damon shrugged. 'She was probably thinking about him and imagined it.' He looked around the table. 'I'll bet ten quid none of you has ever seen a ghost.'

Beth held her breath, but they were still looking at each other, in a slightly giggly manner, like teenagers trying a Ouija board for the first time. Tentatively, she said, 'I had a strange experience, not long ago.'

Sarah's mouth dropped open. 'Did you see a ghost?' she asked.

'I thought I heard one.'

Suddenly, the atmosphere changed. Quietly, Ali asked, 'In the nursery, Beth?'

'No. It was at Calshot Castle.'

Damon responded in a low voice. 'Did it moan like this — ooooh? Or just rattle its chains?'

Ali flashed him an angry look. 'Oh, do shut up, Damon,' she muttered, then turned back to Beth. 'Was that why you fell down the steps? Because the sound frightened you?'

'Yes. I heard a voice, calling to me. But there was no one there.'

'What kind of voice?' Ali persisted.

'A young woman's voice. With a country accent. It was as though she was trying to tell me something.'

'Such as?'

'I didn't stop to find out. I just ran from the room. That was when I tripped.'

Gavin leaned towards Beth, his expression serious. 'Did it just happen on one occasion?' he asked.

'No, twice. I expect it was just my imagination.'

Damon laughed. 'Or too much vino with your lunch. Which reminds me . . . ' He held up the empty wine bottle. 'Shall I get another one?'

'Please do.'

There was a moment's awkward silence before Ali said, 'You didn't say anything about it at the time.'

'No. It was when . . . you know . . . I felt you would think I was going out of my head.' Her laugh was short. 'To be honest, *I* thought I was going out of my head.'

Sarah looked sympathetic. 'You should have told us,' she said. 'We would have understood.'

'I know. I wouldn't have mentioned it now, but talking about ghosts and things reminded me, and I was curious as to whether anyone else had ever — had ever had a similar experience.'

Again they looked at each other, but all shook their heads. Then Gavin said, 'But I don't think we can ever say things aren't so, just because we haven't experienced them.' He smiled at Beth. 'I expect it has put you off visiting the castle, though.'

Beth smiled back. 'Actually, I have been back — just to see if anything happened again.'

'And did it?'

'No. Nothing at all. So it must have been either imagination, or my black mood earlier.'

Gavin nodded. 'Ali told me about your little girl. I'm truly sorry.'

'Thank you.' Feeling strangely comforted by his simple words, Beth stood up. 'I'll make the coffee. Shall we stay out here, or do you want to come inside?'

They opted to stay outside a little longer. Later, as she watched her friends over her coffee cup, she realised she hadn't felt so relaxed and comfortable for months. The candlelight reached into the darkening shadows of the garden, flickering warmly on their faces, and seeming to enhance the perfume of the roses and honeysuckle that she had been training to climb over the pergola above their heads.

Having made two trips to the bathroom, Sarah looked rather drawn, but she had declined Beth's offer to lie down, saying she'd rather be out in the fresh air, thanks, but they wouldn't stay too late. She found it difficult to keep awake with this child. Fortunately, Damon was very understanding — and helpful — and Lorraine and Mrs Hosey, who came in two mornings a week, insisted that she rest in bed as much as possible. Sarah was grateful that Beth and Jane had taken over the routine running of the business and was sure that once this wretched sickness eased, she would be back in harness again, at least until the baby was due. Looking at her friend's swollen ankles and shadowed eyes, Beth wasn't so sure, and hoped that the scan next Tuesday would not reveal anything amiss.

Damon was recounting a tale about going to a wrong address, taking a washing machine to pieces and finding nothing wrong with it before discovering he should be in the house next door. The story was highly embellished with irate husbands and neighbours, but told with great panache, to the delight of all, even Ali. Almost as tipsy as Damon, she laughed with such gusto that she was in danger of tipping backwards on her chair, and would have done if it hadn't been for Gavin's protective arm. Bryn had been furious once when Beth had been only slightly merry at a party, whisking her off and complaining all the way home that she had probably ruined his hopes of any sex that night. Remembering the incident, Beth realised that Bryn had always referred to their making love as sex, an expression she found lacking in tenderness, like his own love-making. He was quite good at arousing her but, once his own needs had been satisfied, that was it. When he complained about her silly mood after the party, Beth had made matters worse by giggling and reminding him that he had once had a severe case of 'brewer's droop' after an anniversary dinner. But he continued to sulk for days, so she made sure after that to restrict her alcohol intake to one glass of wine with a meal. Gavin, however, didn't seem at all bothered by Ali's behaviour, just winked at Beth and moved a candle to safety, away from Ali's flapping, inebriated hand.

For the first time, Beth felt as though she was living a perfectly normal life, not being hampered by what was expected of her, just enjoying herself with a group of friends.

As they kissed her cheek before they drove

away, Beth was grateful that so many ghosts had been put to bed that night. Not just Eliza, but Bryn. Perhaps she would look at the divorce papers tomorrow. She didn't feel the need for another relationship, but neither did she feel lonely as she waved a final farewell to the retreating rear lights and closed the front door.

She had friends — very good friends — and that was enough.

8

The sounds of Sunday drifted into Beth's barely conscious mind, distant bells urging one to hurry. Those not scurrying along the church path could turn over and sleep on, but not Beth. Reluctant to leave her warm bed, she lay there, savouring each precious moment, waiting for the ping of her digital alarm, wondering whether to have a leisurely bath, or a shower, which would give her more time to browse through the paper over her toast and coffee. Gradually, she became aware of another sound, drumming against her window-panes, and with low heart imagined her prospective clients clutching the glossy brochure with an artist's view of very des-res 'Seascape Homes' set in a field of dreams, while staring at a sea of mud. She would have her work cut out to convince them that the quagmire would eventually be transformed into well-drained, tarmac roads and landscaped gardens, just like the pictures. Sighing, she turned her head to check the time. An electronic eye blinked back, smugly informing her that she didn't have time for a cup of coffee, let alone — oh, hell! She must have switched off the alarm an hour ago. Sitting up sharply, too sharply, a grandmother of a hangover began to thunder inside her head, and Beth knew without doubt that today was going to be a struggle.

Profusely apologising to the tight-lipped couple waiting in their car outside the showhouse, Beth handed them her umbrella and led the way across duckboards already sinking into puddles, forcing a bright smile into her voice as she described the benefits of the 'Sea Anchor' houses, and assured them that flooding would not be a problem on the finished site. She hoped they didn't notice her fingers crossed behind her back.

By the time the third potential buyers had handed back the soggy umbrella, Beth had given up any hope of remaining dry and clean, dashing back into the showhouse to quickly towel dry her hair before the next appointment and wringing out the bottoms of her muddy jeans. Perhaps it was just as well she hadn't had time to press her suit and blouse. Making a mental note to bring a change of clothing, hairdryer and wellington boots, Beth went in search of an aspirin to soothe her still pounding head, muttering to herself as she opened empty bathroom and kitchen cupboards. There must be a first-aid box somewhere.

Her next appointment was late. Good. Might be time for a cup of coffee. And while the kettle was boiling she could renew her hunt for anything that would ease the throbbing in her head. Nothing in the desk drawers. Perhaps her handbag?

She tipped the contents out on to the desk. Ah, yes. Amongst the keys, pens, stamps, airmail letter from her father and polo-mint, together with accumulated fluff, was a soluble aspirin pack. Very flat — and very empty. 'Shit!'

'Oh, dear. We are in a mood, aren't we?'

Beth peered out from under the towel at the site foreman, grinning down at her from the other side of the desk.

'What's up, Beth?' he went on. 'Didn't you get laid last night?'

'For goodness sake, Dave. Don't you ever think of anything else?'

'Not if I can help it.' He leaned a little closer. 'You look bloody awful. Hangover?'

'If you must know — yes. And I'm out of aspirin.'

'I've probably got some back in the van. Do you want me to drop them in?'

Her anger evaporated. 'Oh, yes, please. It's one of those 'never again' heads.'

'Tell me about it. It'll cost you, of course.'

Beth reached for her purse, but Dave laughed.

'Not money. I'll settle for a kiss. Unless you'd rather have a quickie in the back of the van.'

'In your dreams, Dave.' Now it was Beth's turn to laugh, even though it hurt. 'What did you want to see me about, anyway?'

'Only to give you the progress update and new schedules.' Still grinning, the foreman dropped a pile of damp papers on her desk. 'Won't get any outside work done today, of course, but we should be able to catch up on some of the inside painting.'

Frowning, Beth scanned the sheets. 'What about the plasterers? Shouldn't they be working on the 'Seahorse' terrace?'

'Greg's phoned in sick.'

'Again?'

'Afraid so.' The foreman chewed on a fingernail.

'And Trevor?'

'He'll try and get in later. Stag night or something last night, I reckon.'

Beth knew why he couldn't look her in the eyes. She had seen the plasterers working on an extension to a large private house near Beaulieu a week or so ago, when Greg was supposed to be in bed with summer 'flu, and Trevor out of action with a football injury. No doubt Dave was well aware that they were moonlighting, and Beth guessed the reason.

Greg's eldest son wanted to go to university, and Trevor was getting married next month. By rights, she should report them to Sarah, but they worked well when they were on site, and there really wouldn't be much satisfaction in getting them sacked. However, it was her responsibility to keep an eye on the deadlines.

Quietly, she asked, 'What's the completion date now, then? The realistic one, I mean. Sarah will want to know.'

'They'll all be ready on the 26th.'

'You're sure? Only the Macmillans were not best pleased when they had to cancel their removal people last week. Neither was Sarah.' And neither was I, she thought. Mr Grainger telephoned every day to ask when they could move in to 'The Cherries'. 'You know what will happen if there's another delay.'

He nodded. 'I'll have a word with the lads.'

'Good.' Beth switched on the desk lamp and ran her finger down the page of her desk diary. 'I do wish people would keep their appointments,' she murmured. 'You'd think at least they'd have the decency to phone if they're held up. Most of them have mobiles these days.'

'There's a car outside, but no driver. Maybe they're wandering around on their own.'

'What! They are supposed to come here first.' Irritably, she sighed. 'He won't be able to get in. I've got the keys. What a prat!'

A slight movement from the corner of the room caught their attention. The combination of overcast skies and a huge conifer outside the window made it a dark corner, but now she could see a man standing there. 'Who . . . ?' she began, then stopped as he stepped forward.

'I'm the prat,' he said, his voice completely devoid of humour. 'Waiting for the keys.'

The silence was almost unbearable, until Dave murmured, 'I'll get those tablets for you, Beth,' nodded in the direction of the man, and beat a hasty retreat. She still couldn't think of the right words to say, and her apologies sounded to her ears like the blabberings of an idiot.

'Oh, dear. I'm so sorry. What can I say? It's just that — I didn't see you, Mr — ' She glanced down at her diary, 'Mr Masterson.'

'Doctor Masterson.'

'Of course. Can't read my own writing. Sorry.'

'And I am a scientist, not a GP. So please don't tell me about your ailments.'

Beth forced a polite smile as she murmured, 'Thank you for explaining.'

The man had his back to the window, and

she couldn't see his features, but she felt an aura of displeasure as he held out his hand.

Thinking he wished to shake hands, Beth held out her own hand. But he didn't move any closer to the desk, just said, in a weary voice, 'The keys, please?'

'Oh, I see. Sorry.' She knew she had to stop these futile apologies. 'That's all right, I'll take you down there.'

'No need. I can walk, if you will tell me how to find Admiral's Way.' As Beth hesitated, he added, 'Does that give you a problem?'

Beth felt her cheeks burning. 'Not at all.' She pointed at the site plan laid open on her desk. 'There — right by the shore. But you'd better let me accompany you. It's quite muddy at the moment.'

'I assume there are duckboards?'

She nodded.

'Then it shouldn't be a problem.' His glance took in the wet towel draped around her neck, and the rivulets of water running into her eyes. 'You will be of more use to the next — client — if you finish mopping yourself up and do something about your headache. Make yourself another cup of coffee. That one must be cold.'

He was gone before she could warn him that the duckboards were slippery. Serve him right if the patronising bastard did fall over, she thought, rubbing furiously at her hair.

Ten minutes later, her hair was still wet, her head still aching and the second cup of coffee had grown cold after a run of telephone enquiries. The only thing that lifted her jaded spirits was the sight of Dr Masterson standing in the doorway. It was apparent that the slippery duckboards *had* proved to be a problem after all.

'Oh, dear,' she said, desperately stifling an urge to giggle. 'Would you like to use the cloakroom? The water is hot.'

At first she thought he was going to refuse, but the filth on his hands obviously had to be removed. With a curt, 'Thank you,' he followed her pointing finger and turned into the doorway opposite her office, giving Beth a satisfying view of his mud-soaked posterior.

When he returned, he had removed most of the mud from his trousers, but they were still looking uncomfortably wet. His stance was peculiar, to say the least.

Reaching into a desk drawer, she removed her sandwich lunch and handed him the empty supermarket bag. 'You might need this on the seat of the car,' she said, still struggling to control her twitching lips.

It obviously pained him to thank her, and for a moment he stood frowning, then asked,

'Do all the houses in Admiral's Way have only four bedrooms?'

'No. The two 'Sea Lord' houses at the end have five. Internal walls are completed on the ground floor, but not the first floor.' She couldn't resist pointing out, 'They are marked on your brochure.'

'Unfortunately, the incompetent receptionist at the hotel forgot to give me my mail until this morning, just as I was leaving. And if you dig deeply into the mud by the dangerously slippery duckboard where I fell, you might be able to retrieve it.'

Beth handed him another brochure. 'All the details are in there, Dr Masterson, and if you wish to make another appointment for your family to view, my telephone number is on the back.'

'Why should you assume I have a family?'

Because his head was lowered, flipping through the pages of the brochure, it was difficult to see his expression, but he seemed to have recovered his composure, and his hostility.

'Five-bedroom houses are usually only of interest to families,' she answered, equally abruptly.

For a moment, he studied the Admiral's Way details without speaking, then said, 'Actually, I think I would prefer to speak to

Mrs Martin. Will you make an appointment for me to see her tomorrow morning?'

Resisting the urge to throw the heavy desk diary at him, Beth shook her head. 'I am afraid that Mrs Martin is not making morning appointments at the moment.'

Dr Masterson raised his eyebrows.

'She is pregnant.'

He sighed heavily. 'Then will you please make an appointment for me to see her deputy. I assume she has one.'

'I am her deputy.' Beth deliberately kept her gaze on the diary. She didn't want him to see the anger in her eyes.

'Really? Well . . . I'll telephone you at nine-thirty.'

'Ten o'clock is the earliest I can speak to you, I'm afraid.' Beth scribbled the time and date on one of her business cards and pushed it across the desk.

'For goodness sake! Can't you come in early for once?'

'Actually, I shall be here at eight-thirty, Dr Masterson. But I have appointments until ten o'clock.' She wrote his name on the page, added 'TEL' in capitals, then closed the book. 'Good morning.'

It wasn't until later, when she snatched a quick sandwich break, that Beth was able to look up the details of the wretched man.

Sarah had spoken to him originally, but there was not much to go on. Just a temporary address at one of the better hotels near Southampton. Beth made a note of all the relevant information she might need when he telephoned. With luck, he wouldn't be interested in Admiral's Way, and she needn't see him again. Still, Sarah was a little concerned about selling those houses, the most expensive on the development, so it would be quite a *coup* if she could pull it off. The bonus would be welcome, too.

★   ★   ★

The rain had stopped, but dark clouds threatened more of the same, so Beth took another umbrella along to the site the following morning. At least she would be able to keep her new suit dry. The umbrella had belonged to Bryn, but he hadn't noticed it in the utility room when he collected his belongings.

The young family with the nine-thirty appointment were taking a second look at the three-bedroom semis. They had been living with parents and this was their first house purchase, so they were very unsure of the procedure. When she brought them back to the showhouse, she noticed the red light winking on her answering machine. Obviously, Dr Masterson had already telephoned. Well, he would have to wait. The Clarkes were bombarding her with questions, and the children needed to be kept amused by emptying the toybox she had provided in the hall.

After twenty minutes of carefully answering their questions, Beth was able to write Mr and Mrs Clarke's name on the site plan and make an appointment for them to see Sarah to discuss the mortgage options before sending them on their way with a handful of brochures and sweets for the children. She was crouched on her haunches, searching for a missing teddy bear, when it was thrust into her hand.

'Is this what you are looking for?'

Startled, Beth nearly toppled backwards. 'Thank you.' She took the toy from Dr Masterson, who had mysteriously appeared from the same dark corner as yesterday. Did he just lurk there, waiting to catch her unawares, she wondered? She glanced at the telephone.

'I thought . . . '

'Yes, we did have a telephone appointment,' he interrupted, 'but I changed my mind. Needed to have a better look at the houses. My attempts yesterday were rather rudely interrupted.'

Was that a little smile, Beth wondered, or indigestion? As with new-born babies, Dr Masterson's expression was difficult to fathom. This time she was able to look at him more closely. No rain running into her eyes.

He was taller than she remembered. Even wearing her high heels, she had to look up into his face. Not as tall as Gavin, though, probably just under six feet, and his hair was dark, slightly tinged with grey. Couldn't tell the colour of his eyes in this light. Nothing particularly outstanding about his features. If he didn't scowl so much, he might be considered quite good-looking.

Suddenly, she realised that he was staring back at her, as though waiting for her to speak. Just in time, she stopped herself from saying, 'Sorry,' and picked up a small bunch of keys from her desk. 'Do you wish to look at the 'Sea Captain' houses again?' she asked.

'Yes.' He cleared his throat. 'Would you accompany me this time, Mrs Lewis?' he asked. 'There are certain specific questions I wish to ask, and I think they can be explained more easily on site.'

'Of course, but . . . ' Beth hesitated. 'I only allow fifteen minutes for a telephone appointment, so I have another client coming at ten-fifteen.' Her hand moved towards the telephone. 'And I really should play this call back, in case it is urgent.'

'Actually, it is a cancellation of your ten-fifteen appointment. Came through while I was waiting. It appears that Ms Edwards and Mr Havelock have found another property.' He slightly stressed the 'Ms' as though he found it distasteful.

'Oh. Right. That gives us more time, then.' Beth slipped the keys into her pocket, put the Ansafone back on and picked up her bag.

As she walked around the desk, his eyes noted her open-toed, sling-back sandals.

'Surely you're not going out on site in those?' he commented.

'Of course not.' Feeling rather smug, she kicked off her sandals in the hall and pulled on the wellingtons, already well coated with mud. 'Do you want to come in my car? Or walk?' She locked the front door, turned the 'Open' sign round to read 'Back soon', and waited.

He elected to go by car as it would be quicker. Beth was pleased. It meant fewer slippery duckboards to negotiate. She parked outside the first house in Admiral's Way.

'All the 'Sea Captain' houses are of a similar size and layout,' she began.

'I can see that from the brochure.'

With a steely smile she ploughed on, 'And

this one has a larger garden, which catches the sun for most of the day, and has a fine view of the . . . '

He held up his hand. 'Let me make it quite clear, Mrs Lewis, that I will not be pressured into making a purchase by any kind of sales talk. As you say, those details are in the brochure. I shall only require your opinion on other, more specific details.'

Gritting her teeth, she vowed that she would not say another word, except to answer his questions.

Three of the four-bedroom houses were inspected in silence, punctuated only by Dr Masterson's irritating habit of tapping his pen against the brochure as he checked room sizes. Then they walked in and out of the shell of the two larger houses, not once, but twice. After that the questions began.

'I see that only the master bedroom is en-suite, but I am looking for a house with all the bedrooms en-suite.'

Beth was tempted to ask him why he didn't buy a hotel. Instead, she studied the house plans. 'Bedrooms two and three are larger than average, so it should be possible. I am not so sure about the other two, although . . . ' She hesitated and checked the measurements again.

'Although . . . ?' he prompted.

'The end house has a slightly larger landing, because of the different angle. It is possible that a small en-suite with a shower cubicle could connect the two rooms.'

His smile was wry. 'You obviously do not have teenage daughters. Access rights would be a nightmare.'

So he had teenage daughters. Bad-tempered like their father from the sound of them. Then Beth had another thought.

'The bathroom is large and would not be essential if each bedroom had its own facilities. I'm not sure if the developers would agree, but it would solve your problem, and there is a cloakroom on the ground floor.'

Thoughtfully, he looked again at the first-floor plan in the brochure, then turned back a page. 'If the downstairs cloakroom could be enlarged to include a bath or shower cubicle, I might be interested in that option,' he said.

For goodness sake, couldn't they bath or shower upstairs, Beth thought, as she drew a rough plan on her notepad. 'There is room for it to be extended alongside the kitchen wall over there,' she replied, 'although a decision would have to be made fairly quickly, while the builders are still working on this level.'

'I have my own deadline to meet, which is

sooner rather than later.' He glanced back at the 'Sea Captain' houses. 'When will they be ready?' he asked.

'Two or three weeks. But, of course, it is too late for any major alterations.'

Frowning, he looked around at the piles of bricks and window-frames, waiting to be inserted into the larger houses, which did not even have a staircase. 'And I suppose you will tell me that it is impossible to give a completion date for this one, given the unpredictability of an English summer, not to mention the unpredictability of English workmen.'

'The weather I can do little about, but I am quite capable of reminding the builders of their penalty clause when necessary.' She consulted her schedule. 'The two 'Sea Lord' houses are estimated for completion by the end of next month. However . . . ' Now it was her turn to tap her pen. 'The extra work will mean extra time for the plumbers and electricians as well as the builders.' She looked up. 'All I can promise is that I will keep the work moving as fast as possible.'

For a moment he turned to stare straight into her face. Then he nodded. 'Provided your builders will agree to the adaptations, at an acceptable price, I will arrange for my mother to view the site within a few days.'

'Your mother?' Despite herself, Beth could not refrain from asking, 'And your wife . . . ?'

'My wife is in America. She will rejoin me when I have found a suitable property, but has told me exactly what she requires.' He put the brochure back into his pocket. 'However, my mother will be living with us, so she will obviously want to be consulted.'

'Obviously.' Beth repressed a shudder as she imagined three generations of arrogant Mastersons. She sketched her impression of the first floor, with the new measurements. 'Of course, so many adaptations will hike up the price considerably,' she commented.

'Of course,' he snapped, taking the drawing. 'I'm not a complete idiot, Mrs Lewis. How quickly can you let me have the new quotations?'

Returning stare for stare, Beth said, 'I can fax them through to the hotel on Wednesday, Dr Masterson. Is that quick enough for you?'

He nodded.

'Good.' She took her car keys from her bag. 'Now, unless there are any other alterations you haven't yet mentioned, I would like to get back to my office.'

'Actually, there is something else.' He walked towards the back of the plot. 'I would like a conservatory somewhere along here, where Mrs Masterson can enjoy the view. Do you have brochures?'

'Mrs Martin has contact with an excellent local firm. You would have to deal directly with them, but I can arrange for their brochure to be sent to you.'

'Thank you.' At the door of the car, he hesitated, looking away from Beth, across the site. 'And will you please add ramps to the modifications. One front, one back. For wheelchair access.'

Beth scribbled furiously on her notepad. Why on earth didn't he buy a piece of land and have an architect design a house to his specific requirements, she wondered. It would have been much easier, and cash didn't seem to be a problem.

A little smile touched her lips as she thought about how pleased Sarah would be if Beth could sell the biggest house on the site, with all those expensive modifications. And her own bonus would be . . .

Another thought brought her down to earth, as she drove the silent Dr Masterson back to his car. If he bought the house, they would be neighbours. Not close neighbours, thankfully. Her own humble little abode was on the other side of the development. But the thought of living anywhere near the surly Dr Masterson, his bossy American wife, two squabbling teenagers and grumpy granny in a wheelchair, was enough to wipe the smile from anyone's face.

9

For some moments, Beth sat looking at the photograph, gently stroking the print with her thumb. It had been taken by a nurse, moments after Katie had been born, and it was the only photograph she had of her child. Within days it had become apparent that something was very wrong, although at first view, she appeared perfectly normal. Bryn had suspected, and made excuses not to hold the baby, but said nothing to Beth. It wasn't until she spoke to his mother that she had discovered just what he feared. Even then, the old woman had tried to blame the problem on Beth's gypsy blood, but once Bryn had let slip the truth about his aunt, Beth was able to investigate the disease, and realised it had skipped a generation. Poor little Katie.

Gently, she closed the baby album, with so few precious memories, and wrapped it in tissue paper before placing it in the box with her other personal effects. Tomorrow she would leave her dream house in the eager hands of the Grainger family. She hoped they would have better fortune.

Stretching her aching back, she lifted the

clock from the wall. That had been a wedding present from a friend in her office, so Bryn had allowed her to keep it. It was a good clock, but she must check the battery. That couldn't possibly be the time. Almost two-thirty? Her wrist watch confirmed. God! No wonder she was tired. But there was still the kitchen stuff to pack, and she couldn't go to bed until she had scrubbed the grubbiness out of her skin and washed the dust from her hair.

An hour later, she lay back in the bath and closed her eyes, her thoughts meandering over the events of the past few days.

After extended negotiations between herself, Sarah and the developers, she had faxed the final figures through to Dr Masterson's hotel late on Wednesday evening. Her own removal preparations had been put on hold. With contracts being exchanged on two other properties, and completion on another, not to mention new enquiries, Beth and Jane were working flat out. Sarah had originally agreed that Beth should have the rest of the week off, but now she had complications of her own. The scan had revealed not one baby, but two. Sarah's excitement was clouded with fear. The amnio test was still to come. If it revealed that one of the babies was handicapped, Sarah and Damon would have

116

to decide whether to risk an abortion. It could harm the other foetus but, on the other hand . . .

Beth knew only too well the anguish they were facing, but there was little she could do to help, except to take on even more responsibility for the business. So she suggested that she have just one day off, leaving Sarah to man the showhouse. As it happened, that was the day Dr Masterson chose to bring his mother to view the site, but he had decided he didn't need accompanying, they would drive down, take a look, then go away to make their decision. Beth couldn't really care less whether he bought the house or not, despite the dangling carrot of the bonus. She was only too thankful that she didn't have to put up with his company.

★ ★ ★

Unsurprisingly, dark clouds full of rain scowled at Beth as she drew back the bedroom curtains for the last time, and strong winds whipped through the branches of the young cherry trees that had given the house its name. 'Flaming June!' she muttered as she shivered into her jeans and sweatshirt. This end wouldn't be so bad. At least there was a wide drive to walk on, but the new house still had duckboards where the short drive would be laid at a later date. Better sweeten the removal men with a cup of tea before she packed the last of the groceries.

'Thanks, love. Three sugars, please.' The big guy with tattoos from wrists to elbows grinned appreciatively at Beth as he man-handled her mattress down the staircase.

'Have you got any custard creams?' The owner of the muffled voice was out of sight behind the unwieldy mattress.

'Oh, Lord.' Beth knew the cupboard was almost bare but had intended to shop after she had moved in. 'Sorry. I'm out of sugar and biscuits. Give me half an hour and I'll pop down to the shops. I need some other things, anyway.'

Might as well get something for my supper while I'm about it, Beth thought, throwing a frozen chicken tikka into the trolley on top of the sliced loaf and packet of ham she had earmarked for lunch. The flower display near the exit splashed colour into a dull day. On impulse, she bought two bunches of scarlet carnations, a disposable vase — and two bottles of wine.

After the removal men had been refreshed with sweet tea, biscuits and currant buns, Beth put one bunch of flowers into the little vase, and scribbled a note for the Graingers, wishing them luck in their new home. She hoped they remembered where they had packed their bottle opener.

Barely time to dash through the house with the vacuum cleaner and duster before the last dining chair was taken out, and the 'Sold' sign thrown into the back of the van. Very little time to say goodbye to the memories in each room, but perhaps that was just as well. Nobody out in their gardens to wish her well. Just a twitch of curtains as the old lady who lived with her daughter next door fluttered a frail hand. Returning her wave, Beth put the car into reverse gear, then drove quickly away, in the wake of the furniture van. She didn't look back.

Sarah looked pale and drawn as she discussed a purchase on the telephone. A couple sat on the other side of the desk, carefully reading the contract in front of them. Putting her hand over the mouthpiece, Sarah whispered, 'Busy day. See you later.'

Nodding, Beth put the spare keys to 'The Cherries' on the desk, and tucked the 'Sold' sign out of sight in the corner, half expecting to find Dr Masterson hiding there, waiting to catch her out. Anxious to be far away from the possibility of bumping into him, she almost ran back to her car.

The tiny patch of earth in front of her new

house was well and truly sodden, and the duckboards gave scant protection. As Beth opened the front door, the smell of brand new carpeting wafted down the staircase. She had ordered a couple of rugs for the wood block flooring downstairs, and arranged for the fitters to come in first thing and lay a plain beige carpet in the two bedrooms, bathroom, landing — and stairs. But the stairs were still uncarpeted, and not a sound of hammer on tack disturbed the silence.

'Hallo. Anyone there?' Beth called as she climbed the stairs. The landing was uncarpeted. So was the bathroom and one bedroom. The other bedroom, her bedroom, was full of rolls of carpet.

'Bloody hell!' The tattooed removal man had followed Beth upstairs. 'That's a bummer if you like.'

Beth shook her head in disbelief. 'They promised faithfully they would be finished and out before we arrived.'

'Well, they're certainly out, but it doesn't look as though they've started, let alone finished.'

'But where are they? It's hardly a day for having a tea break on the beach.'

'Probably down at the pub.'

'At this time of day?'

'Some of them open at ten.' He pulled

open the roll of carpet nearest the door. 'Did you fancy a change?'

'Sorry?' Beth had wandered over to the window for better light, hoping she had the carpet firm's telephone number in her bag, and not in the box on the van.

'It's a bit different to the one you left behind at the other house. Nice and bright, though.'

How could beige be bright? As she turned, Beth froze. The carpet wasn't beige. It was orange. Not even a subtle shade of rust, or terracotta, but bright, bright orange. Her voice rose an octave. 'That's not my carpet!' she cried.

The man nodded, sagely. 'Didn't think it was quite your taste. Better check the other rolls.'

They were all orange, with a hideous geometric design in black. Beth riffled through her handbag, searching for the receipt. 'Look!' She waved it under the man's nose. 'It says quite clearly, plain beige. I'll kill them when they do turn up.'

'Never mind, love. Look on the bright side.'

'What bright side?' She glared at him.

He grinned. 'At least they didn't put it down.' He peered over her shoulder at the receipt. 'What's that say there?' He pointed to the handwriting at the bottom.

'It's only the address.'

'Is it the right one?'

'Yes. Plot three, Mariner's Close.' She looked closer. 'Oh. I think I see what you are getting at.'

'Well, that three looks a bit like an eight to me.'

'And if their copy was wet, the ink might run and . . . ' Thoughtfully, she looked out of the window. 'There's another removal van, along the road. I think that's plot eight.' She zipped up her anorak. 'I'll run along there and find out what's going on. Can you start on the downstairs, please? The boxes are marked.'

The shouting and yelling that exploded from the house on plot eight was ominous. As soon as Beth saw the smaller van in front of the huge removal van, she guessed what had happened. The logo, 'Fitted to Perfection', added insult to injury.

After knocking twice on the open front door, Beth ventured into the hall. A trio of brawny males sat on a settee in the front room, arms folded. They looked at Beth without interest, and silently pointed upwards. They had seen it all before.

She made her way upstairs, calling as loudly as she could, but nobody answered. The four people screeching at the top of their voices had reached mega decibels. Not only were they noisy, they were standing on a beige carpet. *Her* beige carpet. When they noticed her, the silence was as sudden as a turned-off volume control.

The woman glared belligerently. 'Who the hell are you?' she asked.

Her husband recognised Beth. 'It's the woman from the showhouse,' he said.

'Well, if you've come to see if we're settled in comfortably, we aren't!' The woman gestured wildly towards the other two men. 'Thanks to those two bloody morons, the removal blokes can't bring our stuff upstairs. You'll never guess what they've done.'

Beth remembered the woman as being a difficult client, and frantically sought in her memory bank for a name. Thankfully, she found one. 'Actually, I know what has happened, Mrs Porter,' she said. 'They've delivered the wrong carpet.'

'Too right they have.' Mrs Porter stopped, and stared at Beth. 'How do you know?' she asked.

'Because this carpet is the one I ordered. And I suspect I have several rolls of your orange carpet in my house.' She showed the receipt to the fitters. 'At plot number three.'

The fitters studied her receipt, compared it with the one Mrs Porter held, and stared at each other. Neither said a word, but Mrs Porter still had plenty to say.

'Well?' she asked. 'What are you going to do about it?'

The older of the two frowned and fidgeted before he answered. 'We've already fitted it in two of the bedrooms,' he muttered, 'but there's not enough for the third one. I think we've got another roll back at the depot, if you'd settle for that, then this lady could keep yours.'

'No way!' Mrs Porter spluttered. 'We paid for Axminster. I don't want this cheap rubbish.' She glanced at Beth. 'No offence intended.'

'None taken,' Beth murmured, feeling very offended. 'In any case, I wouldn't want to swap. The orange one is not to my taste.' She flashed a brief smile. 'No offence intended.'

The fitter shrugged his shoulders. He seemed to have run out of ideas.

'I can understand why you might have confused the two plot numbers,' Beth said, 'but I don't understand why you left the orange carpet in my house before coming down here.'

'Ah, well. It was raining, like, so we stopped at your house first and had our tea break. Then Robbie here saw on the worksheet that these people were moving in an hour before you. So we thought we'd better get down here first, in case they got here a bit early, like.'

'God, give me strength,' Mr Porter muttered.

'I'm sorry, mate, but we thought we had plenty of time to do both. But we sort of run out before we'd finished here.'

'Sort of run out!' Mrs Porter was ready for another explosion. 'If you were any good at your job you would have realised you didn't have enough before you started. Call yourselves carpet fitters? You couldn't lay a doormat!'

Beth realised she would have to think of something, before war broke out again. 'Can you take this carpet up and relay it in my house?' she asked the fitter. 'My two bedrooms are slightly smaller, so there shouldn't be too much work involved.'

The man looked at his worksheet, then shook his head. 'Your bathroom is a different shape, and we've already cut this one to fit round the loo here.'

'That doesn't matter. First make sure there's another roll of beige, then you can do my bathroom tomorrow. The main priority is getting carpet down in the bedrooms as quickly as possible so that the removal men can unload. If Mr and Mrs Porter will agree to having the bathroom and stairs fixed tomorrow, I think that's the best solution?'

Slowly, the Porters nodded, but the fitter shook his head. 'Sorry, missus, but we're scheduled for Southampton tomorrow.'

Mr Porter leaned towards the man until they were almost nose to nose. 'Then you'll have to reschedule, won't you?' he demanded. 'Unless you want to finish up in court.'

The man looked suitably impressed, but made the mistake of looking at his watch.

'And if you're thinking about a lunch break,' Mr Porter warned, 'forget it. Neither of you stops — not even for a pee — until my bedroom carpet is down.' He looked at Beth. 'What time are you moving in?' he asked.

'Ten minutes ago. The removal men are there now.'

'Christ.' Mr Porter turned back to the men. 'What are you waiting for then? Move your arses.' He smiled sheepishly at Beth. 'Sorry about the language, love, but I've really lost my rag over this lot.'

Beth had hoped she might get her carpet down first, but decided it was best to humour the Porters. After she thanked her removal men for putting down sheets of newspaper to protect the floor, she suggested they take a lunch break while the carpet fitters worked on plot number eight. Eating a lonely ham

126

sandwich while the men sat in the van with their lunch boxes, listening to pop music, did little to lift her spirits. She couldn't even be bothered to look for her own radio, so began to unpack the boxes and find new homes for her spice jars and food containers. It didn't take long. This kitchen was minuscule compared to the one she had just left, and the cupboards were soon full.

As she filled the vase with water, Beth paused, stared at the flowers, tipped the water back into the sink, and made two fresh mugs of coffee for the men outside.

'I have to go out,' she told them. 'The carpet fitters are getting in their van now, but I won't be long.' Then she unlocked her car, put the flowers on the passenger seat and left the site.

The pretty little cemetery nestled at the edge of the New Forest, tucked away so shyly, many people did not know it existed. She had not visited Katie's resting place for some weeks, and the flowers she had left last time had died. After she had tidied the tiny grave, Beth crouched in silent prayer for some moments, hoping for a feeling of peace, but none came. All she could feel was a sense of loss. It was as though she had lost everything and everyone that mattered. Her child, her husband, her parents, her home.

Looking up at the heavy sky, she murmured, 'I suppose you've taken the phone off the hook,' and went back to her car.

She had intended to stop off to speak to Sarah, but Dr Masterson's car was parked outside the showhouse, so Beth drove straight past. Her bedroom furniture had been crowded into the larger room, and the carpet fitters were working in the smaller bedroom, their expressions morose.

'Where are my rugs?' Beth asked.

The older man glanced up. 'Rugs? What rugs?'

Beth showed him her copy of the order. 'Those rugs,' she said.

He compared her paperwork with his own. 'Nothing about no rugs on my worksheet,' he finally said, then turned back to the beige carpet.

Through gritted teeth, Beth ordered him to telephone the depot on his mobile and make sure the rugs were on the van tomorrow.

Downstairs, the tattooed man waited, invoice in hand.

'I've told those geeks upstairs they'll have to give you a hand carting the rest of the stuff into the spare room when they've finished. Sorry we can't hang on but we've got to start on an overnight job. Someone moving back to Liverpool. Don't ask me why.'

They had stayed long after the planned time, and cleared away all the rubbish and muddy newspapers. Beth felt they deserved a generous tip.

'Thanks very much.' The man glanced around. 'It'll look better once you've got the curtains up.'

Beth nodded. The curtains and carpets had all been part of the sale of 'The Cherries', and the new ones wouldn't be ready for a few days, so she would have to improvise for the time being. The naked windows left her feeling exposed and vulnerable.

After the van had rumbled away, she busied herself making up the bed and unpacking. Very reluctantly, the carpet fitters carried the surplus tea-chests and boxes into the second bedroom, glumly agreeing to return first thing in the morning to finish the job — and bring the missing rugs.

Beth wandered from room to room, aching with tiredness and longing to stop but knowing she had to do as much as possible today as she would be back on duty in the showhouse tomorrow morning. For a moment she stood by the window, looking out over the houses, only a few inhabited. Everything was too new to have any sense of character yet. Twilight would come early this evening. Already one or two lamps were being switched on in an attempt to dispel the gloom, but Beth was reluctant to plug in her own lamps until she had found something to cover the windows.

The bare floors and windows added to the feeling of loneliness, and Beth hoped that Sarah would soon lock up the office and come down, even though she wouldn't be able to share the bottle of wine that waited in the almost empty fridge-freezer. Not much point in waiting. Might as well take a short break before tackling the next task. Browse through the gardening book that was too large to fit on the bookshelf. A birthday present from Ali when Beth had such plans for 'The Cherries'. Hopefully there might be a design for a pocket handkerchief garden.

As she sank back into the armchair, her muscles threatened that they would never allow her to rise again. Perhaps it had been a mistake to stop before she had finished. But the wine was cool and heady, and Beth was too tired to resist the temptation to close her eyes for a moment.

'Beth.' The voice was soft.

'I'm in here, Sarah.' She must have left the front door ajar. Then she felt the chill. Not the cool air of an unseasonable June evening, but a damp, unpleasant chill.

'Beth.' The voice was still soft, but insistent.

It wasn't Sarah. Beth knew it wasn't Sarah. It sounded like . . . but it couldn't be . . . not here. Perhaps she was dreaming. Beth opened her eyes.

The room was hazy, just as the room at the castle had been. No one else in the room. Just the voice, calling, 'Beth. It's me. Eliza. You remembers me, don't you?'

'No.' Beth's mouth was dry, her voice little more than a whisper. 'It can't be happening again. This isn't the castle.'

'This was where I lived 'afore I was wed. They had to pull down our old home so they could build your grand new houses. I did try to warn you.'

10

'Warn me? What do you have to warn me about?' Beth still searched for the owner of the voice as she spoke.

'This house. You mustn't stay here, Beth.'

'Why not?'

'Because it's cursed. I means it.'

Beth tried to laugh, but only managed a strangulated sound. 'Don't be ridiculous,' she said. 'The house is brand-new. There's no way it can be cursed.'

'Aunt Bazill cursed all the land, as well as the dwellings. Mr Purkiss on the end didn't believe in gypsy lore, till he stuck that pitchfork in his foot. Lockjaw be a dreadful way to die.'

'Well, yes, but it doesn't mean it was because of anything your aunt did.' Beth couldn't believe she was arguing with a disembodied voice, but she had to ask, 'Why should she want to curse the land, anyway?'

'Because of the monkshood.'

'I still don't understand.'

'It grew in the garden, Beth.' The voice sighed. 'Granny Wells lived next door with her sister, Gatherell. Crazed, she were. In the blood, Aunt Bazill reckoned.'

'Did she live next door, too?'

'On the other side. Anyways, it were coming up to harvest supper, and Granny was making a broth. Sent her sister out in the garden to gather the vegetables. Silly old biddy dug up the monkshood roots as well, and chopped them up to go in the broth with the rest.'

'Oh, my God!' Beth remembered. 'That's aconitum, isn't it?'

'I don't know about that. Some folks calls them wolfsbane. Pretty flowers to look at, as long as you doesn't eat them.'

Beth was almost too afraid to ask, 'What happened?'

'Granny had been tasting it all along, so she were the first to go, poor old soul. Then the babies. Ma never got over losing Charity and William, and Aunt Bazill lost all her little'uns.'

'What about the other grown-ups?'

'We always fed the nippers first. They made such a fuss when they were hungry. So, by the time our turn comes round, the babies had started being sick. Terrible, it were.'

'So you didn't eat the broth yourself?'

'Only a couple of mouthfuls.' There was a pause, then the voice dropped to a tearful whisper. 'But it were still bad enough to make me lose the child I was carrying.'

After a moment, Beth asked, 'What happened to your great-aunt?'

'Oh, she sat down with the children, so she didn't last long. Just as well.'

'What a dreadful thing to happen.'

'And it didn't end there, neither. The curse made bad things happen for years.'

'Were you all gypsies?'

'Only on Ma's side. She were content enough, living in a proper house. But Aunt Bazill never settled. So she left Uncle Matthew and went back to the others. Forest gypsies they was. In the end, folks was too feared to live here, so the houses fell down.'

'And is that what you were trying to tell me?'

'I didn't know then that you were going to live here. There is something else I wants you to know. About the castle.'

Would it never end? Beth passed a hand wearily over her brow. 'Is that cursed, too?' she asked.

'No. I haven't the power. But it should be. You'll think the same when I tells you about my husband. Francis . . . '

The voice suddenly faded, and Beth became aware of a rattling sound, and a man's voice. It came from outside the front door.

'Beth! Are you there? Let me in.'

Beth flew across the room and flung open the door, almost knocking Damon over in her haste. The sound of the bottle smashing down on to the step and the sight of his flowers strewn amongst the broken glass and red wine was too much for Beth. She burst into tears.

'Please help me,' she cried. 'I don't know what . . . ' She knew she was gabbling, but couldn't help herself.

'Hey, hey. Easy, now.' As Beth's knees buckled, his arms tightened around her. 'Found another rat, have you? Let's get you back inside, then I'll take a look.'

All Beth could do was wail and shake her head, as Damon examined every corner of the room, then searched the tiny kitchen thoroughly.

'Nothing there, Beth. Whatever frightened you, it's gone.' He picked up her wine bottle. 'Haven't you got anything a bit stronger? A drop of brandy would do you good. Wouldn't do me any harm, either. You gave me quite a fright, you know.'

Somehow, Beth found her voice. 'That's all I have, I'm afraid. But do help yourself. I'm sorry I broke your bottle — I must clear up the glass before . . . '

'Stay there. I'll do it in a minute.' He

glanced around at the boxes still waiting to be unpacked. 'Glasses?'

She couldn't remember. 'Oh — I think there are some in the kitchen.'

He came back with a tumbler. 'This will do.' After he'd drunk half in one gulp, he refilled both their glasses, then sat beside Beth on the settee. 'Drink up, love. You need to get some colour back in your cheeks. And don't worry about the rats or mice or whatever. We were infested with them when we moved into the cottage, and I've still got some of the poison pellets left. Polishes them off in no time.'

'It wasn't rats.' Beth struggled to find words that would sound credible.

'What then?' Damon put his glass down on the small table. 'An intruder? Is that what frightened you? An intruder?'

Beth shook her head. 'It's difficult to explain,' she murmured.

'Take your time.' Damon held Beth's hand. 'Try breathing deeply, then tell me what happened — when you're ready.'

'Do you remember when I told you all about the voice I had heard at Calshot Castle?'

Damon stared at her. 'You're not telling me you've heard it again, are you?'

As Beth tried to explain what she had

experienced, she realised how pitiful it sounded. No wonder he looked at her in disbelief. When she had finished, Damon drained his glass, then turned towards her, still holding her hand.

'Tell me something, Beth,' he said eventually. 'How long did you sit in that chair before you heard the voice?'

'Not long, just a few moments, really. I intended to have a look at my gardening book. Why?'

'Bear with me.' He picked up the book from the coffee table, glanced at the open page, then raised his eyebrows. 'Look at this,' he said. The page featured aconitum, known as monkshood. 'All parts of the plant are poisonous,' he quoted.

'Oh,' was all she could manage.

Damon smiled. 'You've probably not had much sleep lately, have you?'

'No.'

'And I bet you haven't had a proper meal today.'

'I was going to have something later on.'

He picked up the almost empty wine bottle. 'Shall I tell you what I think?'

Sipping her wine, Beth nodded. She guessed what he was about to say.

'I think you were suffering from the effect of plonk on an empty stomach and an exhausted mind and body. It would be like — like taking a Mickey Finn.'

'So you think I fell asleep.'

'I'm sure of it. And you'd read enough to trigger off a weird dream.'

For a while she pondered the thought. It was possible, but . . . 'But all those names? Surely I couldn't have remembered so much detail. I never remember that much about dreams.'

'Neither do I as a rule. But sometimes I have one that is so vivid it stays in my mind for hours. You must have had that happen to you before?'

'Yes — but — never quite like this one.'

'By the time you've finished that bottle, you won't remember anything about it. Now, where's your dustpan and brush?'

'Under the sink.' Beth stood up. 'I'll do it.'

'OK. And what about some music to cheer us up? Do you have a CD player or something?'

'Just a cassette player. It's part of the radio. There's a box of cassettes on top of the sideboard.'

It pained Beth to throw such lovely flowers away, but there were splinters of glass among the foliage, so she carefully wrapped everything in layers of newspaper.

Damon looked up as she walked through

the house with the bulky package. 'I like this old Sinatra one. It's got some real smoochie numbers on it. Wonderful to dance to.' Smiling, he moved towards her.

'Careful! This is full of broken glass.'

'No problem. I can wait until you've dumped it.'

Beth realised that Damon was just a little drunk. Not enough to be a nuisance, but she'd had enough problems for one day, and she still felt slightly shaky from her experience. 'I need to wash that step, make sure there's no glass left lying around,' she called out as she placed the wreckage in a black plastic bag, then went on, 'Does Sarah know you're here?'

'I put my head round the door on the way in. She's tied up with someone at the moment but said she'll come down as soon as she's shut up shop.'

He was still rummaging through the cassettes when Beth carried the bucket of hot water and mop back through the living room. 'By the way,' she said. 'Thanks for the thought. I assume the flowers and wine were meant for me? Sorry I vandalised them.'

'Just a little house-warming something. I'll get some more later.' Damon had plugged in one of the lamps and hummed along with Sinatra while Beth washed the step. Then he tried again. 'Come on, love. Life's too short to clean steps. Let's dance.'

Beth side-stepped him as she took the bucket back into the kitchen. 'The only dancing I can do is to gallop around this house and finish unpacking.' She laughed to soften her words. 'I'm back on duty tomorrow — but you can do me a favour, if you like.'

Damon had followed her into the kitchen and went down on one knee in a dramatic pose. 'Ask away, my pretty lady.'

'If I can find a couple of blankets . . . '

'Now that sounds like an offer I can't possibly refuse.'

Beth really wasn't in the mood for this, but she didn't want to sound churlish. 'Good.' She smiled down at him. 'Would you please put them up at the windows for me? My curtains won't be ready till next week, and I feel a bit like a goldfish, especially with the lights on.'

'Does it matter? Most of the other houses are still empty.'

'I know. But one or two across the road are occupied. Look, there's someone having a gawp now.'

It was true. Across the road a woman had just parked her car and was peering, quite unashamedly, into Beth's window, squinting a little to see what was going on. Suddenly, to Beth's horror, Damon turned up the volume on the radio full blast, grabbed Beth, and swept her across the room in an exaggerated tango-style dance, spinning her around before turning to the window and bowing with theatrical flourish to the onlooker. The poor woman was so flustered, she dropped her keys.

Switching off the lamp and lowering the volume of the cassette, Beth shook her finger at Damon. 'That was outrageous,' she protested. 'I haven't even met the neighbours yet, and here you are . . . '

'Serves her right for being so nosy.'

Beth had to admit he had a point, but she didn't want an argument, so she went upstairs for the blanket and a curtain wire. Between them they managed to drape it over to cover the best part of the window, then back upstairs to give some degree of privacy to the bedroom with the other blanket.

'Thanks, Damon. Some jobs really need two people.'

'So that's why you've still got a double bed.' His voice and expression were full of innuendo. 'If you want any more odd jobs done in the bedroom, you only have to ask.'

'For goodness sake! You're as bad as Dave.'

'Dave?'

'Site foreman. Excuse me.' Beth tried to move past Damon to the door, but he blocked her way. She wasn't quite sure whether it was deliberate, or his slightly tipsy state that caused them to trip. Whatever, the end result was the two of them sprawled across the bed, Beth underneath, with Damon's heavy weight pinning her down.

'For God's sake, get off!' Beth cried, but Damon was laughing like a hyena, and didn't budge. Eventually, she managed to wriggle out from under his body, to find herself staring at Ali and Gavin, standing in the doorway.

Gavin looked nonplussed, but Ali's face was thunderous. 'Still at it, I see, Damon,' she said, then turned to Beth with a questioning eyebrow.

Beth smoothed down her skirt. 'Damon was helping me fix up the blanket at the window,' she said, 'and we — fell over.'

Ali's expression relaxed a little. 'I see,' she said. 'Not that it's any business of mine.'

With an effort, Damon managed to sit up. 'That's right, pally Ali,' he smirked. 'So you just butt out. We weren't up to any hanky-panky, were we, Beth?'

Beth could have sworn Ali murmured, 'Well, that'll be a first,' but Damon was braying again, so she couldn't be sure.

Two bottles of wine and more flowers awaited Beth downstairs, plus a large pile of take-away Chinese foil cartons.

'We guessed you wouldn't have found time to cook anything, so Gavin suggested we bring something in,' Ali explained. 'And Sarah will be here any minute. She's just locking up.'

Beth hadn't really fancied eating a chicken tikka alone in front of the television, so she was delighted to have company, and moved by the thoughtfulness of her friends. While they were sorting out plates and spare ribs, Damon opened both bottles and slurped wine into five glasses.

'Good job Sarah is driving me home,' he said, as he raised his glass.

'What about your van?' Ali queried.

'Oh, Beth won't mind me tucking it in behind her car — will you, Beth? Then Sarah can drive me over in the morning.'

Beth opened her mouth to protest, then resignedly closed it again.

Ali wasn't so easy. 'You really are a selfish bastard,' she said, spooning out a sweet and sour pork dish.

'I love you too, darling.' Damon mouthed a kiss towards Ali. 'In fact, I love you all, including Beth and her ghostly voices.'

All eyes turned towards Beth, who

continued to shove empty containers into the black sack, trying hard not to appear embarrassed. She had decided she wouldn't mention her strange experience, but now felt compelled to repeat Eliza's words to her friends.

'Damon thinks I must have fallen asleep,' Beth added, hoping that would close the issue.

Ali and Gavin looked at each other thoughtfully. 'Do you think you fell asleep?' Ali asked.

'I was certainly tired enough. Actually, I suppose it's the only logical answer.'

'You could be right.' Ali frowned. 'But you will tell us if it occurs again, won't you?' She picked up the empty vase, still on the draining board. 'This has water in the bottom,' she commented, looking at Beth.

'Ah, yes. I did buy some flowers for the new house, but took them to Katie's grave instead.' They exchanged a sad little smile. 'So I'm very pleased to have some more. Thank you, Ali — and you, Gavin, of course. I didn't know you were coming down mid-week.'

'There are one or two businesses I want to take a look at that might be of interest.'

'Well, it's very kind of you to come over. By the way,' Beth reached for her handbag. 'How much was the food? Might as well pay you now, before I forget.'

'My treat, my pleasure. And no arguments.' Gavin slipped his arm around Beth's shoulders and gave her a friendly hug. 'Reckon you've had quite a day, one way and another. Now you need to relax for a while.'

Before she could answer, the front door was pushed open and Sarah called out. She, too, had a bottle of wine and a miniature rose bush. 'This can go out in the garden next year,' she said. 'It'll need a bit of digging over first, though. The fronts are going to be landscaped, but I'll bet the builders have buried every bit of rubble in the back gardens.'

'Bound to,' Damon said. 'But fear not, Beth. I'll come over and give you a hand.' Then, with a hasty glance at Sarah, he added, 'When I've finished our rockery, of course.'

Ali scoffed. 'Quite the little Sir Galahad, aren't you?' Again, Beth wondered why there was so much acrimony between them.

By the time they had eaten, and pitched in to unpack a few more boxes and leave the house relatively straight, the frightening incident had been pushed further back into Beth's mind. And after the wine bottles were emptied, and they had taken their leave, she really began to feel Damon must have been right. There was no other explanation.

Yet, as she crawled into bed, quite exhausted and sure she would sleep like the proverbial, her fading consciousness was haunted by a bizarre thought.

What if it hadn't been a dream? Would she have to share her new home with a ghostly voice?

11

There was no other way around it. Reluctantly, Sarah had decided that they would have to close the showhouse on Thursday, for most of the day, anyway. Jane was on holiday, and the temp couldn't be expected to run the office or the showhouse while Sarah was at the hospital. It could take hours. All day if the results of the tests weren't good. Beth crossed through the page in the diary, noting that Thursday was the day Dr Masterson would be moving in. Thankfully, the builders had completed all the modifications in time and there had been no major problems. The few hiccups had been swiftly dealt with by Beth. She scrawled a reminder on a yellow post-it note to give him the keys on Wednesday. His wife wasn't arriving until Friday, so Beth would go along later that day, to make sure everything was OK. She'd been a little surprised to learn that he was bringing his mother and daughters with him on Thursday. Surely an elderly invalid in a wheelchair would be a hindrance? Perhaps she was another awkward customer, and had insisted on seeing what was going on so she could make sure the removal men didn't scratch her precious furniture.

Then Beth had another thought. Where was the furniture coming from? He had already arranged for the carpet and curtain fitters to collect a key on Tuesday but, even if he had been renting furnished accommodation in America, there would be personal effects, and items in store in the UK. Perhaps he was buying everything brand-new, like the curtains and carpets. Still, it was none of her business, and she had more important things to occupy her mind.

Most of the houses had been sold by now, but there were still many aspects to keep her busy. Contracts, mortgages, referrals, pouring oil on troubled waters when conveyancing didn't go through quickly enough, putting properties back on the market when the purchasers couldn't get a loan or lost the sale of their existing home — and the relentless phone calls. How was the building progressing? Was she certain they would be able to move in on time? Could they move in before completion date? Would she check the measurements of the bathroom window? And could she please recommend a removal firm, gas-fitter, electrician, plumber, landscape gardener and odd-job man? One woman even asked Beth to take care of the cat and its litter of five kittens for a couple of days before they moved in, as the stress of the upheaval might affect moggie's milk. Beth tactfully convinced the woman that there would be more upheaval with clients and their children in and out of the showhouse, then turned her attention to the next enquiry.

Her evenings were filled with trying to turn her own house into a home. The removal men had collected the large packing cases, but she still had a number of boxes stowed in the spare room. The living room looked better now the curtains were up, but the walls were rather bare, and the house hadn't yet developed its own character. Give it time, she thought, but time was the enemy — in some respects, at least, although she was glad she hadn't time to dwell on the fact that the house might possibly be haunted. There had been no further whisperings or strange experiences, but Beth had decided she would check up on those names as soon as she had a chance.

For now, she was happy enough to have sorted out most of her financial difficulties. The difference in the two mortgage payments was substantial, and heating costs were bound to be cheaper in such a small house. Sarah had given Beth a generous bonus for selling the most expensive house on the site to Dr Masterson. It was such a relief to have sufficient money to pay the standing orders. She had even begun to think she might be able to afford a holiday next year.

She was just writing another reminder to tell Dave about the closure on Thursday when the man himself appeared.

'Ah, just the person I want to see.' Beth crossed out her note.

'Great! Your place or mine?'

'Idiot.' He was so outrageous, Beth couldn't keep a straight face. After she'd explained about the closure, she asked if he would pop down to Admiral's Way on Thursday and make sure everything was functioning in the big house.

Dave pulled a face. 'I was hoping I could keep well clear of that lot.'

'Why, has he given you any hassle?'

'Not really. But he's a bit of a miserable sod, isn't he. Still, I'll show my face round there and hope to God he hasn't found something to complain about.' He took a strip of chewing gum from his pocket. 'Wonder what his wife is like, poor cow,' he mused. 'Have you seen her?'

'No. She's flying over from the States, won't be here till Friday. Which reminds me, Dr Masterson's mother will be with him on Thursday. I think she's an invalid, so some kid glove treatment wouldn't come amiss. I'm sorry I won't be here to greet them myself.'

'So am I. If she's anything like her son, she'll be another bundle of laughs.' Dave winked. 'You do realise you owe me one now, Beth?'

She sighed. 'I might just treat you to a pint, if you promise to behave yourself.'

'I'll hold you to that.'

As Dave turned to leave, Beth suddenly remembered, and called him back.

'You've lived in the area most of your life, haven't you?'

'Fawley born and bred. Why?'

'What was this site before the developers bought it?'

'Nothing, as far as I can remember. It was just a big field. Probably part of a farm once upon a time.'

'Do you remember seeing any buildings on this site?'

'Farm buildings and so on? I don't think so.'

'No cottages?'

'Wait a minute.' Dave screwed up his eyes in concentration. 'When I was a nipper there was a couple of derelict cottages here. No roofs. Just broken walls. Used to play around them with me mates. They pulled them down ages ago.'

'And you've no idea who they belonged to,

or who'd lived in them?'

Slowly, Dave shook his head. 'I could ask my Dad. He was a builder, too, before he retired. Why do you want to know?'

'Just curious as to what it was like in the 'olden days', as my grandmother used to call them.'

The foreman paused by the door. 'Tell you who probably does know. The old boy who lives along by the coastguard's cottages. I do a few odd jobs for him now and again. Ninety if he's a day. Always telling me yarns about the refinery being built and things like that. I'll have a word.'

'Thanks, Dave.'

He licked a grubby finger and drew a vertical line in the air. 'That's another pint you owe me,' he said. Then he grinned and shook his head. 'Reckon old Aaron will know about the cottages if anybody does. He's always bragging that there's been Purkisses around these parts since Good King Hal built the Castle!'

* * *

Beth checked the contents of the box. Maps of the New Forest and the Waterside area. A comprehensive local guide advertising services. Two newspapers giving details of summer fêtes, the New Forest Show and entertainment between Southampton and Bournemouth. Bus and ferry timetables. An assortment of money-off vouchers from local shops and restaurants. Finally — wine, locally made chocolates and a small floral display in a basket.

When Beth had mentioned her mother taking 'welcome' gifts from the church to newcomers, Sarah had liked the idea and persuaded the developers to fund the wine, chocolates and flowers, as a goodwill gesture. It had proved to be very popular already and had certainly helped to soften Mrs Porter's fury over the carpets. Beth hoped it would have an equally soothing effect on Mrs Masterson. Jet-lag and moving into a property you've never seen wasn't exactly a stress-free scenario, and no doubt a mother-in-law and teenage girls wouldn't help matters.

So, with a fifteen-minute gap in her appointments at four-thirty on the Friday afternoon, Beth pressed the button on her Ansafone, hung a 'Back soon' sign on the door, and drove down to Admiral's Way, feeling just a little apprehensive.

At least the weather was fine and, for a moment, she paused to admire the view across the water as she parked the car. Then she turned back to the house. It really was rather splendid, even with the messy front garden. High-spirited voices spilling out from the open windows gave life to the house.

Raising her hand to knock on the front door, Beth was almost knocked flying by a young girl in brief denim shorts, all arms and legs and swirling blonde hair.

'Oh, my God, I'm so sorry. I didn't see you there. Haven't hurt you, have I?'

The girl looked so concerned, biting her lip and glancing over her shoulder, that Beth was equally anxious to reassure her. 'Only a little stirred, but not shaken,' she laughed.

'You're sure? Dad's always telling me to slow down. I just didn't think. Sorry.'

'Don't worry. I've had worse. And at least I didn't drop this.' Beth shifted the box to the other arm. 'Are your parents around?'

The girl looked at Beth, then at the box. 'Are you Mrs Lewis?' she asked. 'The lady who sold Dad this house?'

'That's right.'

'You're not a bit like I imagined you to be.'

Beth didn't dare ask her to explain. Goodness knows what Dr Masterson had implied.

'I'm Cassie.' The girl thrust her hand towards Beth. 'Cassandra, really, but everyone calls me Cassie. Do come in.' She led the way back into the hall. 'Isn't the house great? I've always wanted to live near the sea.'

Well, at least she had one satisfied customer, Beth thought, as she followed the teenager into the house.

'I think Mum and Dad are in the conservatory, being terribly English and having tea. Shall I get another cup and saucer?'

'Thanks just the same, but I have to get back.' As Beth smiled at the girl, she noticed a photograph on a small table. The woman had the girl's radiant smile and blue eyes, and was holding aloft a large trophy.

'That's Mum,' Cassie said, with obvious pleasure. 'She was quite famous once.'

Beth noted the numbered vest and sweat band of an athlete. 'I was never any good at sport myself, but my father was keen on athletics,' she said, looking closer at the picture. 'The face is familiar, but I don't remember the name Masterson.'

'She always used her maiden name, Vanessa Rhodes.'

'What distance did she run?'

'Three thousand metres until they allowed women to run ten thousand back in the eighties. She actually got up to Olympic standard, but had to drop out because of a hamstring injury.'

'That must have been tough. Did it keep her out of action for long?'

Cassie grinned. 'Not as long as having two babies did.'

'Did she ever run again?'

'Not on the track. It's difficult to maintain that peak after a long break, but she found she had the stamina for the marathon. Won races all over the world. Come and see her cups.'

Not sure that she should be doing this, Beth followed Cassie into the main living room, where a display cabinet was filled with gleaming cups, statuettes of runners and shields. 'My goodness! I'm really impressed. You must be proud of her.'

'We are.' A different voice answered. Standing in the doorway, a slightly older girl held out her hand. 'I'm Nadine, and I've come to rescue you from my horrible little sister. Young motormouth here will do your head in if you give her half a chance.'

As Beth introduced herself, she quickly realised that Nadine was a complete opposite to Cassie and definitely her father's daughter with her dark hair and grey eyes, but her serious expression lit up like a lamp when she smiled, as she did now. Briefly, Beth wondered if the father looked as attractive when he smiled.

The girls pretended to spar, then Cassie decided to go in search of her parents, racing out of the door. Nadine shook her head, with all the wisdom of a mature adult, although she couldn't be much more than fifteen. 'My sister never walks like normal people,' she said, then turned back to the cabinet. 'Not many people can leave such a legacy.' Her voice was a little sad.

Beth thought it was a strange comment for a young girl to make, but Nadine went on, 'I'm sure my grandmother would like to meet you,' she said. 'I'll just call her.'

'Oh, please don't disturb her if she's resting,' Beth protested.

'Thora resting?' Nadine laughed. 'You wouldn't say that if you knew her. She never stops. Cassie gets all her energy genes from Thora.'

Beth had a quirky vision of being knocked over by a frenetic granny in a wheelchair.

'You can judge for yourself,' Nadine went on. 'Here's the grand dame in person. Thora, this is Mrs Lewis, who sold Dad this lovely house. She thought you might be resting.'

Nothing could have prepared Beth for the surprise as she turned around. Standing in the doorway was a woman who was not just attractive, but quite stunning. Tall and slim, she had the eyes of her son and older

157

granddaughter, and the trimmest figure anyone could wish for, whatever their age. Even in shorts and casual top, her thick grey hair caught back with a bright scarf, she exuded elegance. And legs to die for, Beth thought, green with envy.

'Not much chance of resting, with so much to do.' Another warm handshake. Head on one side, she appraised Beth. 'You're much younger than I imagined.'

'Really?' Again Beth wondered what the man of the house had said about her.

'Only because Tom was so impressed with your efficiency, and he usually doesn't think anyone under the age of forty can be efficient. Silly, isn't it?'

Surprised by his approval, and not a little pleased, Beth said, 'I hope you like the house as much as your granddaughters seem to, Mrs Masterson,' she said.

'To use their vernacular — it's real cool.' Thora Masterson's voice was low and her chuckle was throaty. 'And do call me Thora,' she added. 'Everyone else does. Helps to make me feel less ancient.'

This lady would never be ancient, Beth thought, warming to her as she murmured her own name. Thora Masterson must be at least sixty, but could easily pass for ten years younger. So why did they need the ramps?

Perhaps another relative was an invalid. But no time for wondering.

Beth held out the box. 'Should I leave this with you?' she asked. 'It's just a few things that might help you all to feel a little more at home, compliments of the Seascape Development Company.'

'What a lovely thought, and such pretty flowers — but I think you should give it to Vanessa. I told her I'd bring you through.' Thora Masterson led the way across the hall and into the room that had been especially converted to lead into the conservatory. Then Beth understood.

Dr Masterson stood behind his wife, who was as beautiful as she appeared in the photograph. But now her eyes were shadowed with fatigue. And she sat in a wheelchair.

12

The experts on the screen examined pieces of porcelain and furniture, delighting some owners with their valuations, disappointing one who had treasured a Monet, only to be told the painting was a fake. Usually it was one of Beth's favourite programmes, but now she paid scant attention to the beautiful and less than beautiful objects displayed. Her thoughts went back again and again to the house at the far end of Admiral's Way, and the woman in the wheelchair.

Not for the first time, Beth wondered what had caused Vanessa Masterson to lose the use of her legs. A sporting injury? Somehow, she didn't think so. Rugby players or horse riders were more at risk from spinal injuries than track runners. More likely to be an accident off the track — perhaps in a car. Whatever, the look in her eyes had haunted Beth for the past two days. The desperation had seemed to reach out as Beth shook the hand that was so weakly offered. Even now, the memory of that touch sent a chill down Beth's spine, and she shivered.

Then the close-up of a magnificent piece of

Fabergé jewellery caught her eye. The joy in the woman's expression when told how much her 'little trinket' was really worth brought a smile to Beth's face, and once more the room was filled with warmth. It really was too fine an evening to dwell on sadness, she thought, especially as Sarah was so happy with the result of her amnio test.

Jumping up, Beth switched off the television and decided to go for a walk before the sun set. The beach embraced every water sport imaginable, and the less energetic watched with interest as inexperienced sail-boarders were dunked into the water time after time, no doubt envying the more skilful who turned the mischievous waves to their own advantage. Most of the bathers were briskly towelling themselves dry, shivering slightly, although a group of children pleaded with their mother for 'just a little longer — please', despite the cooler breeze. Nearly everyone was talking to someone. Very few were alone.

Perhaps she should consider buying a dog. She had a few more weeks at the showhouse, so might even be able to take a puppy to work, once it was house-trained. By the time she found another job, and she knew she should start looking soon, the puppy would hopefully be old enough to be left alone without creating too much havoc. Beth didn't really fancy driving fifteen miles into Southampton again each day, and if she could find a decent job locally, she would be able to go home lunchtime so that the dog would not be left alone for too long. She decided to ask Ali to keep her eyes open for a suitable vacancy.

Engrossed in her thoughts, wondering what breed of dog could live happily in her small house, Beth didn't realise she was heading for disaster until she found herself flat on her back, with a human windmill lying on top of her. Only slightly winded, she lay still for a moment, while the girl rolled off and knelt by her side.

'Are you OK? I'm so sorry — oh, it's you! Oh, God! What must you think of me? Here, let me help you up . . . ' The words gabbled out in a torrent as Cassie Masterson tried to apologise and drag Beth to her feet at the same time.

'I'm fine,' Beth assured her. 'Just let me get my breath.'

'Cassie!' Dr Masterson's voice was firm, but not angry. 'Leave Mrs Lewis alone for a moment before you do any more damage.'

'I'm sorry, Dad.' Cassie's voice was almost tearful. 'It was all my fault. I was running backwards to catch the ball, and . . . '

Nadine interrupted. 'It was as much my fault for throwing the ball so hard.'

Her father looked down at Beth. 'Are you sure you're all right?' he asked.

'Really, I'm OK.' Beth was too embarrassed to look at him. 'Please don't worry. I wasn't looking where I was going, either.'

As she tried to stand up, Beth knelt on a sharp stone and lost her balance. The next moment, Dr Masterson was behind her, and with one sharp heave she was on her feet.

'Ouch, that looks painful.' Cassie stared at Beth's knee, which was bleeding profusely. To make matters worse, it was the knee she had injured earlier in the year.

'It looks worse than it is,' Beth said, trying not to wince. 'I'll just go and wash it in the sea.'

'Not unless you fancy a mud bath first,' Dr Masterson said. 'The tide's going out. Look.'

Beth followed his gaze to where the bait catchers were busy digging up worms, ankle-deep in mud. Then she dabbed at her knee with a tissue. It was soon saturated.

Dr Masterson produced a handkerchief from his shorts' pocket and crouched to bind it around her knee. 'Come back to the house and you can bathe it properly and put a dressing on it.'

'It's not far for me to walk home. I can

manage, honestly.'

'Nonsense.' His tone of voice allowed for no argument. 'If you walk home like that, someone will be phoning for an ambulance. Our house is much nearer.'

Cassie took hold of Beth's arm. 'I'll help you,' she said.

Beth could have walked more easily on her own, but the child was so eager to help.

'Oh, look! There's Thora.' Nadine waved to her grandmother, further along the beach. 'I expect she's wondering where we've got to.'

After the greetings and explanations, Thora Masterson shooed her younger granddaughter away from Beth. 'You're dragging the poor girl over sideways,' she observed.

Dr Masterson looked anxious. 'Is Vanessa all right on her own? Supposing the phone rings?'

'Vanessa is quite comfortable in the conservatory, I put the Ansafone on, and if someone rings the doorbell they'll have to wait for a couple of minutes. So stop fussing, Tom.' Thora went on, in her matter-of-fact tone. 'Actually, she asked me to come down and let you know that supper's ready. I think she's feeling peckish, so that's a good sign.'

'Look,' Beth paused. 'It's obviously an inconvenient time. Why don't I just walk home?'

Thora looked at her in astonishment. 'Washing your knee and sticking a plaster on it won't take a jiffy. In fact . . . ' She glanced at the others with raised eyebrows. 'If you haven't any plans for the evening, you're very welcome to join us.'

'Oh, no. I couldn't. It's very kind of you, but . . . ' Beth stumbled over her words.

'But what?' Dr Masterson asked.

'Well, look at me.' Beth glanced down at her faded denim shorts. 'I'm not properly dressed, for one thing.'

Thora Masterson snorted. 'It's only cold meat and salad, my dear, so I shan't wear my tiara.'

Cassie giggled. 'Please say yes, Mrs Lewis, then I won't feel so awful.'

For a moment, Beth couldn't think what to say, and the Masterson family took it as an acceptance.

'Well, then, that's settled.' Dr Masterson motioned his younger daughter. 'Cassie, run on and tell your mother — and see if you can find the first-aid box.' He smiled at Beth, and she discovered that it did transform his face. 'We'll soon have you patched up, Mrs Lewis,' he said.

'For goodness sake, Tom,' his mother remonstrated. 'Don't you think we should dispense with the formalities? After all, we are neighbours.' She pointed at him, then herself, then Beth. 'You Tom — me Thora — her Beth. There. That's the introductions.'

At first, Beth thought that Tom Masterson was horribly embarrassed, as he shook her hand without speaking, his face perfectly serious. Then she noticed the twitch of his lips as the girls exploded into laughter.

The next couple of hours passed swiftly, and far more pleasantly than Beth could have imagined, aided by a couple of gin and tonics and a bottle of rather good Chardonnay. Vanessa didn't seem to resent the intrusion, although she said little, just quietly smiled at the good-humoured banter between her daughters and their grandmother as they sat in the conservatory to make the most of the late evening sun. The back garden was still a shambles, but Beth agreed to arrange for a jobbing gardener to call on the Mastersons and sort it out. Tom Masterson was attentive towards his wife, discreetly cutting her food so she could eat it with her fork, American fashion.

They talked of America, which the girls found exciting when they visited for holidays, and their new school, which they would be joining in September. At one point, Cassie asked Beth about her husband, and she answered honestly that they were separated. A significant look from Tom prevented any more personal questions from the inquisitive girl, and the conversation changed to the new TV costume drama series, dogs, and where were the nearest riding stables? They didn't mention athletics, or Vanessa's illness.

It was quite dark when Beth said she had some work to sort out before the morning and, despite her protests, Tom Masterson insisted on walking her home. 'The roads aren't made up yet, so we don't want you stumbling into a pothole,' he said.

After she had said her goodbyes and thanked Thora for the meal, and the plaster and the loan of her cardigan, Beth left with Tom Masterson. He seemed quite concerned about her knee, although she tried not to limp.

'Don't you think you should see your doctor in the morning?' he insisted.

'Not really. It's just . . . I had a bit of a fall earlier in the year and it's still a bit sore, that's all.' She wondered how he would react if she told him about her ghostly encounters.

For a while they walked in silence, then Tom said, 'In case you are wondering, Vanessa is suffering from motor neurone disease.'

It stopped Beth in her tracks. 'Oh, my

God,' she whispered. 'That's dreadful. I'm so sorry.'

After a moment he said, 'Yes. It is dreadful,' and walked on. His face was turned away so she couldn't see his expression. 'That's why we chose this house.'

Beth wasn't quite sure what he meant, so didn't answer.

'Vanessa wants to die in England,' he went on. 'And the girls want to spend as much time with their mother as possible. They asked if they could leave their boarding school and switch to a day school, despite exams and friends and all that.'

In a tight little voice, Beth said, 'They are wonderful daughters. You must be incredibly proud of them.' She wanted to scream at the injustice of it all.

'Yes. Yes I am. And as for my mother . . .' He turned back to Beth with a tiny smile. 'Well, you've seen her, so you know what I mean.'

Beth nodded. 'She's wonderful. Truly wonderful. You would think Vanessa was her own daughter.'

'Oh, yes. Vanessa's parents died years ago, so she regards Thora as her mother. In fact, she listens to Thora much more than she does to me, or the girls.'

'Perhaps she needs to have someone like that.'

Tom looked down at Beth. 'I think you're right. My wife hasn't many friends. Now we are back in England she is going to need all the companionship we can give her.'

Thoughtfully, Beth asked, 'Do you think it would help if I called in sometimes?' He was silent for so long, Beth feared she had offended him. 'Although you may feel she would prefer to just be with her family.'

'No. Not at all. I'm sorry if I gave that impression. It's . . . ' He was still looking at Beth, but his back was to the street lamp and she couldn't see his expression. 'It's an extremely kind thought, but — with the hours you work surely your free time is limited — and full?'

Beth wasn't sure whether he was trying to put her off, or just questioning. 'Not that full,' she quietly said. 'But it's up to you — and Vanessa, of course.'

'Oh, I have no doubt that Vanessa would be happy to see you again. She needs to feel she is leading as normal a life as possible for someone in her situation. So please do call if you have the time.'

'I'll be glad to.'

'There's just one thing . . . ' Again he hesitated. 'Please don't mind if she doesn't talk too much. Her speech is only just beginning to be affected, but she does like to listen to other people.'

'I understand. It must be a terrible situation for all of you — not just Vanessa.'

'It is particularly hard on the girls, seeing their mother deteriorate and knowing there is no cure. Sometimes I think it would have been better for them if we had stayed in America, even though the medical costs were horrendous. But I'm not sure how the girls will handle it when things get worse.'

'They'll find strength from somewhere.' Beth's voice was low. 'When my mother had cancer I didn't think I could bear to watch her die, but I kept going for her sake, and I know I would have felt far worse if we hadn't been together.'

'I hope you're right.'

They were now at her house, and he waited for her to put on the hall light before he turned away. Then Beth remembered.

'Tom . . . '

'Yes?' He turned back.

'I almost forgot Thora's cardigan.' She handed it towards him. 'And thanks for walking me home.'

'It was the least I could do after we had been thoughtless enough to knock you off your feet.' In the light from her doorway she glimpsed his smile again. Then he was gone.

As she closed the door, Beth wondered

about Dr Tom Masterson. Her first impressions had been of an obnoxious stuffed shirt. He was certainly very formal and matter-of-fact, sometimes quite brusque. Even his attentive attitude towards his wife was dispassionate. But there had been those brief moments when he smiled, and she had a momentary vision of another man. A man with warmth buried deep in his soul. A man afraid to show emotion. Perhaps the shock of his wife's illness had locked all feeling inside him. But she mustn't dwell on their tragedy for too long. She had work to do.

It wasn't until later, when she put aside her file and turned out the bedside lamp, that another memory, even more disturbing, returned. A memory of the strength of a man's arms when Tom Masterson had hoisted Beth to her feet on the beach. It was a long time since she had remembered Bryn making love to her, or imagined any other man making love to her, or even wanted to. That was probably the only thing she and the ambiguous doctor had in common. They had both been forced to repress their emotions by their nearest and dearest. But Vanessa could not help her situation, whereas Bryn had deliberately and cold-bloodedly destroyed their love.

A tiny tear trickled from beneath Beth's

closed eyelids, moments before she fell asleep, and when she awoke in the morning, her first thought was of a dream she couldn't quite recall. Like most dreams, the recollection was fuzzy around the edges, but she was sure it had been about Eliza. And something else . . . but it was so vague.

13

For some time Beth lay with her eyes closed, willing herself to remember the dream. Had she actually seen Eliza? All she remembered was that soft voice, telling a sad story. It must have been sad, a tear still dampened Beth's cheek. Fragmented parts of the dream flashed in and out of her mind. Eliza falling in love with the handsome soldier. An ambitious soldier, who aimed at promotion. Once he was a master gunner he could apply for a post in a better garrison. Their first year together was happy enough, but the miscarriage and grief over the family tragedy left Eliza desperately ill. Soon her husband took to riding down to the port of Hythe, coming back the worse for ale and smelling of whores.

When Thomas Pitman fell ill with the pox, Francis appointed himself acting governor, moved into the gatehouse, and ordered Eliza to nurse their stricken friends in the keep.

As the dream began to fade, Beth concentrated on the voice. She had to remember the ending. Never before had she so wanted to recall every detail. Then she gasped, as the full horror of the tale unfolded.

Francis had locked his wife in the keep with the dead and dying. Just a small amount of food and water. Eliza begged him to send one of the men to Hythe, to fetch a doctor. He laughed as he refused. No one bothered to visit Calshot, and the gunners wouldn't go near the sickroom. That was when she realised he wanted her to die. And he told her why. He'd found a more comely girl. One who could read and write. With someone like that at his side, he might even become a captain.

Eliza's voice had sobbed as she told how his final words twisted the knife in her breast as surely as the key he turned in the door. His new love came from a family of respected merchants. She would bear healthy children, not brats who might turn out like great-aunt Gatherell.

So Eliza had bathed the fevered heads of her friends, given them sips of water, tried to ignore the stench of the dying, and waited. She was the last to die.

The memory of that heart-broken voice remained with Beth for some moments as her conscious mind returned to reality.

She opened her eyes as the increasing sound level of her alarm clock intruded. The light filtering through the gap in the curtains was bright with sunshine. And it was time to get Monday on the move down at the showhouse, however sad she felt.

While she was showering, Beth tried to turn her thoughts into other, happier directions; the Mastersons, a puppy, her next job, Sarah's babies. But each time her mind insisted on recalling that hushed voice, and she knew she would have no peace until she investigated further.

As soon as she had unlocked the showhouse, Beth scanned the desk diary for the week. Surprisingly, Friday morning was free. Later, she dialled the office. Sarah should be in by now.

After giving her the results of the morning's appointments, one promising, one maybe, the others just sightseeing, Beth asked if she could take the morning off on Friday. 'I still need a few bits and pieces for the house. Could you cover the showhouse for a few hours?'

'Why don't you take the whole day?' Sarah suggested. 'After all, you didn't have the few days I promised you when you moved.'

Beth glanced down at the diary. 'There are only two appointments so far in the afternoon, and I have a feeling one of those won't turn up. Thanks, Sarah. I'll take you up on that.'

'Fine. I'll sort it out with Jane for this end. Are you looking for anything in particular?'

Beth hesitated. She could hardly say that she was looking for old parish records without inviting awkward questions. 'Oh, this and that. Things to brighten up the place a bit really.'

'Paintings and cushions and such-like?'

'Yes.' Beth had another thought. She wouldn't need to spend a whole day in Winchester. 'And I might call in on Ali. See if she knows of any jobs that might be coming up when I've finished here.'

There was a brief silence at the other end of the telephone, then Sarah said, 'Actually, Beth, I was going to talk to you about that when I come in on Thursday.'

'Oh?' Beth wondered if Sarah had another housing development in the pipeline.

'I had intended to continue working until the last possible moment, but I'm feeling more and more like a wallowing hippo, so I'd really like to pack it in earlier. Not only that, I want to spend some time on my own with Jamie, before my two little monsters make their entrance.'

'That's understandable. So do you want me to help Jane out in the office for a few weeks?'

Again a hesitation, then Sarah said, 'I'd like

you to take over as manager.'

'As manager? But I'm not qualified to handle mortgages.'

'I know. But there are independent advisers we can use for referrals until I'm back — unless you want to do the training, of course.'

Beth knew it would take at least two months before she could give advice, and another four months to be able to handle the mortgages. 'How long are you planning to be away?' she asked.

'I haven't worked it all out yet, but I honestly don't think I will be coming back to work six weeks later, like I did with Jamie. My blood pressure is high and the doctors are suggesting I might have to have a Caesarean. Then there's Lorraine to consider. She's wonderful with Jamie, but I get the feeling she's a bit anxious about caring for new-born twins as well.'

'So you could be taking a few months off?'

'At least six I would imagine. Once we have established a routine, and Jamie is at nursery school every day, I'll be in a better position to think about it. But I do need to know the office is in good hands while I'm knee-deep in Pampers.'

'What about Jane? Won't she expect to take over?'

'Jane is a super secretary, but she doesn't have your legal knowledge and she's not as good at dealing with the public as you. We have talked about the situation and she said she'd be much happier if you took on all the responsibility and hassle and left her to get on with the admin side.'

'I see.' Beth's mind whirled around all the aspects. She would still have to look for another job eventually, but it would solve the immediate problem. 'When are you thinking of leaving?'

'As soon as I can shut down the 'Seascape' showhouse. There are only half a dozen properties unsold, so it shouldn't take long. You don't have to answer now. Anyway, you'll want to know more details about salary and so on. Can you leave it until Thursday to make up your mind?'

'Of course. And Sarah . . . '

'Yes?'

'Thanks for having faith in me.'

'There's no one could do it better.'

⋆   ⋆   ⋆

Parking was never easy in Winchester, particularly when the city was thronged with tourists, but Beth was fortunate enough to find a space behind the library, only to be informed that the Fawley parish records were now in the county records office. It wasn't far to walk and, after she had signed in, been issued with a security badge, and explained what she needed, she was in luck. They had a hard copy of the dates she needed, so she would not have to queue to use the micro-film machine.

As Beth waited, she read the notice requesting that users ask to borrow a cushion to protect the more delicate documents, and suddenly felt awestruck as she looked around at the people poring over yellowed pages in ancient languages. These papers had survived wars, fires, storage in attics and cellars, political intrigue. They told stories that would otherwise be lost for ever, and deserved to be treasured and protected. Modern technology was all very well, but it couldn't match the experience of handling the real thing.

The book she was handed was divided into baptisms, marriages and burials, each entry painstakingly written by the clerk of the parish, sometimes in beautiful copper-plate writing, sometimes in barely literate hand.

What were the dates Mr Brooke had given? Beth consulted her notes, then turned to the last section of the book. There were quite a few burials registered in the early part of the eighteenth century. Ah, yes, here was a name

179

she had written down. 10th May 1709, Thomas Pitman, Master Gunner, Calshot Castle. The next entry was on the following day — Elizabeth Mintern, daughter of Thomas Pitman. Beth shook her head. Mr Brooke had only mentioned one daughter, Mary Pitman. Her entry was next, she had died on the 12th of May. Then Mary Seal on the 15th, and . . . Beth caught her breath as she read the entry for 20th May: Stoyl, Elizabeth, wife of Francis, Calshot Castle.

Beth recounted the entries. Five, not four. She tried to remember Eliza's words, but her memory was clouded, although she felt certain that Eliza hadn't mentioned the number of deaths. Mr Brooke had mentioned four, but perhaps he had missed the entry for Elizabeth Mintern. She may even have been a married daughter.

Suddenly, Beth realised the way her thoughts were leading. It was as though she believed she had actually had a conversation with a ghost, not a dream. For a moment, she sat still, looking at the page, feeling slightly peculiar. Then she pulled herself together and decided to read some of the other entries, around the same dates and area, see if any pattern emerged.

Not many between April and June. One at Leap, that must be Lepe. Three in Exbury.

No mention of cause of death. Nothing significant there. Out of curiosity, she turned back to the baptisms section. March 1696: John and Edward, two bastards of widow Melza. Ouch. Very much a stigma in those days, and no support groups or DSS to help. Probably the families were the only ones who helped, and if they couldn't — or wouldn't — heaven help the widow Melza. Beth flicked through the pages. Other entries were also interesting, but no clear link. Perhaps the marriages section? Ah, the marriage of Richard Serle, widower, to Elizabeth Thorn, in September 1709 might be significant. The surnames were frequently spelt differently, so it could be Richard Searle, Seale or — Seal. If his wife had died in May, he would probably remarry quite soon, particularly if there were children to care for. But Mary Seal could have been his daughter, not his wife. No mention of any further baptisms of that name, but a burial in 1723 of Elizabeth Searle, wife of Richard and, in 1756, of Mary, daughter of Richard. That could mean that a daughter was born to Richard's second wife, but not baptised.

She found no record of any marriage of Francis Stoyl, either to Eliza or the new girl. The old family names made fascinating reading, and their various spellings, or misspellings. Stoyl could be Stoyll or Stowell, even Stoel. It seemed to depend on the measure of education afforded by the parish clerk of the time. One very common surname was Purkes, also written as Purcas, Purchase, Purkas and Purkiss. Wasn't that the name Dave had mentioned? Old Aaron was right. There had been Purkisses around for centuries, however they spelt their name. It could quite easily have been one of his ancestors who lived at the end of the terrace of cottages.

Some of the Christian names were also interpreted in a variety of spellings. Ursulah, Margarere, Amey, Bridgett, Joane, Rachell, Symon, Gyles. Many good old biblical names, still popular today, and some very unusual ones. Anstace she remembered from the book of names she had bought when she was expecting Katie, but the spelling there had been Anstice. Goodness, here were a couple of unusual male names: Gerrit and Zachona. Maybe some of the pop stars studied old parish records before lumbering their off-spring with their rather strange names. Charity was quite sweet and could always be shortened to Cherry, and — Gatherell. Yes, there it was, plainly enough. A name Beth was sure she had never heard of, until . . .

But it still didn't really prove anything. All

she had done was to confirm that some of the names existed in the eighteenth century. There was no mention of smallpox, but it was definitely odd that five people should have died at Calshot Castle within the space of a few days. That had to be an epidemic of some kind, surely?

Deep in thought, she left the building and walked down the hill to the traffic lights. Almost on auto-pilot she crossed with the small crowd that moved to the flashing instruction of the 'little green man', and was surprised to find her way blocked on the opposite pavement. Even when she tried to side-step the tall man in front of her, he side-stepped in the same direction. Irritated, she raised her eyes to his face.

'Gavin! Sorry. I didn't see you.'

He laughed. 'Well, as I'm usually told I'm big enough and ugly enough, that's got to be a first.'

'I suppose it does sound a bit stupid.' She shook her head. 'I was miles away. Just not looking.'

'Well, at least you didn't cross on the red light.' Gavin took her arm. 'I think we ought to move out of the way, don't you?'

For the first time, Beth became aware that other pedestrians were now having to side-step, and some didn't look too happy about it.

'What are you doing in Winchester?' they both asked, almost in unison.

'You first,' Gavin said, laughing.

'Just shopping.'

'In the county records office?' There was a whimsical smile on Gavin's face. 'I saw you come down the path. That's why I waited. Guessed you would cross here to go back to the city.' As Beth hesitated, he went on, 'Whatever you found in there, it was totally absorbing.'

'Yes, it was. But I'm not really sure that I can explain it. Not without sounding completely paranoid, that is.'

'Something to do with the Calshot ghost?'

Beth nodded.

For a moment, Gavin stood looking down at her. Then he looked at his watch. 'Shall we lunch?' he asked. 'Then you can tell me about it. Only if you want to, of course.'

She stared up into his face. His expression was sympathetic and sincere and she really needed to talk to someone. 'I'd like that,' she murmured.

'Good. Do you know the watering holes in Winchester?'

'Actually, I was on my way to the Cathedral refectory.'

'Then lead on, Macduff.' As they walked along Jewry Street, Gavin chattering on about his favourite foods, Beth realised that she still didn't know why he should be in Winchester.

14

Murmuring her thanks, Beth took the cup of coffee from Gavin. It was her second cup. Although the Cathedral refectory was busy, they had been lucky enough to find a small table by the window overlooking the terrace, which gave them a certain amount of seclusion. They must have been talking for almost an hour. Correction — *she* had been talking. Gavin was a good listener. He hadn't interrupted, just allowed her to tell him the whole story, not only about Eliza, but her own feelings about Bryn's desertion, Katie's death, her suicide attempt. She hadn't even told Ali that she had intended to walk into the sea that day — and keep walking. Afterwards she had felt too ashamed to tell anyone. So what was it about Gavin that made it so easy for her to open up? Her feelings of desperation, guilt, isolation and fear poured out as though she were in a confessional. Small wonder that Ali was so smitten with this gentle giant.

'What frightens you the most, Beth?' Gavin's voice broke into her train of thought. 'Wondering whether you are going off your trolley because of all the dreadful things that have happened to you? Or finding out that Eliza really is someone from the spirit world, trying to get through to you?'

It was a question she hadn't yet asked herself, and Beth stared back at him for a moment before she dropped her eyes. 'I'm not sure,' she murmured. 'A little of both, I think. But . . . ' She raised her eyes again. 'Do you think it is possible that I *did* hear her voice?'

He took his time before he answered. 'Let's just say that I don't think you are going off your trolley. Some of the incidents could be put down to a dream, but there is a consistency in the tale that makes me wonder.'

'So you think it's possible?'

His gaze wandered out through the window to a table where a woman sat discreetly breast-feeding her baby, while two older children tucked into their ice-creams, a huge umbrella creating almost a surrealist effect of light and shade. As Beth followed his gaze, the woman dipped her finger into one of the ice-creams and licked it, provoking laughter from the children. The cosy little scene tugged at her heart as she remembered how she had felt when breast-feeding Katie. It hadn't mattered that Katie was different.

All that mattered was the love that flowed between them. Bryn denied it but Beth had treasured those special moments, knowing that they couldn't last.

She glanced across the table at Gavin and they shared a smile, then the moment was shattered by a tut-tutting comment from a woman sitting nearby. Beth turned to look the woman full in the face and was not surprised to see that she was elderly, with disapproval oozing from every pore, and almost hissing the words 'indecent' and 'shouldn't be allowed' to her companion, who looked more embarrassed than indignant.

Beth hoped her words reached the woman. 'Why do people make such a fuss about something so perfectly natural?' she asked Gavin. 'It's not even as though you can see anything.'

'Personally, I think it's a very beautiful sight.' Gavin smiled again as one of the little girls wiped her hand across her face, smearing chocolate ice-cream everywhere. 'Perhaps it's wishful thinking?' he added.

'Or sour grapes.'

Gavin's attention came back to Beth. 'You seem to have a lot of common sense, and I'm a great believer in what my mother used to call her 'woman's intuition'.'

'So?'

'What does your gut feeling tell you about the voice?'

After a pause, Beth said, 'My gut feeling tells me it's for real. But my common sense tells me it's out of the question.'

'Why?'

'I don't know. Logic, I suppose.'

'Once upon a time logic told man that the world was flat. And certainly there was no logic that explained the miracles of Christ, or dreams that warn of disaster. Who knows what mysteries we might take as normal in a thousand years' time?'

'So you think Eliza could be for real?'

'Whether or not she is real, I don't think you will forget her until you do something about it.'

'But what can I do? I've found out as much information as I'm likely to from the records, but there is no real proof that the dream was anything other than . . . well, just a dream.' Beth paused, thoughtfully sipping her coffee. 'Yet I can't help feeling there must be a reason behind the dream, and the voice, imagined or otherwise.'

'Do you have any idea what the reason might be?'

'I'm not sure. The story in my dream was about a man cold-bloodedly planning that his wife should catch smallpox, knowing there was little chance of her surviving the dreadful disease, and no one would suspect it was murder. If that happened to me, I wouldn't be able to rest in peace until the truth was told.'

'Then do just that.'

'What?'

'Write everything down, from the very first words, to the facts you have just checked in the records.'

'Then what?'

'Hmm.' He stared down at the table for some moments, then suggested, 'You could try writing it as a short story. Or an anecdote. Perhaps then you could both have a bit of peace.'

Beth wondered if he was merely trying to humour her, but his smile was sympathetic. And he had given her troubled mind some food for thought. 'Yes,' she said slowly. 'I could do that, I suppose. It's the next step that's the problem.'

Gavin nodded, then said, 'What about the chappie you went to see? The one who talked to the writers' group.'

'Mr Brooke? The local historian?'

'Yes. Or you could ask Ali. After all, she was a member for a while. She might come up with an idea.'

'I think I'd rather not involve Ali at this

point. I still feel a bit self-conscious about it. And I'd be grateful if you wouldn't . . . '

'Not a word, I promise.' He sat back in his chair. 'You and Ali go back a long way, don't you?'

'From schooldays. She's still my best friend. Don't know what I would have done without her when I lost Bryn and Katie.'

He nodded thoughtfully, then asked, 'What made her set up her own secretarial agency? It's a very competitive business.'

'You know Ali. She thrives on a challenge. Even when we were doing our secretarial course together, she said she would only work for someone else long enough to get experience.'

'Who did she work for?'

'The Brook Street Bureau. As a temp while she took a personnel course.'

'It was a brave step to strike out on her own in a city like Southampton.'

'Very brave. Ali was only twenty-one, but she had a game plan from the day we left college. Always believed that a small agency could succeed alongside the nationals, and she was right.'

'Didn't the big companies ever try to buy her out?'

'One or two made overtures, but she soon sent them packing with a flea in their ear.'

'What about funding? It must have cost her a bit to get started.'

'Oh, she had it all worked out. Her first office was a tiny but cheap room down by the docks. The bank was a bit cautious, so her father loaned her the money for an advertising campaign, and she blew her birthday endowment money on a desk, typewriter and clapped out old banger.'

Gavin smiled. 'And now she has a very nice office overlooking Town Quay, and drives a Saab.'

'It wasn't easy, though. For the first two years she did the prime assignments herself, until she had acquired a small team of first-class secretaries.'

'Hence the name, Quality Temps.'

'Exactly. It wasn't until she landed a contract with one of the largest firms of solicitors in Southampton that the business really began to move up.'

'And is that why she specialises in legal secretaries?'

Beth nodded. 'She's highly respected in the area. Law firms know they are going to get the best when they hire through Ali. And she was voted 'Business Woman of the South' about five years ago.'

'I didn't know that.' Gavin sounded impressed, then asked, 'Does she supply permanent jobs as well as temps?'

'Sometimes. She placed me with Prestwicks. But her main business is with temps.' A thought crossed Beth's mind. 'Do you talk to Ali about the business?'

His laugh was a little self-conscious. 'To be honest, our weekends together are so brief, we don't have a lot of time for talking about our work.'

'So why ask me?'

'I'm interested in everything Ali does. Everything she has done. What makes her tick.' He fiddled with his teaspoon. 'Do you think she would ever want to give up the agency?'

Beth stared at him. 'After all the work she has put into it? No, I don't — unless it was for a really good reason.'

'Such as?'

'Marriage. Starting a family.' She remembered his expression when he looked at the mother with the baby, and became excited. 'Is that why you are asking all these questions?'

'Sort of.' He hesitated. 'But it's early days yet, and we're very happy the way things are. So please don't even hint . . . ' Gavin looked at Beth appealingly.

'Now it's my turn to promise to keep my mouth shut — and I do hope things work out well for both of you.' She drained her cup. 'There's a bit of a queue waiting for tables, and I ought to take a look around the shops while I'm here. Sarah won't believe me if I go back empty-handed.'

Gavin glanced at his watch. 'Goodness, is that the time? I must be on my way as well.'

'By the way,' Beth asked. 'What *are* you doing in Winchester? Ali told me she wasn't expecting you until later this evening.'

He hesitated, then said, 'Just someone I needed to see first. I'd rather not tell Ali, if you don't mind. It's a business errand for my boss, and a bit delicate.' He picked up his lap-top computer, commenting, 'I don't like leaving this in the car. Too much hassle if it was stolen.'

They walked through the terrace, past the visitor centre and out into the Close. Thronged with sightseers, many of them taking photographs, or sprawled on the grass, it made an attractive vista with the backdrop of the ancient cathedral. 'Ali is trying out her new Italian cookbook tomorrow night, so I'll see you then,' she said, offering her hand. 'And thanks for being such a good listener.'

'My pleasure.' He took her hand, but leaned down to kiss her on the cheek before he turned away. Then he came back. 'I just want to say . . . ' Gavin looked across towards the cathedral, as though seeking inspirational words. 'Whatever happens, Beth, I want you to believe . . . ' He still seemed to be struggling before his final words came out in a rush. 'I really do care about Ali.'

Before Beth could answer, he was gone, his long legs swiftly taking him through the crowds, along Great Minster Street and out of sight, leaving Beth wondering.

★　★　★

There were plenty of items Beth would have liked to buy, but either they were way out of her price range, or completely unsuitable for her tiny home. It took another hour before she saw the watercolour prints of an Edwardian square in each of the four seasons, just right for her lounge. Then, just like buses, three more items appeared on the scene, flaunting themselves from their shop window perches. Eventually, she settled for two patchwork cushions, and a lustre vase that was pleasing even without flowers. The onyx lamp would have to wait for another visit, and another bonus.

It was when she paused to shift the bags to a more secure hold that she saw Gavin again. On the other side of the road, he was standing on the pavement, looking up and down the street, Beth wondered if he had seen her, but, as she raised her hand to wave, a tall blonde, wearing a smart suit, hurried towards him from a doorway between two shops. For a few moments they remained in deep conversation then, as the girl became a little agitated, Gavin smiled, took her arm and they walked away, her long stride matching his.

Stunned, Beth watched their disappearing figures. Oh, Ali, she thought. You've done it again. Fallen for the wrong guy. But we were all so sure he was different. Even me. Especially me. I really trusted him.

Then she remembered Gavin's words, 'Whatever happens, Beth, I want you to believe that I really do care about Ali.' In that case, what was he doing meeting an attractive blonde in Winchester? And smiling warmly at her. Yes, his smile had definitely been warm, not just polite.

Curious, Beth crossed the road and walked to the doorway between the two shops. Probably leading to suites of offices above the shops, she thought. But there was only one name printed on the door. Wessex Secretarial Services.

Now Beth was more confused than ever.

15

Beth had intended to get down to her notes about Eliza that evening. Anything to try and take her mind away from worrying about Ali and Gavin. But the telephone rang while she was putting her key in the front door. It was Sarah.

'Saw you drive past,' she said.

'And couldn't wait to find out what I'd bought, I suppose.' Beth hoped her voice sounded suitably light-hearted.

'Actually, no — and yes.'

'Would you like time to think about it?'

'Of course I want to know what you've bought, idiot. It's just a case of first things first.'

'Right. I don't understand, but do carry on.'

'It's about dogs.'

'Dogs?'

'Yes. Those little furry things with a leg on each corner and something that wags around the bum.'

Beth sighed. 'I get the picture. So . . . ?'

'So — do you still want a pooch?'

'Oh.' Beth thought for a moment. 'Well,

yes, I think so. But it would depend on the pooch.' She had a terrifying vision of Sarah trying to offload a Doberman or something similar. Sarah had always had a weakness for stray animals, turning up at school with half-drowned kittens, mice, hamsters — even a grass snake once. As for her collection of puppies ... Mrs Biddlecombe had made frequent visits to the local vets to find homes for unwelcome members of Sarah's menagerie. Some of them were returned to their original homes, having not been truly lost at all, just fancied by the little animal lover.

'You don't have to worry about this one,' Sarah went on. 'It's a Westerly.'

'Isn't that a yacht?'

'It sounds something like that. You know, the little white dogs with black button eyes and the cutest expression. Scottish something or other.'

The word 'little' sounded more interesting. 'Sounds like a West Highland terrier.'

'They're called Westerlys, aren't they?'

Beth chuckled. 'Westie, I think. Tell me more.'

'I had to take Busby to the vet's yesterday. He'd been off his food and was literally pooping all over the place — '

'For goodness sake, Sarah, skip the horrible details and get to the point.'

'That's just what Damon said — before he said I couldn't keep it.'

'Keep what?'

'Not what. Who. He's called Hamish. The vet told me his owner had just moved into a retirement home and isn't allowed to take him with her, so the poor little fellow needs a new owner. He's just perfect for you, Beth.'

'Hmm.' Beth pondered, but was cautious. 'Why doesn't Damon want him? Has he got some inappropriate habits?'

'No. He's a real sweetie. But Damon said we already have two Labradors, three cats and a pond full of everything that swims. I might have tried to talk him round, but Mrs Hosey pointed out that it wasn't fair on Lorraine, either. She thought two infants crawling in opposite directions would be quite enough for the poor girl to look after when I go back to work — she's right, of course. So, how about it?'

'How old is — Hamish?'

'Not sure. About four or five, the vet thinks. So you wouldn't have to worry about puddles in the house.'

'True, but . . . ' Beth realised that a lot depended on mutual chemistry, and the previous owner's discipline. With Beth out for most of the day, he might chew everything in sight, especially if he was pining for his previous owner. 'At least I could train a puppy to my way of thinking, not someone else's,' she argued.

'Beth, just come and look at him. I'll bet you a fiver it will be love at first sight.'

'Have you got him there? A *fait accompli*?'

'Of course. And there's no time like the present. I'll put the kettle on.'

There was no arguing with Sarah when she was in this sort of mood, so Beth set off for the showhouse.

Sarah sat well back, her stomach almost creating an extension to the desk, but Beth couldn't see any sign of a dog.

'OK,' she said, looking around the room. 'Where is he? Filed? Hiding in the waste paper basket?'

Grinning like the proverbial Cheshire feline, Sarah motioned Beth to back away to the other side of the room. Still Beth saw nothing, until she followed Sarah's dramatic downward nods. At first Beth only noticed her friend's swollen ankles. Then there was a slight movement as a tiny black nose inched forward from between Sarah's feet, and the brightest black eyes she had ever seen stared up at Beth, the white furry head cocked on one side with curiosity.

'Oh,' breathed Beth. 'He's delightful.' Slowly she pulled a chair closer and eased herself down on to it, prepared to wait until Hamish came towards her. She didn't have to wait long. The wagging rudder propelled the dog towards her feet, which were well and truly sniffed. Sliding her hand down her leg, she waited for the gentle touch of his wet nose. Obviously satisfied that there were no worrisome smells of other beasties, his dainty pink tongue licked her fingers. Then the strangest thing happened. He sat back and looked up at her, raised one forepaw and gave the softest 'woof'. It was as though he was speaking to her.

'What does he want?' Beth asked Sarah.

'I think he wants you to pick him up.'

'Did he do it to you?'

'You're joking! One look at me and he realised that it would be like climbing Mount Everest. But you're different — you've got a lap.'

Another 'woof', just slightly louder, reminded Beth that she should at least try it. Very gently, she placed her hands under his plump belly and lifted him on to her lap. The response was immediate. Hamish stretched his body up her chest until the exploring tongue was just able to reach her chin. Then he eased back, found a comfortable position on her lap, and looked across at Sarah.

'You see,' Sarah gloated. 'If he was a cat he'd be purring like mad.'

'All right, you win.' Beth laughed as she reached into her shoulder bag for her purse. 'One fiver coming up.'

'Keep it. I've bought enough dog food to last for a few days, but he'll need a new collar and name-tag.'

'Thanks. Does he have a basket, or favourite blanket, or anything like that?'

'No. The vet thinks he slept on the woman's bed.'

'That's out for a start.' She wagged her finger at Hamish with mock severity. 'First chance tomorrow we're off shopping for a doggie bed.'

'Where's he going to sleep tonight, then?'

'He'll be fine in the kitchen.'

Sarah snorted. 'You'll be lucky.'

'So where did he sleep last night?'

'Don't ask.' Sarah continued to grin.

For a moment, Beth stared back, then she said, 'It's all a question of discipline. Starting as you mean to go on.'

'Of course.'

Sarah's smug expression was infuriating. Beth turned her attention back to Hamish. 'I just hope you haven't got any other bad habits I haven't been told about.' She raised her eyebrows at Sarah.

'He's been wormed, jabbed and house-trained, if that's what you mean. The vet put everything down here.' Sarah handed Beth a piece of paper. 'Anyway, it's too late now. He's already adopted you.'

Beth pulled a face at Sarah, then looked back at Hamish. It was true. His expression was so adoring there was no way she could have refused to keep him. 'The poor woman must be heart-broken, having to give him up,' she commented. 'Do you think I'd be allowed to take him to visit her now and again?'

Sarah shook her head. 'From what I hear, she has the beginnings of dementia. Put him out in the garden to wee one day and forgot all about him. A neighbour eventually rescued him and phoned the vet.'

'Poor little chap.' Beth stroked his silky head. 'He is a bit on the podgy side,' she observed. 'I'll have to take him to Weight Watchers.'

'Too many chocolates and not enough walkies, I believe,' Sarah said.

'Well, we can soon rectify that. I could do with a bit more exercise myself, and there's no time like the present.' Beth lifted Hamish down from her lap. 'Does he have a lead?'

'Of sorts.' Sarah handed Beth a well-chewed string of leather. 'I think it had belonged to all her previous dogs.'

'Exercising teeth rather than legs, by the look of it.' Beth fastened the rusty clip to the collar, which had also seen better days. 'But it'll have to do for now.'

'Your coffee is getting cold.'

Beth had forgotten about it. 'Thanks,' she said. Then her mind turned to a different direction. 'Sarah . . . ' She hesitated.

'Yes?'

'What do you think of Gavin?'

Sarah looked surprised. 'I don't understand,' she said.

'I just want to know your opinion of him, that's all.'

'He's a thoroughly nice guy, in my opinion. Certainly the nicest of all the guys that Ali has fallen for, by far.'

'Do you think he's trustworthy?'

'In what way?'

'Well, you know what rotten luck Ali has with her love life. I'd hate to see her let down again.'

'Are you worried that he might have another love nest up in Cheshire?'

Before Beth could answer, the telephone rang.

Sarah listened quietly to the caller for a few minutes, then said, 'I think you've made a wise decision, Mr Johnson,' she said. 'I felt your wife really liked that house. And yes, the office is still open. I'll have the necessary papers ready for you.' As she replaced the receiver, she grinned broadly and punched the air. 'Yes!' she cried gleefully. 'I knew they'd have it.'

'Which one?'

'The last of the expensive ones, in Admiral's Way. They came back for a second look this afternoon, and I could see by her face that she was smitten. It hasn't taken her long to convince him that a house near the sea is what he really, really wants.'

'Was he doubtful?'

'Only about the price. It will probably stretch them a bit, but they've already sold their house in Marchwood, and their buyers are getting fidgety.'

'Children?'

'Three, and another on the way.'

'Great spot for a family.' Beth stood up. 'I'd better let you get on.'

'Before you go — what were you saying about Gavin?'

The last thing Beth wanted was to be interrupted by excited house-buyers. 'Nothing,' she said. 'See you at Ali's tomorrow night?'

'Of course. It's great to be eating properly again. Talking of eating . . . ' Sarah reached under the desk for a plastic shopping bag.

'Don't forget Hamish's supper.'

After Hamish had licked the dish clean, Beth decided that a walk in the direction of the beach would be a good idea. At first, Hamish was excited by all the sights and smells of the seashore, straining at the end of his tatty leash. Then he decided he'd had enough exercise for one day, and sat down. Beth tugged gently on the lead.

'Come on, Hamish,' she said. 'Just to the next breakwater, then we'll go home.'

Hamish was having none of it. The more she tugged, the firmer he glued his backside to the beach.

'Please don't do this to me,' she pleaded, but he didn't even look at her. Just sat firmly, panting a little and looking out to sea.

'Beth!' The figure dashing towards her, arms waving wildly, could be none other than Cassandra. Only she could have such energy at the end of a warm afternoon. Smiling, Beth waited, knowing what the reaction would be as soon as the girl noticed Hamish.

'Oh, Beth! Is he yours? Really? Oh, Beth, he's so sweet.' She crouched down to tickle his ears. Hamish looked as though he thought he was in heaven. 'When did you get him?'

As Beth was telling her his story, they were distracted by a jet ski coming in from the sea, rather fast and too close for comfort.

'I wish they wouldn't do that,' Cassie complained. 'It must have frightened the life out of poor little Hamish — oh, Beth — look what he's doing.'

Beth looked at him in dismay. 'I didn't think to bring any plastic bags or anything with me.'

'Not to worry. I'll get something. You wait here.'

Cassie had obviously inherited her mother's love of speed, for Hamish had barely finished his embarrassing but necessary task when she came dashing back, carrying plastic bags and a small trowel.

'Thanks.' Beth rubbed at the trowel with one of the spare bags. 'I'll take it home and clean it properly. Let you have it back tomorrow, if that's all right?'

'Bung it in the other bag and I'll do it later.'

'I couldn't possibly — '

'Nadine and Thora are dying to see Hamish, and I've been given strict instructions to bring you both home now, so it's no problem. Can I take the lead?'

Within minutes Hamish was being petted and cooed over by the two girls and offered a large bowl of water, which he lapped up instantly, then woofed his thanks for the biscuits. Beth wasn't so sure that biscuits were a good idea, but hadn't the heart to spoil the moment. Then Thora wheeled Vanessa into the conservatory.

'Hallo, Beth,' Thora said. 'Cassie tells me you've got the loveliest dog she's ever seen, and — oh, yes — just look at him, Vanessa. Isn't he gorgeous?'

The smile on Vanessa's face said it all. For a moment, she just stared, then beckoned Thora to bend closer and whispered something in her ear.

'I don't see why not, dear,' the older woman said, then turned to Beth. 'Vanessa is wondering whether Hamish could sit on her lap.'

Carefully, Beth lifted Hamish and placed him on the rug covering Vanessa's knees. Very slowly, Vanessa's hand moved from the arm of the wheelchair until she was able to stroke his back. He remained perfectly still, almost as though he knew what an effort it was. Perhaps that was how it had been with his previous owner, Beth wondered. Or just animal instinct.

The smile never left Vanessa's face and, after a few moments, she raised her eyes to Beth, and moved her lips. Although the words were indistinct, Beth knew she was saying 'thank you'.

Eventually, Thora broke the spell, brushing

her hand across her eyes. 'I'm going to make some tea,' she murmured. 'Tom will be in soon.'

Beth stood up, preparing to take her leave, but was promptly shushed back into the chair by Thora and Cassie. So it was that when the man of the house arrived a few minutes later, he was greeted by the sight of his smiling wife stroking Hamish, their two daughters sitting at her feet and Beth looking on.

'Well,' he said, allowing Hamish to sniff at his hand. 'Aren't you a handsome little fellow?' He looked at Beth. 'Or is he a she? I presume he's yours?'

'Yes, and he's a he. Hamish.'

Tom threw back his head and laughed. 'Now there's a name that fits. How long have you had him?'

Before Beth could answer, Cassie burbled out the whole story. Two cups of tea later, Beth declared she really must go home, despite their attempt to persuade her to stay for a meal.

'It really is kind of you, but I've been out all day and have things to do ready for work tomorrow. By the way, Sarah has sold the house next door, so you'll have some neighbours soon.'

Cassie, as usual, was full of questions. What were they like? How old? Children?

'I haven't met them yet. Don't know how old. Yes, lots of children. And they sound like a very nice family.'

Beth said goodbye and, as she reached to lift Hamish from Vanessa's lap, the hand that had been stroking him rested on Beth's hand for a moment. It was obviously a struggle to speak, but the words, 'Come again' were clear enough.

'Of course.' Beth smiled. 'And shall I bring Hamish?'

Vanessa nodded.

'I'll walk back with you,' Tom said.

'I'll be OK, honestly,' Beth protested, laughing. 'I've got my little guard dog to protect me.'

'To tell the truth I could do with stretching my legs. I've been stuck in meetings all day, but I don't feel like getting changed and jogging along the beach. A walk will do me good.'

At first he just made polite conversation about her job, future plans, one or two ideas he had for the garden. Then he said, 'I've never known Vanessa to take to an animal as much as she has to Hamish. Cassie begged for a dog or a horse, but Vanessa always put her off, even when she was quite little. Said our lifestyle made it impossible.'

'I suppose it would have been very difficult,

living in two countries, especially when she was so involved in athletics.'

'Maybe.' He walked on thoughtfully. 'Cassie approached me again about a dog when we bought this house, but I was the one who said no this time.' He reflected for a moment, then went on, 'As Vanessa's disease progresses, she is going to need more and more attention, and when the inevitable happens, the onus will be on Thora to care for the dog while the girls are at school. She has said she doesn't mind, bless her, but I still feel it isn't fair on her, or the animal.'

'I can see your point, but perhaps a small animal would not be too much trouble, and they say that having a pet to stroke is very therapeutic for an invalid.'

'Yes, I can see the reasoning behind that.' Hamish was tiring again, so Tom paused to carry him the last few yards, still talking. 'I don't want you to think that we're trying to poach his affections from you,' he said, 'but if you would like to leave Hamish with us sometimes — perhaps when it's inconvenient for you to take him to work, we'd be very happy to have him, and I think it would please Vanessa.'

'That's very kind of you, Tom, but what about Thora?'

'Thora only wants the best for Vanessa, and

if it will help to make her remaining time with us a little more pleasant, Thora won't mind. The girls would be tickled pink, of course, and it's a compromise that could be of benefit to both of us. Please think about it.'

'I will, and thank you.'

As she watched Tom stride back along the road, Beth wondered how he could speak with such detachment about his dying wife.

★ ★ ★

Later that night, after Beth had sorted out her work for the next day, and written a shopping list for Hamish, she wondered whether she should confront Gavin, tell him she had seen him with the girl outside another agency and wait for his reaction. It wasn't going to be easy. Perhaps she should leave well alone. If Ali was happy, Beth didn't want to be the one to spoil everything. On the other hand . . . whatever, she couldn't do anything about it until tomorrow night. So she pushed all thoughts of Ali and Gavin from her mind, poured herself a glass of wine and wrote down in detail the facts relating to Eliza. On Monday she would contact Mr Brooke, tell him she had checked the records in Winchester, just out of curiosity, and see if he had any further observations to make, anything at all that might be of help to rid herself of the voice, without actually telling him about it. Then she hunted through a box of old clothes she had designated for a jumble sale, found a woollen jumper and settled Hamish down on the back doormat. He looked very sleepy, after all his fresh air and exertions, and she didn't foresee any problems, but left her bedroom door ajar, so she could hear him, should he decide to have a gnaw at the furniture.

She wasn't sure exactly how long she had slept, long enough for her to have gone into a deep sleep, when she heard the soft but insistent 'woof'. Hamish was sitting at the side of the bed, one paw raised. She knew she should be firm and take him back downstairs, but all her good intentions went awry when he cocked his little head on one side and 'woofed' again.

'All right.' Sleepily, she leaned over and scooped him up. 'But you keep to that side of the bed, understand? And it's only for tonight, so don't think I'm a soft touch.'

His gentle 'woof' as he curled up on the duvet told her that he understood every word, perfectly.

16

There hadn't been an opportunity to speak to Gavin during the evening. It was the fault of one small West Highland terrier, who even managed to upstage Sarah's bump. When Beth phoned Ali to say that she was a bit concerned about leaving Hamish on his own so soon, Ali immediately agreed that Beth could bring him. So, having put some of his new possessions into the boot of her car, and dressed him in his spotless red collar and lead, complete with shiny name-tag, they set off.

It was a wonder they managed to have a meal at all. Ali spent more time playing with her canine guest than working in her kitchen, and was only prised away when someone else demanded that it was their turn. As for Hamish, he loved every minute and was impeccably behaved. Even barked at the door when he needed to go out for a 'wee' visit.

Gavin's behaviour was also faultless. Although she watched him closely, Beth couldn't sense any feeling that he was acting a part, or leading a double life. He had greeted her with a friendly kiss on the cheek, asked

214

quietly if she was all right, looking as though it really mattered, then turned his attentions to Hamish. The atmosphere between him and Ali was one of a loving relationship, with affectionate glances and his arm around her shoulders when they were standing together. In fact, Sarah whispered to Beth that it wouldn't surprise her if they announced their engagement. They didn't, but Ali did mention to Sarah that she might be looking for a house before too long. That was the only time Gavin dropped his facade, if it was a facade. He looked away, with a slight frown, then murmured something about refilling the nibbles dishes.

On impulse, Beth followed him into the kitchen. Perhaps if she mentioned that she had seen him again the previous day, she might be able to judge something from his reaction. For a moment or two they silently tipped peanuts into two dishes, then she tentatively asked, 'How did your business meeting work out yesterday?'

Without hesitation, he said, 'Fine, thanks. I managed to sort out the query for my boss. And how about you? Did you find anything you liked for the house?'

'Yes. I bought some paintings and cush-ions.' She was about to add where she had bought them, just to see if he looked nervous because she had been so near to the agency, when Ali came into the kitchen.

'We won't need too many nibbles now, darling, I'm about to dish up.'

'Great.' Gavin beamed at her. 'I'm starving, and it smells delicious.'

'It's got that new sauce that you like.'

'What a woman,' he said. 'Sometimes I think I don't deserve you.' He kissed her lightly on the lips. 'Want some help?' he asked.

'Would you strain the pasta for me, please?'

They looked so happy together, and so right. It was as though Beth didn't exist. More confused than ever, she went into the bathroom. Here was even more evidence of Ali and Gavin being a twosome. His towelling robe hung behind the door with Ali's, his electric shaver and aftershave on the shelf beside the female toiletries. How could she burst this bubble? Beth thought. What if his visit to the secretarial agency and meeting with the girl were perfectly innocent? Ali would never forgive her if she spoiled everything through a misunderstanding, or clumsiness.

The remainder of the evening passed happily enough, although Beth had to remove Damon's hand from her knee at one point. As usual, he had drunk too much wine. Sarah glanced at him once or twice, and finally reminded him that they had a home to go to, but seemed to be in good humour.

As she turned the car in the forecourt, Beth's last glimpse of Gavin and Ali was of them waving from the window, arms around each other, and smiling. She hoped and prayed that she was wrong to have misgivings about him but, apart from an actual confrontation, what could she do to find out the truth?

★   ★   ★

Hamish curled up quite happily on his new bed in the kitchen, but Beth's mind was too full for sleep. She heated herself some milk, added a spoonful of honey, and ran her finger along the bookshelves, looking for something gentle that might lull her into drowsiness. *Little Women.* Beth smiled wistfully as she took down the well-worn book. Even as an adult, she had continued to dip into it from time to time, but she hadn't looked at it since Katie died.

Plumping up her pillows, Beth settled herself comfortably in bed, sipped her hot milk, and opened the book at random. *Chapter 15 — a telegram.* Oh, dear, Beth sighed. *Chapter 15 — a telegram,* was not the most relaxing choice, particularly when she came to the contents of the telegram, *Mrs March: Your husband is very ill. Come at once.*

Suddenly she was a child again, remembering the times when her mother sat on Beth's bed, reading their favourite story aloud, Beth always begging for more. Like Mrs March, her mother had always known instinctively how to react to a difficult situation. She would know what Beth should do about Ali and Gavin. If only she was still alive to listen and advise.

Gulping back the tears, Beth read on, *How still the room was as they listened breathlessly, how strangely the day darkened outside, and how suddenly the whole world seemed to change, as the girls gathered about their mother, feeling as if all the happiness and support of their lives was about to be taken from them.*

No. This would not do. Beth was about to find a happier passage, when she heard Hamish whimper at the foot of the stairs. This time she was determined to have no such nonsense, so she padded downstairs in her bare feet, picked him up and carried him back to his bed, with a quiet but firm order to 'stay'. At first, he just looked appealingly at her, then the strangest thing happened. He began to growl, and scampered up the stairs.

That was when Beth became aware that her feet were icy cold. There was no doubt that woodblock flooring was not as warm as the lush carpets she had left behind at 'The Cherries'. She would have to get into the habit of slipping on her bathrobe and mules to wander around this house in the middle of the night. She shivered. There was a shocking draught. Must be the upstairs window. Even so, the house still felt too cold for a summer's night. Now, if that wretched little dog had managed to clamber up on to her bed . . .

The room was only partially lit by her bedside lamp, but there was no sign of her new pet, until she sprawled full length and peered under the bed. His little white shape was just out of her reach.

'Come on, Hamish,' she called. 'You've got your lovely new bed downstairs. I really can't be doing with this.'

Beth held out her hand to try to coax him towards her, but he backed up towards the wall, making the most peculiar noises, half growling, half whimpering. Then she heard another sound. Weeping. Could it be the next-door neighbour? She crawled out from under the bed and put her ear close to the wall, but it was impossible to hear the sound clearly above the noise Hamish was making.

'Shush, Hamish!' she whispered fiercely, but could only hear fragments. It sounded like a child crying, but they didn't have children next door. Then there was something else. A voice, sobbing. It sounded as though the child was pleading with someone. As Hamish's growls softened to a whimper, Beth detected a few words.

'Please, I beg you.'

What was going on next door? Then Beth's blood ran cold as she heard a name. Her name.

'Beth. Be careful.'

'Eliza?'

Now Hamish began to bark. Sharply and furiously. It was impossible to hear anything above the din. Beth's legs gave way and she slid down the wall to her knees. Had it been Eliza? Not next door, but here, in this room? Was this house not only haunted, but cursed? If so, what could she do? It was her home. She couldn't afford to move again.

A cold nose touched her leg. Hamish was wriggling towards her, still half under the bed. She listened. Silence.

Beth knew she should have taken him back downstairs, but didn't have the heart. Instead, she brought his bed upstairs and tucked it into the corner.

'That's as close as you're getting,' she

murmured. 'Tomorrow, you can sleep on the landing, but tonight — ' she dropped a goodnight kiss on to his furry head, 'tonight I need you as much as you need me.'

* * *

Several hours later, Beth lay staring at the ceiling, listening to the gentle snores of Hamish, and wondering if the whole incident might not have been yet another fragment of her imagination, perhaps triggered by reading that sad *Chapter 15 — a telegram*. But if Eliza really was trying to warn her about living in this house, or an unhappy soul trying to tell someone, anyone, what had happened to her all those years ago, would her unseen presence ever leave Beth in peace?

Suddenly, Beth sat upright, remembering what she had said to Gavin. 'I wouldn't be able to rest in peace until the truth was told.' And he had suggested writing it down — as a short story, or anecdote.

What if she tried to get it published? Would that be the end of the matter?

Snuggling back under the duvet, Beth planned what she would say to Mr Brooke.

17

Mr Brooke was curious as to the source of Beth's story, but she passed it off as something she had stumbled upon in a pub. An old man talking about skeletons in his family cupboard, tales his grandmother had told him when he was barely more than knee high.

'Sounds like he might be spinning yarns to get free pints. I'm not sure you could interest a publisher. It's mainly hearsay. Nothing to back it up.'

'I know, but his great-uncle had been a gardener at a big house, and he'd been on more than 'walking-out' terms with the kitchen maid.'

'So where do the dastardly deeds at the Castle come in?'

'The kitchen maid was the one you mentioned. You know, the story you heard when you were a child.'

'The one Mrs Wheeler told me? About a ghost frightening the life out of the poor girl? Why are you so sure it's her?'

'It has to be. This poor girl had been dumped by her boyfriend when she told him she was pregnant. He had his eye on another girl, of a higher station, so he didn't want to know.'

'That sort of thing happened all the time in those days. Still does.'

'I know, but listen to this. The girl told one of the other maids that a ghost had talked to her, told her about her own experience when she lived at Calshot Castle, and how her husband had abandoned her for someone else — *also of a higher station.*'

For a while there was no sound from the telephone. Then Mr Brooke said, 'I doubt very much whether the servant would have kept a diary or anything like that. She probably couldn't even read or write.'

'But she could draw.'

'Draw?'

'Yes. She had drawn a picture of the ghost.'

'Did you see the picture?'

'Yes.' Beth crossed her fingers as she lied. 'The old boy in the pub showed it to me. It was a rough drawing, but looked like a gypsy girl. Wasn't that what your Mrs Wheeler said?'

Again a silence, then Mr Brooke asked, 'Where was the kitchen maid supposed to have seen this ghost?'

'On the beach, near the Castle.' Beth remembered her first feeling of Eliza's presence and her own despair. 'She had gone there to drown herself. But once she had seen the ghost she rushed back to the house in hysterics and told everyone about it.' Again Beth used her imagination to make the story more plausible. 'She even spilled the beans about the under-gardener and her predicament. He denied it, of course, said she had fantasies about him and wasn't quite right in the head. They believed him, and she was put away.'

'And the gardener kept the drawing?'

'I suppose so.' Beth went on with the true purpose of her phone call. 'It's an interesting tale, don't you think?'

'It's quite a yarn, I agree, and would certainly spice up a collection of local folk lore.'

'That's the reason why I phoned you.' Beth tried to sound less excited than she felt. 'As a local historian, you must know most of the people who publish such stories.'

'Oh, yes.' Mr Brooke sounded thoughtful. 'There have been some very good anthologies over the years. In fact, if my memory serves me right, someone in Lyndhurst is compiling another one at the moment.'

'Really? How can I get in touch with them?'

'Leave it with me, and I'll ask our secretary if she has the address. It might be better if I contact them first, make sure they are still looking for material.'

Beth would have preferred a more direct approach, but wasn't in a position to argue, so she left her telephone number with Mr Brooke and hoped for the best.

Two weeks later, he phoned with the address of Ken and Margaret Beamish, who would be glad to consider the story and would she like to visit them? The last thing Beth wanted was to become even more involved, so she made the excuse of too much work and agreed to send them a typescript that they could use or adapt if they wished. Actually, the work excuse was not too untruthful. The last house on the 'Seascape' development was in the process of being sold, and Sarah was anxious for her to take over the main office as soon as possible.

With a sigh of relief, Beth sealed the envelope and drove to Fawley post office. At least she could now tell Eliza, should she appear again, that the truth about her death had been told at last. And, hopefully, that would be the end of that.

After leaving the post office, Beth bought a bottle of wine at the general store and picked up a selection of fliers on fêtes, open gardens and show jumping events. She had another 'Welcome' box to prepare for the Johnsons, who would be moving in next door to the Mastersons in a few days. As Beth crossed The Square to order the flowers, she heard her name called. It was Cassie, full of beans as always.

'Hi. And hallo to you, too, Hamish.' The little dog had to be hugged and adored before she could continue. 'I'm glad I saw you.' Cassie giggled as the pink tongue found her nose. 'Mum has been asking when she is going to see this little beastie again. We all miss him, and you too, of course. Even Dad asked if you had called in.'

'Oh,' Beth was a little taken aback. Her mind had been so focused on Eliza and Ali recently that she had almost forgotten her promise. 'I'm sorry — I've been rather busy so he's just had short walks round the block, I'm afraid. But I've just sold the last house, so I won't have to work weekends, which will make things easier.'

'Great! Come and see us tomorrow then.'

'OK. I'll ring Thora first, to make sure it's convenient.'

'You really don't have to, you know. We're always pleased to see you.'

'Thanks.' Beth smiled at the girl's enthusiasm. 'I've almost finished my errands. Can I offer you a lift?'

'Actually, I cycled, thanks just the same.'

Cassie nodded towards a mountain bike parked outside the post office. 'Present from Dad. What do you think?'

'I think it's magnificent. Much grander than the old rattler I used to have at your age.'

'It's brilliant. Masses of gears. Just what I need for getting to the stables. Do you ride?'

'I used to. Not for years, though. What about you?'

'Only when I was at boarding school. What with Dad's job and Mum's lifestyle, we never stayed in one place long enough for me to have a pony of my own.'

'Do you think your father will be more settled now?'

'He's got to, really, because of Mum. When he asked to move back to the UK he told the refinery he wanted to stay for several years, at least until . . . ' Her face clouded briefly with unhappiness, then she brightened. 'I really like it here, you know, so near the sea and stuff.'

'Good. It's a nice place for young people, and it won't be long before you and Nadine make friends at your new school.'

Cassie grimaced. 'Not sure about Nadine. She didn't even want Dad to buy her a mountain bike. Said she'd rather spend her time with Mum, or maybe just go for a walk on the beach. Never can tell what she's thinking inside. She's a loner, like Dad.'

Gently, Beth observed, 'It must be dreadful for all of you.'

'Yes, it is. Of course it is. But Thora and I talk about it. Cry on each other's shoulder, whereas Nadine and Dad . . . ' The pensive look crossed her face again. 'If only they could let it out, I am sure it would help.'

'You may be right, but people have their own way of dealing with grief.'

Cassie looked directly at Beth. 'I suppose it was like this when your mother was dying. How did you cope?'

Beth had forgotten she had mentioned her mother's illness. Even after thirteen years, it was still painful to remember those final months. Slowly, she said, 'It wasn't easy, and it hit my father very hard. There were just the two of us, and he couldn't accept that she wouldn't get better. Sometimes I thought he'd never get over it. The best thing he did was to go to Canada and build a new life for himself. It's what my mother would have wanted.'

'But what about *you?*' Cassie persisted. 'Didn't it make it harder for you — to be left on your own?'

Beth smiled wryly as she remembered almost a feeling of relief when her father finally left. His grief had been so overwhelming she had found it difficult to get through her own loss. 'I had married by that time,' she said, 'so I wasn't alone. And Dad is with his brother, and their rather large family. Perhaps one day he'll find someone else to love.' She didn't tell Beth that every phone call and letter from her father was still full of longing for her mother. Even when Katie died, he hadn't been able to face the funeral.

'I'd like to think that Dad will do that, eventually,' Cassie said. 'I don't think people should be on their own, do you? Even if they are as old as Dad.'

Beth suppressed a smile at the thought of someone in their forties being considered too old.

Hamish barked one of his gentle reminders that he had been standing still for quite long enough, and Cassie remembered that she was supposed to be buying shampoo for Thora, and taking it straight back.

★ ★ ★

By the time Beth handed over the keys to the new owners of the showhouse, Hamish had so endeared himself to the Masterson family that Thora asked if they could look after him while Beth was working at the Hythe office.

'I know it sounds like an awful cheek, especially as you are obviously devoted to one another — but if only you knew the difference he makes to Vanessa.'

'It's not a cheek at all, Thora. In fact, it is very good of you. To be honest, although Sarah and Jane are quite happy for me to take him into the office, I am a little concerned about the clients, and how they might react.'

'Surely that's not such a problem? He's such a friendly little chap. Not at all snappy.'

'Yes, but there are people who are allergic to dogs. Then there are the children to think of.'

'I see your point. They could either be scared stiff, or pester the life out of him.'

'Exactly.'

'So does that mean we can have him? Just while you're at work, of course.'

'If you're sure it's not too much trouble. After all, you've got your hands full with Vanessa, and the house to run as well.'

'Hamish will be more help than hindrance. He'll be good company for Vanessa, especially when the girls go back to school. Nadine hardly leaves her side. But, talking of the house . . . '

'Yes?'

'I was wondering whether you know anyone who might come in for a couple of mornings a week to help with the cleaning. It's not too great a problem at the moment, with the girls around, but once they have homework and so on, I can't expect them to do as much as they do now.'

'And it's a very big house to keep in order.' Beth thought for a moment. 'I don't know of anyone off hand,' she said, 'but I'll ask around.'

'Thanks. I could put a card up in the shops, of course, but I'd much rather have a personal recommendation. Preferably some-one who wouldn't be too worried about being alone with Vanessa if I had to pop out to the shops.'

Jane said she'd ask her mother, but it was Sarah who came to the rescue. Her Mrs Hosey had lived in Dibden before she married, and still had relatives in the Waterside area. When asked, Mrs Hosey was sure her sister would be only too glad to earn a few pounds. Her widow's pension didn't go far and she lived down one of the lanes between Fawley and Calshot. No, she didn't drive, but that had never stopped Edie from getting around. If it was too far to walk, she trundled along on her old push-bike.

Fortunately, Edie Cooper and Thora Masterson hit it off from the start and, before the end of summer, a mutually beneficial routine had been established. Even the garden began to take shape as Thora was able to give it more time between the gardener's weekly visits. And Beth soon settled in at her new desk, knowing that Hamish was being cosseted on Vanessa's lap. Each evening she would collect Hamish and take him for a long walk, and she was pleased that he made as much fuss of her as he did of Vanessa. It was as though he knew she was his real owner, and he was on loan to the others. Even when Tom asked if he could accompany her, Hamish stayed close to Beth, and looked to her for instructions. She enjoyed the walks with Tom. They didn't talk much, but it developed into a pleasant companionship.

Soon, she found herself sharing other areas of her life with his family, not just her dog. Sometimes she would be invited to stay for a meal, or Cassie would ask if they could go riding together. It didn't take Beth long to feel quite at home again in the saddle, and she loved the exhilaration of a canter through remote parts of the forest, Cassie always ahead, blonde hair streaming behind her, racing Beth back to the stables. If anything would blow the cobwebs away, after a stressful day in the office, it was those rides with Cassie.

Then, one day, they returned to the stables

to find Tom waiting there. At first Beth was anxious, thinking that something had happened to Vanessa, but his smile put her fears to rest.

'Thora told me you were here, so I thought I'd come over to see how you're doing.' He patted Cassie's horse. 'This one can certainly put on a bit of speed,' he observed. 'Are you sure you're strong enough to handle him?'

'Don't fuss, Dad. Of course I am. And Blaze always does as he's told.'

'She's a very good rider, Tom,' Beth reassured him.

'You're not so bad yourself,' he said. 'In fact, I thought you were going to beat this young tearaway of mine.'

Beth knew she could have beaten Cassie, but she always allowed the girl the excitement of a successful finish.

'Why don't you come out with us next time, Dad?' Cassie asked, as she began to unhitch the saddle.

'I might do that.'

Beth looked up from the strap she was loosening. 'Have you ridden much?' she asked. He had never mentioned it.

'Only in the States. On a ranch, with saddles like armchairs.' He took the saddle from Cassie. 'Expect these things feel a bit different.'

'There's a place near Brockenhurst that specialises in western-style riding.'

'Really!' Cassie was excited. 'I've always wanted to try it.'

So it was that Cassie switched her loyalties to another stables for a short while, and the three of them would ride together once a week, until Cassie decided that she wanted to ride her beloved Blaze again during the last week of the holiday. Tom didn't fancy switching saddles, so asked Beth if they could ride together.

That was when she discovered the true reason for his phlegmatic attitude.

18

For a while they rode in companionable silence, commenting on the sighting of a rabbit or a deer, not really talking, just enjoying the tranquillity. The evening was warm but rather humid and after half an hour or so, they stopped to let the horses drink from a stream, and refresh their own faces with the cool water.

'Is it safe to drink, do you think?' Tom asked.

'I wouldn't chance it. All sorts of nasties have been known to seep into the stream.'

'Rather like the 'something nasty in the woodshed', I suppose. You don't know what it is, but it's there.'

They both laughed, and Beth sat back on a grassy hummock, lifting her face to dry in the sunlight filtering through the leaves. Tom still crouched down on his haunches, his face turned away.

Suddenly, he said, 'How long have you been separated from your husband?'

Surprised, Beth looked at him. She had never discussed her marriage with any of the Mastersons, and they had never asked, not since the day when Cassie had mentioned it. Beth cast her mind back through the calendar of events. 'About a year, I suppose, no — a little longer than that. Time goes so quickly.'

'Had you been married for long?'

'Ten years.'

He swivelled his head round towards her, then looked away again. 'You must have been very young when you married.'

'I thought I was old enough at the time — but, looking back, my father and friends tried to warn me, and they were right. If I'd listened more, and thought more, per- haps . . . ' Her voice trailed.

'I'm sorry. I shouldn't have pried. It's obviously painful talking about him.'

'Not at all. I don't mind talking about Bryn. He was a bastard. Past history.'

Tom laughed. 'You must have thought I was like him when you first met me. I can't believe how rude I was to you.'

'Yes.' Leaning forward, Beth picked up a pine cone and lobbed it at his back. 'And it's a good job you didn't hear some of the names I called you under my breath.'

He turned and grinned at her. 'Trouble was, I'd just had a really bad experience with another estate agent. They hadn't got a clue what they were doing. Gave me details of the most unsuitable properties on the market, even sent me on a wild goose chase after one they had already sold.' He sighed. 'It was wrong of me, I know, but I suppose I assumed you were all tarred with the same inefficient brush.'

'Well, you did catch me on a very bad hair day.'

'I'll never forget my first sight and sound of you mumbling from under that towel, soaking wet, like a bit of flotsam blown in from the storm.'

'Still, I got my own back when you fell bum over tip into the mud.'

'Oh, God! I was mortified.'

For a few moments they sat silently, each smiling at the memories. Then Tom said 'I hope you've reviewed your opinion of me by now.'

'Of course. As long as you don't still think I'm a complete dimbo.'

'Goodness, no! I soon realised that you are very, very good at your job. The way you handled all those adaptations to the house was nothing short of superb.'

'Thanks.'

'And I really am sorry I was such a — a — '

'Cad?'

His eyebrows raised. 'That's an expression you don't often hear now.'

'The worst thing my father could ever think to say about anyone was that they were an utter cad. That was a quaint expression even for his generation.'

'Cassie told me he now lives in Canada.'

'Did she now?' Beth chuckled.

'Oh, yes. I always have to remember not to tell Cassie anything I don't want passed on,' he said. 'Nadine would take a confidence to the grave, but my little chatterbox cannot keep a secret to save her life.'

'She's very young, and so full of life. I truly enjoy her company.'

'Sometimes I think that Cassie will be my saviour. However down I feel about things, somehow she always manages to lift me up.'

'I know what you mean. She has the same effect on me.' Beth sat up and leaned her arms on her knees, idly watching the horses, who had wandered a little way downstream. 'And it's no wonder you feel down at times. I remember feeling so totally helpless when my mother was ill, knowing there was nothing I could do to prevent the inevitable.' She was thoughtful for a moment, then went on. 'Thora is wonderful with Vanessa. Was she a nurse?'

'Yes. Eventually she had her own nursing home, mainly for elderly people, but a few younger invalids who had no family to support them.'

'And she gave it up to care for Vanessa?'

'Oh, yes. As soon as she heard, she put the place on the market so I could bring Vanessa back to England. She didn't want to die in the States and, to be honest, the medical fees out there were taking me close to bankruptcy. I couldn't have bought this house without Thora's financial input — or her offer to live with us.'

'Does Vanessa have any relatives?'

'No — at least, none she has contact with. Her parents were killed in a car crash when she was small and her older brother was brought up by relatives on a remote Scottish island. They don't even exchange Christmas cards.'

'Who looked after Vanessa?'

'Elderly grandparents at first, then various aunts and uncles. Nobody could really cope with her, so she ran away at fifteen. If she hadn't been helped by a man who was into athletics and spotted her potential, she might have finished up on the streets — in every sense of the word.'

Beth was shocked at the calm announcement. Thinking of the frail beauty in the wheelchair, she said, 'You can't really mean that?'

'I'm afraid it's true.' His voice was still emotionless. 'The first man she met when she left home set her up in a flat. During the day she worked as a receptionist in a beauty salon. At night she was the entertainment for the man's business friends when they were staying in London. In other words — a call girl.' Tom looked round at Beth, who was too stunned to speak. Then he went on, 'That's how she met the athletic club manager. Just in time, before her pimp found another girlfriend and threw her out.'

It took quite a while for Beth to absorb his story. Then she asked, 'How did you meet her?'

'Not under those circumstances, I can assure you. I didn't know her background until we'd been married for years.' Tom's smile was wry. 'We met at a restaurant. Vanessa was just beginning to make a name for herself on the athletic circuit and I recognised her, but didn't have the nerve to speak to her. The guy I was lunching with saw me gawping and arranged an introduction. She was so beautiful and vivacious — every man in the restaurant ogled her and the women looked murderous.' Lost in memory, Tom glanced away, then went on, 'To use the old cliché, I fell head over heels in love at first sight. I was really surprised when she agreed to have dinner with me.'

'So the feeling was mutual?'

'In a way. I didn't realise at the time that she was in a relationship with one of the guys in her party, so it wasn't until later that I discovered she had dumped him for me.'

Beth wondered what Tom meant by 'in a way'.

'Naturally, I was flattered,' he went on. 'Who wouldn't be? Even when one of her so-called friends warned me that I might also be dumped if someone more interesting crossed her path, I didn't believe them.'

'But she married you.'

'I think I was the first to offer marriage, and it suited Vanessa to have the support and backing of a husband, and the wherewithal to have a family when her biological clock began to tick.'

Such bitterness, Beth thought. 'You make her sound very . . . ' She struggled for the word.

'Ruthless? She is — was. Sadly, she isn't now in a position to be anything other than helpless.'

'So why did you stay with her?'

Slowly, Tom stood up and arched his back, taking a few steps towards the horses. His voice was so low, Beth could hardly hear him. 'She was the one who left,' he said, 'with her personal trainer. Younger, better looking, and much, much richer.'

'American?'

He nodded. 'That's when I found out the rest of the story. A sort of farewell taunt. So I began divorce proceedings.'

Beth waited for him to turn and walk back. 'She was still competing on the international circuit, but her times began to drop as she found it more and more difficult to stay the distance. At first it was thought she had a virus, although a few reporters she had crossed swords with wrote that she was too old and should retire.'

'But it was the disease.'

'Yes. And as soon as it was diagnosed, the toyboy was off.'

'Did her friends offer help?'

Tom grunted. 'Friends? Vanessa had always been too busy to make friends. She had acquaintances, other competitors, people mainly in the same business. But none you could really call friends.'

'So what did she do?'

'Phoned me. She had no one else to turn to.' Another silence, then he went on, 'I'm not really a very noble person, Beth, but I just couldn't abandon her. After all, I did still love her.'

Now Beth completely understood his

attitude. 'It must be very hard for you,' she said.

'I think it's even harder for Vanessa, because she had to come back, after all that had happened.'

'Do the girls know? About the divorce, I mean.'

'No. Nor does Thora.' He shook his head. 'I think that's the one thing that terrifies Vanessa. More than death, she fears that they might find out she had left them. Despite everything, she really does care deeply about the girls.'

'But there's no reason why they should find out, is there?'

'No. No reason at all.' He smiled, and held out his hands. 'I think the horses are rested enough, don't you?'

After he had helped her to her feet, she expected him to turn away, but he didn't. For a long moment, he looked down at her, still firmly holding her hands. Then he said, 'You are the first person I have ever felt I could talk to like that. I hope I haven't embarrassed you — and I hope it won't spoil your attitude to Vanessa. She needs someone like you as a friend.'

Beth shook her head. 'I'm glad you felt you could talk to me. After all, I chose to fall in love with the wrong person as well. And as far as Vanessa is concerned, I don't think I would have been her friend when she was a different person, but I do like the woman I know now.'

His smile was very gentle. 'I knew you would understand.' He lifted her hands and gazed at them. 'Although, to tell the truth, that wasn't the only reason I told you.'

Beth made no attempt to back away. The warmth of his hands was too pleasant a sensation.

Still not looking at her, he said, 'Vanessa is not the only person who needs a friend.'

Simply, she answered him. 'I'm here.'

When he raised his head to look at her, there was an expression in his eyes that she couldn't quite fathom. An intense expression that couldn't be described. Afraid of breaking the spell, Beth held her breath, knowing she would never forget this moment. The sun dappling through the trees, the leaves whispering in the slightest of breezes, the munching sound of the horses as they found a succulent patch to graze. All would be engraved on her memory for ever.

When Tom lowered his head, she thought for a moment he would kiss her cheek, or even her mouth, but it was the back of her hand he brushed with his lips, as he murmured, 'Thank you.'

Suddenly, a whinny warned that their

seclusion was about to come to an end, giving Beth and Tom time to remount and instruct their horses to 'walk on' before the group of ramblers reached the glade.

As the trees thinned to open heathland, Beth quickly urged her horse into a trot, then a canter, hoping the action would disguise her breathlessness. When she glanced over her shoulder, Tom was close behind and, as he drew level with Beth, he grinned.

'Race you back to the stables,' he challenged.

'You're on!' she cried, wheeling the horse at a gallop. It was a close finish but, just as they always did with Cassie, he held back at the last moment. As Beth trotted ahead through the gate, she was still wondering whether she was sorry or relieved that he hadn't kissed her.

19

Beth checked the date on the office calendar. Exactly three weeks to T-Day, as they called it — the day Sarah's twins were due. They could arrive earlier, of course, twins often did. Certainly Sarah couldn't wait to get rid of all that surplus weight and discomfort. She couldn't even manage her weekly drive to the office now, so was completely housebound, the telephone and e-mail her only link with the outside world, leaving it up to Damon to call in and report back with any documents that might need Sarah's personal attention. There was one such complicated document in Beth's pending tray right now, relating to an ancient listed building which was being converted into luxury apartments. Even Beth's legally experienced mind had found the many covenants difficult to explain. So Damon was due in to take the paperwork back for Sarah to check.

'All right if I go off to lunch now?' Jane's voice broke into her reverie. 'My car's in for servicing, and he said I could pick it up after one o'clock.' She grimaced. 'Hope he doesn't keep me waiting around, like last time.'

'I've brought a sandwich for a working lunch, so it's no problem.'

'Thanks. Perhaps you can go out for a breather when I get back?'

Beth shook her head. 'Too much to do, I'm afraid. I'm trying to get as much work as possible out of the way while I can still reach Sarah on the phone. Don't want her worrying about loose ends.'

After Jane had gone, Beth made herself a cup of coffee and stared at the telephone, thinking of her own loose ends. She had been so busy, there hadn't been time to phone Ali, let alone visit, and Beth was still concerned about the incident in Winchester with Gavin. The last time she had spoken to Ali, her friend had sounded a little distracted, but said it was only because she was working on a new advertising campaign, trying to keep one step ahead of the competition, and she was missing Gavin, who was back up north for a while.

Then there was Tom. Despite her inner warnings, she still saw him almost daily. After all, he had said he needed a friend, she argued with herself. But what did he mean by 'friend' asked her sensible side. Beth knew she was in grave danger of falling in love with him, but that didn't mean he felt the same way. So she nudged common sense into the background, and continued to call in at the Mastersons each day after work, chatted to Vanessa about the day's events while Thora prepared the evening meal, then took Hamish for a long walk. Now that the girls had joined their new school, homework kept them occupied and Cassie soon had new friends to visit and gossip to for hours on the telephone, so it was usually just Tom who accompanied her. He was one of the few people she knew who didn't need constant conversation to be enjoyable company, so it wasn't difficult to keep their relationship on a neighbourly basis, and any conversation was usually based on general happenings. It was as though they had made an unwritten rule not to step over the line into personal thoughts and feelings.

Beth was contented enough to keep it at that level. The person who troubled her the most was not Tom, but his elder daughter. From the moment they had returned from their ride together, Beth had sensed a change in Nadine's attitude. Whereas, normally she would ask where they had ridden, or just listen with an amused smile while Cassie did the talking, on that day she had immediately picked up Hamish, clipped on his lead, and handed him to Beth, in an almost dismissive manner. When Tom gently remonstrated that they hadn't offered Beth a cup of tea, she muttered something about the dog needing a walk after being cooped up all afternoon with her mother, and disappeared up to her room.

That in itself didn't worry Beth too much. Nadine was always a quiet girl who preferred the seclusion of her own room, but later Beth noticed that when she returned from walking Hamish with Tom, Nadine was always there, watchful and waiting to ask her father to help her with her homework, as though anxious to get him away from Beth. Her attitude to Beth was polite, but much cooler than before, and Beth was sure that the girl was beginning to feel threatened by her presence. If it hadn't been for the fact that Thora frequently said how much Vanessa looked forward to her visits, Beth would have backed off for a while and made some excuse to take Hamish straight home. The last thing she wanted was to hurt Nadine, she had enough grief on her young mind as it was. But Tom had needs, too, and she had promised to be there for him, as well as Vanessa.

So she compromised, keeping their walks along the beach, or similar areas still popular with tourists, and only accepting the occasional invitation to join the family for a meal. They hadn't been riding since that day in August, and Cassie's weekends were now a social whirl of cycle rides and barbecues. She was even talking about joining the school drama group, so her interest in horses had been put on 'hold'. But her life wasn't all fun and gaiety. Sometimes, when Beth called in after work, the girl would be reading to her mother, who was finding it increasingly difficult to turn the pages of a book. The expression on Cassie's face gave Beth some idea of the pain inside the bubbly exterior. Pain that a young teenager shouldn't have to suffer. Beth knew how much the girl needed the lively social life to help her forget that pain, and wished desperately that Nadine would also make new friends, but she locked herself away into a small world consisting only of her school work — and her mother.

Sighing at the thought, Beth's hand hovered over the telephone. Should she dial Ali's number? Or would Murphy's Law come into force to interrupt the conversation with house-hunters?

As it happened, it wasn't house-hunters who came through the door, but Damon. 'Hi,' he said. 'Where's Jane?'

Beth replaced the receiver. 'She's gone to collect her car after its service. Did you want to see her about something?'

His grin was a little off-centre, and Beth wondered if he had been drinking.

'Not really. Sarah has drafted some letters

for her. I'll leave them on her desk.' Glancing at the mug on Jane's desk, he asked, 'Any chance of a coffee?'

'Sure. The kettle has just boiled.' As she went through to the tiny cloakroom at the back of the office, Beth called back, 'I've got some urgent stuff for Sarah. Don't go without it. How is she?'

'As fat as a beached whale.'

Beth was surprised to hear his voice immediately behind her, and feel his breath on the back of her neck. 'Damon!' she said. 'There's hardly enough room for one in here.'

'I know. Cosy, isn't it?' Putting his hands on her shoulders, he tried to turn her towards him.

Beth didn't budge. 'Don't be silly, Damon,' she quietly protested. 'I've got a boiling kettle in my hand.'

'Put it down, then.' His voice had a wheedling tone. 'Come on, Beth. We're both adults.'

To her horror, he slid his hands over her shoulders and down her breasts, trying to find a way inside her blouse and nuzzling into her neck at the same time. Now she definitely smelled the alcohol on his breath as he spoke.

'You know I always fancied you at school. And you fancied me, didn't you? Go on, admit it.'

251

Trying to keep calm, despite her rising anger, Beth said, 'We're not at school now, Damon. Like you said, we're adults.' It was difficult to maintain a reasonable attitude while he was putting his tongue in her ear, but she persevered. 'Do I really need to remind you that you now have a very pregnant wife?' she quietly chided.

'For Christ's sake, Beth!' he whined. 'Can't you see that's the problem? I haven't been able to touch Sarah for months.' He fumbled with the buttons on her blouse. 'A man has his needs, and you can't have had much of a sex life since Bryn left you.' Now he tried to turn her face round with one hand, while his wet lips searched for her mouth. 'We'd be doing each other a favour.'

'I don't believe I'm hearing this,' she said, trying to remove his hand from her breast. 'Are you really suggesting we have sex here in the cloakroom? When someone could walk into that office at any moment? For goodness sake!'

'Put the closed sign on the door. It won't be for long.'

He really was serious, Beth thought, as she felt his body thrusting against her. It was amazing that he could become so aroused when he was obviously too drunk to think clearly. Her mood changed. She didn't feel at risk of being raped, but she sensed that Damon was losing control through alcohol and lust, and he really believed she wanted to have sex with him. She had to get him out of the kitchen and as far away from her body as quickly as possible, before it all got out of hand.

'Damon!' Her voice was sharp. 'This is ridiculous. Stop it. At once. Before Jane comes back.'

Even the prospect of the young secretary walking in upon them wasn't enough. Damon shifted his grip so that both his arms were tightly around Beth, pushing her further into the tiny cubby hole and trying to close the door behind him with his foot.

Beth tried another tactic. 'Damon, you've obviously had a few drinks,' she said, hoping he would see reason and take the excuse she offered. 'Why don't you go back into the office, and I'll bring you a cup of black coffee.'

'I don't want a bloody cup of coffee. Black, white, or whatever. I want you.'

Oh dear. This was going to be more difficult than she thought. Beth had no room to manoeuvre, and one hand still gripped the kettle. She had to make him relax his grip before she would be able to push him back into the office. But how? If only the phone would ring.

The solution was swiftly taken out of her hands, but it wasn't a telephone call. Damon was even more unstable on one leg than two and, as he lurched sideways, boiling water from the kettle splashed on to his hands. Yelping with pain, he released her and stared at the burn.

'You scalded me!' he cried. 'What did you want to do that for? I wasn't going to hurt you.'

Beth couldn't believe how quickly the passionate man had become a hurt little boy. 'I'm sorry,' she said. 'I didn't realise I was still holding the kettle. Here.' She pulled him into the cloakroom and held his hand under the cold water tap. 'Keep it there for as long as possible. It will take the sting out of it.'

'Will it blister?' he asked, peering at the red mark.

'Not if you keep it under the tap.'

Meekly, Damon did as he was told. 'I hope it won't scar,' he muttered anxiously. 'Do you think I ought to go along to the hospital?'

Beth examined his hand. 'It's not too bad,' she decided. 'I think the cold water is doing the trick, but it needs a bit longer.'

'Will you drive me home, Beth? It hurts quite a lot.'

'I'm afraid I can't, Damon. Too much to do here. But I'll call a taxi for you when you're ready. Where have you parked your van?'

'Jones Lane. On the short stay bit.'

'Give me your keys and I'll move it later.'

'How am I going to get it in the morning? That's if I feel well enough to work.' Again he peered closely at his hand, which showed little sign of redness.

'I'll think of something. Now, let's make your coffee.'

It was over. He was more concerned about his sore hand than a bit of nookie on the quiet. The incident hadn't frightened Beth. She had always felt in control. But it had disturbed her. Mainly because of Sarah.

Somehow, she didn't think this was the first time that Damon had allowed his sexual urges to get the better of him. With his type of work, calling on households during the day when women were often alone, maybe — just maybe — there had been opportunities for him to be unfaithful. Opportunities he would grab without a thought for his wife.

There was no way she could tell Sarah what had happened, given her present circumstances. But was ignorance really so blissful for their marriage? Beth sighed as she realised that now she had two secrets to keep to herself. Damon and his embarrassing groping, and Gavin and the blonde. She still desperately hoped that there might be some perfectly innocent explanation, but it did appear as though both her friends had partners who cheated on them.

Her worrying thoughts were interrupted by Jane. She was so angry, she didn't notice Damon at first.

'He's done it again!' she exploded. 'The car's still not ready. So I've got to catch the bus home, and I promised Mum I'd take her to Tescos tonight.'

'Has he said when it will be ready?'

'Tomorrow at noon. Promises, promises.' Jane's tone was scornful. 'I'm going to try someone else next time.'

'My garage is usually pretty reliable,' Beth suggested. 'At least they offer a lift if the work isn't finished on time.'

'They certainly can't be any worse than this chap. I think he leaves my car till last because I'm a woman. Thinks I'm too soft to argue. Well, today he found out he was wrong.' Jane turned to tuck her bag under her desk. 'Oh, hallo, Damon,' she said. 'Didn't see you there. How's Sarah?'

'She's OK,' he muttered. 'Why don't you ask how I am?'

Jane glanced at Beth with raised eyebrows. 'Sorry,' she said. 'How are you, Damon?'

'My hand hurts,' he grumbled. 'Look.'

Jane peered at the hand he thrust towards

her. 'What did you do?' she asked. 'Sprain it? No, there's no swelling.'

'It's a burn. Can't you see how red it is?'

After a slight pause, Jane said, 'Oh, dear. How did you do that?'

Quickly, Beth picked up the telephone. 'Let's get the taxi, Damon,' she said. 'Jane, there's a package for you from Sarah. Could you check it in case anything is urgent?'

Ten minutes later, Damon was bundled into a taxi, with the reassurance from Beth that she would phone him later about his van.

Jane looked up from her work as Beth picked up the empty mug and carried it through into the cloakroom.

'What happened to Damon's hand?' she asked. 'I couldn't see any mark.'

'It was nothing really, but I didn't think he should be driving. Hence the taxi.'

'Ah. I thought he was rather unsteady on his pins.' Jane looked thoughtful. 'What's going to happen about his van?'

Drying her hands on the towel, Beth stood in the doorway. 'Actually,' she mused, 'your wretched mechanic might have done me a favour. If I drive the van, could you drive my car to Sarah's? Then I can take you home.'

'Sure. I'll just phone Mum to tell her what's happening.'

Fortunately, there were no late afternoon

house-hunters, so they were able to lock up promptly at five and drive across the forest to 'Hawthorns'.

Sarah was so huge it was obviously uncomfortable for her to walk far. 'I was so pleased that Damon decided to come home by taxi,' she said. 'Sometimes he takes chances when he's a bit over the top, but I'm glad he's seeing sense at last. Don't want him losing his licence — or worse.'

'Of course not.' Beth held out the keys. 'Where is he now?' she asked, 'Sleeping it off?'

'Yes.' Sarah opened the door wider. 'Coming in for a coffee or something? Jamie would love to see you.'

'Sorry, but I've got to take Jane home and then take my hound dog for a walk.'

Sarah nodded, then said, 'Did you bring those deeds for Estuary House? Damon couldn't remember anything about it.'

Beth handed over the envelope. 'Hope you can make more sense out of them than I did.'

'I'll go through them this evening. Better get it sorted before these two decide to make an entrance.' Laughing, she tapped her stomach, then became serious. 'By the way, Beth. Damon complained about a scalded hand, but I can't see anything. Do you know what he's talking about?'

'He got a bit of a splash from the kettle when he was making coffee. Ten minutes under the cold tap soon sorted it out.'

'Damon making coffee in the office? That must be a first.'

Beth leaned over the bump and kissed her friend on the cheek. 'Take care of yourself,' she said. 'I'll phone tomorrow.'

Sarah smiled warmly. 'Thanks for coming all the way out here,' she said. 'You, too, Jane.'

After Beth had dropped off Jane, she decided to go home before she picked up Hamish. She wanted to phone Ali.

For once, it was Ali herself who answered, not the electronic message taker. She seemed pleased to hear from Beth, and for a while they chatted about this and that. When Beth enquired about Gavin, Ali merely said that he phoned her when he could, but she didn't know when he would be down again. Then Beth told her about Damon, and the incident in the office. There was a long silence before Ali answered.

'I wondered how long it would take him to try it on with you.'

'So you know what he's like?'

'Oh, yes. I know what he's like all right.' Ali sighed. 'I suppose I should have warned you, but I hoped he'd learned his lesson.'

'You sound as though you've had a similar experience.'

'I think every woman who has been within grabbing distance of Damon has had a similar experience, including the au pair.'

'Lorraine?' Beth was shocked. 'In his own house?'

'Afraid so. It wasn't attempted rape, or anything like that, but the poor girl didn't know what to do, so she told Sarah and gave in her notice.'

'Sarah knows!'

'Oh, yes. She doesn't know that he prospected me when she was pregnant with Jamie, but she does know that he had a brief fling with one of his customers about the same time. The husband turned up threatening to sort him out.'

'Oh, my God! What happened?'

'Sarah managed to calm the man down, and he probably went home and beat up his wife instead.'

'But what about Sarah and Damon?'

'Apparently, he apologised profusely, said he had succumbed to temptation for the first time, and promised that it would never happen again. And she believed him.'

'So that must have been before the incident with Lorraine?'

'Yep.' Ali paused for a moment before she

went on, 'You can imagine how she felt when she found out he'd tried to kiss the au pair.'

'Yet she still forgave him?'

'Oh, no. She kicked the little rat out, and Lorraine stayed on. I don't know how long they were separated, but she phoned me one day and said she'd thought it all over very carefully and decided to take him back.'

'I can't believe that Sarah could be so stupid. She's usually so sensible.'

'My feelings exactly. But Sarah said that she felt more miserable without Damon than with him, despite his weakness. So she laid down some ground rules, particularly relating to Lorraine.'

'Are you telling me that she's accepted him back into her bed, knowing that he might have affairs? I don't think I could do that.'

'Nor would I. If it was Gavin, he wouldn't know what had hit him. But her view was that she also has a child to consider. Jamie needs a father as well as a mother, and so will the twins. Sarah has always been a realist. She knows there won't be many eligible men beating a path to the door of a woman with three young children.'

'That's true, but . . . '

'The main thing is that she is the one in control, not Damon.'

'How?'

'By making it quite clear that any shenanigans in their house are definitely not acceptable, and he mustn't go near Lorraine.'

'And she's prepared to turn a blind eye to anything else?'

'Yes. Provided she doesn't know about it, and there are no angry husbands or unwanted pregnancies to deal with.'

'What about the risk of Aids, or similar diseases?'

'Oh, Sarah has thought of everything like that. And she said she still loves him, so I suppose they are happy enough in their own . . . ' Ali's voice tailed off, then she said, 'Mind you, I'm not sure how she would react if she found out about today's little howdy. Unknown floosies are one thing, close personal friends another.'

Quietly, Beth said, 'She won't find out from me.'

'I thought that's what you would say.' Ali's laugh was a little bitter. 'And Damon certainly won't mention it, even if he remembers what he did, given his inebriated state!'

After she'd hung up the phone, Beth sat for some time, mulling over all that she'd heard. How could he behave so badly, she thought. Didn't he realise how lucky he was to have someone like Sarah as a wife? Beautiful, intelligent and much more understanding than he deserved. Beth wondered whether she could have forgiven Bryn, given the same circumstances. She didn't think so, and yet, if Katie had lived, perhaps she too would have needed the security of a husband and father.

Then Beth thought of Ali. She had made it clear that she would certainly not tolerate any indiscretions from Gavin. But there was no proof that he was seeing someone else, just a brief meeting with a pretty girl in Winchester.

Why was it that people could be so attracted to someone who was prepared to hurt them so badly, Beth wondered? Look at her own experience with Bryn. She'd had no idea that he would abandon her and their child. And now, there was Tom.

Tom. He appeared to be so kind, and had overlooked his wife's adultery because she was dying. Beth wasn't sure that he had forgiven Vanessa. Like Sarah, he was a realist, and had the welfare of his children at heart. But Beth wondered whether he, too, would indulge in extra-marital activities, should he be suitably encouraged. Although it would be more understandable than Damon's indiscretions, it would still be adultery, and it would still be wrong.

A tear rolled down her cheek as she knew that, in spite of her beliefs in the sanctity of commitment and marriage, and her affection for his family, she probably would not be able to resist if he opened his arms.

Oh, God, she thought. Why does life have to be so difficult, and so painful?

20

Shaking herself free from her reverie, Beth glanced at the clock. Goodness! Hamish's walk was well overdue. It would have to be a short stroll along the beach tonight. Let him explore all the exciting smells, chase a seagull or two, then back home. If Ginger Tom was sitting on the gatepost at number twenty-one, Hamish would feel it his duty to give a token bark. Not that it brought much response, just a slow movement of the head, a disdainful stare, then a leisurely whisker wash. There was no real animosity between them, but Hamish seemed to enjoy the game of pretence. Perhaps he thought he was defending Beth against the sharp claws of Ginger Tom.

On her way upstairs, Beth noticed a join in the carpet that did not fit as securely as it should. Ruddy cowboy carpet fitters! Probably safer to fix it herself rather than call them back in. Making a mental note to look at it again later, she took a lightweight anorak from the wardrobe. The wind could be a little chill on the shore at this time of evening.

Beth was never quite sure exactly what

happened next. She remembered turning towards the dressing table, to look for a tissue, her foot catching in something, and her shoulder hitting the wardrobe with such force that the door swung open. Unable to stop herself from sprawling on the floor, she lay there for a moment, wondering what she had tripped on.

'Beth! Mind out!' The warning cry was so shrill, she looked up to see the huge suitcase sliding from the top of the wardrobe towards her head. There was barely time to roll out of the way before it hit the carpet, spilling out its contents, the full set of *Encyclopaedia Britannica* — a birthday gift from her parents.

Whether it was a shock reaction to her near-miss, Beth wasn't sure, but she found herself quite unable to move. It was almost as though she was paralysed. If that voice hadn't warned her, she could now be lying with serious head injuries, perhaps dead. The suitcase itself had metal corners — she'd bought it at an auction years ago because it was so sturdy, almost as heavy as a trunk.

Trying to collect her thoughts, Beth looked around the bedroom. The rucked up carpet told her how she had tripped, but not who had called out. The bedroom was empty. Then . . . who?

Eliza. It had to be Eliza who had warned her. Oh, God, the house really was haunted. She might imagine a whisper, but not that loud cry.

Now Beth began to shake, but still couldn't move her limbs until the doorbell triggered her into action. Still shaking, she made her way slowly downstairs, clinging to the banisters and carefully avoiding the dodgy piece of carpet. By now, her visitor was banging on the door, and shouting. It was Tom.

Flinging open the door, she fell into his arms, vaguely aware that Hamish dashed past her and ran indoors.

'What on earth is going on?' Holding her at arms' length, Tom tried to peer into her face, but she clung to him like a limpet, burying her face in his jacket.

'Oh, Tom. Am I glad to see you.'

'I can't hear what you are saying.' He tried to lift her face from his shoulder. 'What on earth has happened?'

'I was so frightened . . . ' Still trembling, Beth glanced over his shoulder and realised that they were being watched. The lady across the road, the same lady who had seen her dancing with Damon, was unashamedly staring. Open-mouthed and with the chamois leather dripping water down her arms, she appeared to be oblivious to the unattended patches of suds on her windows.

Tom followed Beth's gaze and pushed her back through the door. 'Christ! The neighbours will have a field day with this.' Closing the front door with his foot, he led Beth to the settee. 'Stay there. I'll get you a drink and you can tell me what has frightened you.'

'No! Please don't leave me.' As Beth pulled Tom down on to the settee, her emotions began to change gear. The fear of the unknown had subsided, replaced by emotions just as strong. The touch of Tom's hand on her hair, her shoulder, her face, was enough to awaken sensual feelings that she had thought never to experience again. Echoing her emotions, his lips sought her eyes, her cheeks, her lips.

He didn't say a word. He didn't need to. The hungriness of his kisses told her more about his feelings than words. It was as though they had both abandoned themselves to their needs. The only sound she made was when he unbuttoned her blouse and found her breast. Not so much a low moan, more a catching of breath. For the second time today a man's hand caressed her breast, but this time she had no intention of resisting. Beth wanted the moment, the exquisite delight that shuddered through her body, to go on and on

— to the inevitable conclusion.

'Damn the woman!' Tom had shifted his position. 'I swear she has long-range contact lenses.'

Beth raised her head and looked through the window. The neighbour was now pretending to clean her car, which gave her an excuse to move a few feet closer. Her head darted backwards and forwards as she attempted to peer through Beth's picture window, then she furiously wiped the same patch on the boot of her car.

Tom ducked his head and kissed Beth again, at the same time trying to unfasten her bra, not an easy task while trying to keep a low profile on the small settee. 'Do you think she'll give up and go indoors?' he asked hopefully, as the first hook was loosened.

'No. She's got stamina, that one.'

'Well, I can't wait for ever.' Tom wrapped his arms closely around Beth. 'Hold on,' he warned, and rolled them both on to the floor.

'Ouch!' Beth's head had made contact with the table leg.

'Sorry.' Tom tried to unbuckle his belt, but his legs were too long to easily extricate from his trousers and his foot jammed under the settee. 'This is bloody stupid,' he muttered, collapsing on top of Beth. 'I haven't contorted myself so much since my back seat of the Mini student days.'

Beth didn't answer. She couldn't. Her mouth was full of his jacket sleeve, the one she'd managed to free from his arm.

'Let's go upstairs.' Tom raised his body. 'At least we'll be more comfortable.'

'We'll never get past the window without Mata Hari spotting us.'

'Keep down and follow me.' Tom rolled off Beth, and crawled on all fours towards the door.

What a ridiculous pair we make, Beth thought, as she followed him. Tom with one arm in, one arm out of his jacket, and me with my boobs all over the place.

Try as she might, she could not resist the low chuckle that threatened to destroy the passion.

'What?' Tom looked startled as Beth collapsed at the foot of the stairs, stuffing her knuckles into her mouth.

'Nothing.'

'Don't give me that. You're practically blue in the face. I'm glad I give you such amusement.'

'I'm sorry. It's not you, Tom. It's the whole situation. I was just thinking about Bryn.'

'A fine time to be thinking about your husband, I must say.' Now Tom really sounded miffed.

'Oh, Tom. Please don't be cross.' Beth took his face between her hands and kissed him fervently.

'That's more like it.' He looked puzzled as he pushed back a strand of her hair from her eyes. 'But I still don't understand why you should be thinking of your husband.'

Beth giggled. 'It's just that . . . Bryn was so pompous — and very proper. He'd be horrified if he could see me now, actually enjoying this . . . this . . . '

'Bloody ridiculous situation?' Tom filled in the missing words.

'Exactly.'

'Then can we please go upstairs and fornicate in a bed. I hope I'm not as pompous as your ex, but I can be much more passionate without a draught whistling through the letter box.'

'Spoil sport.' As Beth sat up, she heard Hamish's gentle woof from the stairs, reminding her that he hadn't had his nightly walkies.

'Go away, Hamish,' Tom commanded. 'It's bad enough having the neighbourhood witch making notes, without you.' He helped Beth to her feet. 'Anybody else likely to be watching us upstairs?' he asked. 'Detective with a camera, perhaps?'

It was just a light-hearted comment, but

enough to burst the bubble. In a split second, the magic had gone. Beth was reminded that Eliza might be — the thought that she might be in the bedroom — invisibly observing, was too unnerving.

'What's wrong?' Tom seemed to sense the change in Beth as she turned away from him.

Still confused, Beth said the first thing that came into her mind. 'It's a mess,' she gasped. 'The bedroom. It's a terrible mess. Books all over the place.' Even as she talked she knew how pathetic it sounded. There was no other way. She'd have to tell him the truth. 'I'm sorry, Tom. I can't. It's the house.'

'What about the house?'

She took a deep breath. 'It's haunted.'

For a moment, he just silently stared at her.

Beth knew it sounded crazy, but she had to try to explain. 'That's why I was so frightened when you arrived.'

'You'd seen a ghost?'

'Yes. No. At least I'm pretty sure I heard one.'

'This isn't a very funny joke, Beth. For Christ's sake, what are you playing at?'

'I'm not joking. And I'm not playing. I'm sure this house is haunted, and that's why . . . ' Her voice trailed.

The expression on his face was one of utter disbelief. 'Are you seriously trying to tell me

that we can't make love in this house because
it is haunted?'

'Yes.'

'And you're afraid the ghost might be
watching us?'

'Eliza came to me in a dream, and told me
the house is cursed. She tried to warn
me . . . ' Beth's voice faltered as she realised
what it must sound like to him, but she
couldn't get the words straight.

Tom exploded. 'I've never heard such crap
in all my life. You're like a child inventing a
mysterious alter ego who does all the naughty
things. You've even given her a name!'

'I didn't name her,' Beth cried. 'Eliza *is* her
name. She told me.'

Taking her by the shoulders, Tom shook
her backwards and forwards until she cried
out. Beth had never seen such anger.

'Why couldn't you be honest with me?' He
was still shouting. 'If you didn't fancy me,
you should have said so, not giggled like a
silly teenager and then invented a voyeur
ghost.'

'I am being honest.' Now Beth was
weeping. 'I really wanted to, Tom, but I can't.
Perhaps another time . . . '

Tom had stopped shaking her but still
gripped her by the shoulders. So tightly it
hurt. Intense fury was in his face and his

voice. 'If you really think I'd chance having you make a fool of me again . . . ' He flung her back against the wall and tried to get his arm back into the empty sleeve of his jacket. 'There's a name for girls like you, who lead a man on, and then . . . '

'I'm sorry, Tom,' Beth sobbed. 'The last thing I want to do is to hurt you.'

'Hurt me?' he yelled. 'Don't flatter yourself. I'd have to care about someone before I could be hurt again. Oh, shit!' Giving up the struggle, he pulled his jacket off violently so that both sleeves were now inside out, and was equally unsuccessful in attempting to open the front door.

'Please don't go,' Beth pleaded. 'Just let me tell you the whole story.'

'I've heard enough stories this evening to last me a lifetime, thanks very much.' His voice was quieter, but bitter. 'So I'm going home, to take a cold shower.' Finally succeeding in mastering the door, he flung it open, then turned back to Beth. The expression on his face was more hurtful than a slap. 'I've had quite a few of them over the past few years, but never for such a despicable reason.'

The door slammed behind him with a resounding bang.

21

In the silence that followed, Beth recognised that her laughter and tears had been part of the hysteria that had been building up since the fall in the bedroom. If she didn't do something rapidly, it would turn to screams that she might not be able to control. Deep breathing. That had helped when she was in labour with Katie. Big, deep breaths. In. Out. Slow down. Fight the panic with calm thoughts. What calm thoughts? Her life was in chaos. She couldn't think of anything serene or peaceful.

Hamish saved the day. A few woofs and she was able to look down and concentrate on his dear little face, looking up at her with such devotion, his head first on one side, then the other.

'Oh, Hamish, thank you,' she cried, gathering him up into her arms. 'Thank you. Thank you.'

Her body juddered once — twice — again and again. But not with sobs. The tears had been replaced by violent hiccups. Good. Hiccups she could cope with. Hysteria was more difficult. She didn't attempt to cure the hiccups.

Still holding Hamish, she walked back into the living room. The small overturned table was a painful reminder of what might have been. She didn't want to think about it any more than she wanted to think about Eliza. And certainly she didn't want to think about the fact that the house might be cursed.

All she wanted to do was to get out of this house. But where should she go? A hotel? Perhaps, but really she needed to talk to someone. A friend. One who would understand.

Beth's mood lifted as she dialled a number. The Ansafone told her brightly that Ali would get back to her as soon as possible if she left a message after the tone. Damn! Ali, where are you? Not still at work, surely?

'Quality Temps. How may I help you?' Ali's voice trilled.

'Why are you . . . still in the . . . office at this . . . time of night?'

'Oh, hi, Beth. Just trying to catch up on VAT while it's quiet. What's up with your voice?'

'Hiccups.'

'Try drinking from the other side of . . . '

'I don't want to.'

'Oh.' Ali sounded nonplussed. 'A shock

276

often does the trick. Give me a moment and I'll think of something.'

'No, thanks. I've . . . had enough . . . shock for one day. Listen . . . Ali, can you put me up . . . for a night or so?'

'Sure. When?'

'Tonight?'

'Well, yes. Of course I can. What's the problem? Death watch beetle or something?'

'I'll explain later. What time . . . do you reckon to . . . be home?'

'Not for at least another hour. Best make it later than that, to be on the safe side.'

'You're a gem. Thanks.'

'Actually, I'm glad you phoned. There's something I want to run past you — it's about the business. Tell you more later.'

As Beth replaced the receiver, she wondered what Ali wanted to talk about, and whether there would be a chance to discuss her own problems. Then she wondered how she could fill in the time. Drawing the curtains against the inquisitive neighbour, who was now sweeping her front path, Beth began throwing things into her overnight case, and packing a smaller bag for Hamish. Then she switched on the radio, turning up the volume. She really didn't want to hear any more voices, whispering or otherwise.

It took some moments for her to hear the

shrill ring of her telephone. It was Thora.

'Sorry to interrupt, Beth. Are you having a party?'

'No, it's just the . . . radio. Hold on a . . . moment.' Beth switched it off. 'Sorry about that,' she said. 'I hadn't realised . . . it was so loud.'

'I see. Right. Beth . . . '

'Yes?'

'This is rather difficult. I need to ask you a favour.'

'What is it?'

'Well — I've got tickets for the Nuffield Theatre tonight, and the girls are out.'

'Go on.'

'Tom was supposed to be here to keep an eye on Vanessa, but he decided to bring Hamish down to you before I left, as you were a little later than usual.'

'Hasn't he come back?' Beth had no idea where Tom might have gone after he left her.

'Oh, yes, he came back all right.' Thora's laugh was without humour. 'In the foulest mood imaginable.'

'Oh, dear.' Beth waited for Thora to continue.

'He dashed upstairs. I think he took a shower. Then he dashed out again without a word, and roared away in the car.' Thora sounded embarrassed. 'I phoned to see if you could sit with Vanessa for a little while. She's very upset about Tom flouncing off like that.'

The last person Beth wanted to see was Vanessa. Not after almost making love to her husband, and certainly not after that flaming row.

'Beth . . . ' Thora broke into the silence. 'If it was just me, I wouldn't mind so much, but I'm taking Edie Cooper. It's one of those special late evenings with supper, and the chance to talk to the actors. To be honest, I don't think she has ever been to the theatre, apart from a pantomime once at the Mayflower, and I hate letting her down. So if you could help me out till the girls come back, I'd be really grateful.'

Beth sighed. The Mastersons had been so good to her, looking after Hamish. She could hardly refuse without seeming totally selfish. And the girls had school tomorrow, so shouldn't be out too late.

'I am going over . . . to Ali's later on and . . . staying the night, but . . . I could come for an . . . hour or so if that's . . . any help,' she suggested.

'Nadine shouldn't be too long, she's taking an extra curriculum computer studies course and usually comes straight home.'

'OK.'

'Bless you, dear. You've saved my life. Tom

knew I've been wanting to see this play for ages. Just wait till he comes home.' Thora sounded understandably cross. 'Do you have any idea what has got into him?'

'No,' Beth lied. 'I'll be . . . down in a few minutes.'

'Thanks. Beth, have you got hiccups?'

'Yes . . . I expect they'll soon pass.'

It was with a feeling of great relief that Beth locked the front door behind her and bundled Hamish into the back of the car. But the relief turned to anxiety as she parked in the Mastersons' curving drive. If only she could have gone straight to Ali's and poured out her heart to her friend. Anything would have been easier than this.

Thora was waiting at the front door, car keys in hand.

'Vanessa is in her room,' she said. 'See if you can cheer her up. She's very down.' Thora glanced at her watch. 'Sorry I'm in such a rush, but I promised Edie I'd pick her up five minutes ago, and she's a terrible worrier. Help yourself to whatever. You know where everything is.'

Bracing herself, Beth knocked gently on the door to Vanessa's room. The wheelchair was positioned in front of the computer and she half turned to beckon Beth into the room. Her anxious expression brightened a little as

Hamish ran into the room. After Vanessa had fondled his head with her right hand, the only part of her that still functioned reasonably normally, he sat between his two friends. They had often been amused at Hamish's token of loyalty. When he was alone with Vanessa he was usually to be found curled up on her lap. At home with Beth, he was never far from her feet, whatever she was doing, but when Vanessa and Beth were together, he found a point almost exactly midway between them, and there he sat, looking from one to the other with such devotion.

'Thank you for coming.' Vanessa's voice was weaker than usual.

'My pleasure.' Beth leaned forward to stroke Hamish so that she didn't have to look into Vanessa's face.

'Can we talk on the PC?'

Startled, Beth looked up. Then she understood what Vanessa meant. She knew Tom had rigged a pad to support Vanessa's right hand, so that she could log on to the Internet and keep up to date with the athletic world, but she hadn't realised that it was also used to hold conversations.

'It's easier for me, than talking.'

Beth could hear that speech was becoming a greater effort, so she nodded.

'You speak. I'll type,' Vanessa suggested.

She was surprisingly adept at finding her way around the keys with one hand, and Beth watched with fascination as the messages flashed up on to the screen.

Tom wouldn't speak to me. And Thora won't tell me what is wrong. I'm very frightened.

'Don't be,' Beth said, trying to sound calmer than she felt. 'You have nothing to fear from Tom.'

I know he would not harm me, but why is he so angry?

Again Beth lied. 'I don't know. Perhaps he had a bad day at work.'

Slowly, Vanessa shook her head. *He was all right when he first came home. Then he became worried when you didn't call for Hamish. He said he would take him back to you and see if everything was OK.*

'Sorry about that. We had a bit of a panic in the office, and then I had to drive Damon home.'

Vanessa thought for a moment, then typed, *Was he drunk?*

'Just a bit over the limit, I'm afraid.'

Sarah must be a very patient wife. How is she?

'Anxious to get rid of the two lumps as soon as possible.'

Vanessa smiled, a sympathetic little smile.

Then she returned to her own problem. *Do you have any idea where Tom might have gone?*

'No.' That at least was true. 'He'll be back before long. I'm sure it's nothing to worry . . . about.'

Vanessa's head turned towards her, then back to the PC. *You've still got hiccups.*

'Almost gone.'

With a thoughtful expression, Vanessa typed, *Sometimes they are caused by a shock, as well as cured.*

Beth didn't answer, just smiled a tight little smile.

Again Vanessa turned her head towards Beth and studied her, with a quizzical expression, before she sent her next message. *I think Tom isn't the only one who is upset this evening.*

'What makes you think that?' Beth knew her voice was tremulous, the tears perilously near.

When some of our senses are taken away, others are stronger. I can tell you are unhappy. What is it, Beth?

Beth shook her head, trying to blink back the first wayward tear.

I'm your friend. You know that. Perhaps it will help just to talk to me?

Oh, Lord. It was getting worse. 'I'm

supposed to be cheering you up, not the other way around,' she protested, trying to appear light-hearted.

If I can help you, that will cheer me up! At least I'd feel I was doing something useful. I don't often get the opportunity. Vanessa's fingers speedily tapped their way through the message. *Please tell me what is wrong.*

How could she explain that she was in love with Vanessa's husband, Beth thought. And how could she tell her that, less than an hour ago, they had both been rolling around on the floor in complete ecstasy. In fact, if it hadn't been for Eliza, they would have well and truly consummated their passion by now. Only the thought of being watched over by a three-hundred-year-old spirit had got in the way. Oh, yes. She would be as likely to believe the story as Tom. No one would ever believe her. Not even Ali. They would have her sedated and locked in a padded cell before the night was out.

Now the tears refused to be blocked. They ran down her face, her neck, into the collar of her blouse. Choking, strangling tears.

Vanessa looked more anxious than ever. She motioned towards a box of tissues on the side table, then turned back to the PC.

Talk to me, Beth. You must talk to me.

No words could push through the heart-rending sobs. Beth reached across Vanessa and typed, *I can't. You'll never believe me.*

Try me. Or we'll both go mad.

Still sobbing, Beth tried to think how much she could tell, without distressing Vanessa even more. But the words wouldn't come.

Pour yourself a drink, Vanessa ordered. *And one for me.*

I can't. I'm driving. And you're on medication.

Boll . . . I nearly typed a very rude word then! One drink won't hurt either of us.

By the time Beth had poured some wine into Vanessa's special cup, the sobs had subsided enough to allow her words through.

I'm waiting, Vanessa typed, after she'd had a couple of slurps.

'It's not easy. I think . . . my house is haunted.' Beth watched Vanessa's face for signs of disbelief, but she merely nodded.

Go on. I won't interrupt.

That was when the words began to flow, until they poured out in a never-ending rush, like a waterfall. She told Vanessa everything about Eliza, from the first visitation in Calshot Castle, until today's episode. Then she sat back and drained the remains of her glass of wine.

For some moments, Vanessa sat with her

eyes closed, a frown on her forehead, as though deep in contemplation. Then she opened her eyes and reached for the walking stick that hung nearby, the one she used when she needed to get from the wheelchair into the car, or the bathroom. Turning it around, she used the crook to hook on to a small bookcase and drag it towards her. Beth hadn't realised that the bookcase was on casters. She had noticed it before, and noted some of the books on the top shelf. Some of her own favourites by Jane Austen and Dickens, a couple by Dick Francis, three contemporary novels and several biographies of sporting icons. But it was the bottom row that Vanessa pointed to, and those titles really surprised Beth. There were books on every religion under the sun alongside works by great philosophers. The final section, at the end of the shelf, covered every aspect of supernatural beliefs, including one by Sir Arthur Conan Doyle.

'That one.' Vanessa struggled to make herself understood as she pointed to the furthermost book on the shelf.

Beth handed the book to Vanessa, who shook her head, and motioned for Beth to look at it. It was a book of various accounts of sightings of ghosts, obviously well read, with several pages turned down at the corners.

Puzzled, she looked back at Vanessa. 'I didn't realise you were interested in all this.' She indicated the various subjects on the bottom shelf.

Vanessa smiled and turned back to the computer. *Thought I'd better find out what might be in store for me,* she typed.

Beth didn't answer. Her heart was too full. There was no answer that would suffice.

That one has some incredible stories. Would you like to borrow it?

'Yes, please. I've never read anything, or thought about it much, until . . . '

I know. We don't do anything much until we're faced with a problem, do we?

Beth smiled agreement, then asked the big question. 'Do you believe?' She tapped the book on her lap.

Vanessa thought for a moment, then tapped out, *How can we be sure whether this moment is real, or in our imagination, like a dream? There are too many questions without logical answers for me to decide that ghosts do not exist.*

'So you don't think I'm insane? Or making it up?'

When Eliza lived in that cottage, anyone who prophesied that man would walk on the moon would probably have been burned at the stake. Vanessa touched the screen lightly.

If I can visit America on this, why should you not be able to log on to a spirit wandering around in limbo?

Beth breathed a deep sigh of relief, and placed her hand over Vanessa's, afraid to use too much pressure in case she cracked a bone. 'Thank you, Vanessa,' she whispered. 'You don't know what it means to me.'

It means a lot to me to be of some use in this world before I leave it. Now tell me again about the gypsy curse.

Vanessa listened intently as Beth repeated Eliza's words, then typed, *I think I might be able to . . .*

Before she could continue, they heard the sound of a key in the front door.

Vanessa quickly logged off the computer, and leaned back in her chair as Nadine came into the room. Nadine's eyes flashed from her mother to Beth, and she frowned in anger.

'Why are you still here?' she asked, her voice hostile. 'Can't you see what you are doing to my mother? She's totally exhausted, talking to you.'

'Nadine!' For all her weakness, Vanessa managed to convey her disapproval of her daughter's attitude.

Quickly, Beth stood up. 'Thora asked me to come down and stay with Vanessa,' she said. 'I'm sorry if you feel I've overtired her.'

'Isn't my father here? He can usually manage all right on his own.'

'No. He went out. And I'm going now.' Beth placed her hand on Vanessa's shoulder. 'Thank you for the loan of the book.'

Picking up Hamish, and tucking the book close to her so that Nadine couldn't see the title, Beth left the house. It was bad enough having quarrelled with Tom Masterson, without having another confrontation with his daughter.

22

Ali was slicing tomatoes when Beth arrived.

'Have you eaten?' she asked, as soon as greetings between two friends and one dog had been taken care of. 'It's only cold chicken from the deli and salad, but there's more than enough for two.'

Suddenly, Beth realised that she hadn't eaten since breakfast, and that had only been a slice of toast. Thanks to Damon and his drunken attempts at seduction, she hadn't fancied the cheese sandwich she had made for her working lunch. It remained, quietly wilting, in her briefcase. Cold chicken and salad sounded much more appetising.

Hamish had his nose buried in his favourite doggie nosh before the girls sat down at the table. Driving over, Beth had decided that she would wait and see what Ali wanted to say first. Talking to Vanessa had released some of the urgency over her own problems. If the opportunity was right, she would bring up the subject later.

'What did you want to talk to me about?' Beth asked, after they had mulled over the Damon incident again and agreed that he ought to be castrated and hung out to dry.

A tiny frown crossed Ali's face as she poured them both another glass of wine. 'It's about the business.'

Beth waited.

'As you know, I've always wanted to keep it small enough for me to cope with on my own. But now I'm wondering whether I should consider . . . ' Ali paused to sip her wine before she continued, 'Do you think it would hurt me, or the business, to go public?'

Surprised, Beth looked up from her plate. 'Do you mean becoming a limited company?'

'Yes. What do you really think of the idea?'

'I'm not sure. You've always been against expansion. Why now? Is the business in the doldrums?'

Ali shook her head. 'Actually, I've had quite a good summer, and I've bookings for holiday temps for a few more weeks.' She popped another mouthful of salad into her mouth and chewed slowly. 'But it usually quietens down in the autumn and I'm always on tenterhooks a bit until the 'flu epidemics create another panic, but you can't guarantee that.'

'Doesn't Christmas bring you extra work?'

'It used to. But now, so many firms close down for at least a week that they seem to manage. It's such a swings and roundabouts decision. I'd really value your opinion.'

Beth thought seriously about the matter before she answered. 'I don't know much about the benefits or otherwise of going public. On the face of it, I suppose you'd get a financial input from the sale of shares, but you would lose overall control.'

'That's what I told Gavin.'

'Gavin? What's it got to do with him?'

'He was the one who brought the subject up. Actually, he's been on at me for some time now to consider it. Reckons it will attract more business from larger industries if I have plc or whatever on the notepaper.'

'It might, but is it what you want? You've managed pretty well so far.'

'I know, but . . . ' Ali studied the chicken on her fork. 'Gavin thinks I've got into a rut and ought to be more forward-thinking. Maybe he's right. It's a competitive business, and I'm not competitive enough.'

'What about your advertising campaign? Any new business from that?'

'One or two, but it's only just got off the ground. I've placed a regular order with the *Echo* and I'm now working on mail shot, but it's making a big hole in my resources. Which brings us back to square one, of course. I need to invest money to make money.'

'Have you spoken to your accountant about it?'

'Not yet. John's on holiday at the moment, and I pooh-poohed the idea when Gavin first mentioned it. But now I'm seriously beginning to wonder whether I should look into it.'

'I wish I could give you some constructive advice, but I really know little about it.'

'It's just a general reaction I'm looking for. Am I being an idiot for even considering it, or should I be a bit more — adventurous?'

After a moment, Beth said, 'I don't think you're a fool for considering it, but you do need to know *all* the risks involved. When I worked for the accountants, I remember that one or two companies went to the wall after they went public, but others thrived. And, of course, there were people going bankrupt who hadn't moved with the times.' She laughed. 'I'm not much help really, am I?'

Ali smiled back. 'Only that you are echoing my own thoughts. And it does help just to talk to someone.'

'Good. Actually, I can offer a more positive token of help.'

'What's that?'

'Jane is going on holiday the week after next, and I'll need a temp for three weeks, just for the office, no negotiating.'

'Isn't that when Sarah is due?'

'Unfortunately, yes, but Jane had booked the holiday ages ago, before Sarah knew she was pregnant. She's taking her mum to Australia, to visit her sister. Big family gathering or something, so Sarah said to leave the dates as they were. I should have organised it earlier, but it slipped my mind. Sorry.'

'No problem. I've one or two girls who might suit, if they are free. Hang on a moment.' Ali fetched her briefcase and took out her engagement diary. 'That's a nuisance,' she murmured, as she ran her finger down the page. 'They're both booked out. Ah . . . this girl might fit the bill. Computer literate and she's done reception work, so shouldn't be frightened by the great British public.'

'Great.' Beth reached for her own briefcase. 'What's her name?'

Squinting, Ali deciphered her own writing. 'Amanda something. Oh, yes, Whitehorn. Amanda Whitehorn.'

'What's she like? As a person, I mean.'

'Don't know. She's new. Has an appointment first thing tomorrow to register.' Ali made a brief note in her diary, then looked up. 'Tell you what, come in with me and you can interview her. If she's no good, I've got other girls on the files.'

'OK.' Beth snapped shut her briefcase. 'It's only a little drop in the ocean of Quality Temps corporate business, but every little helps.'

'As the old lady said.'

The girls grinned at each other, then took their empty plates into the kitchen and chatted amiably while Ali half-filled the cafetière. She was obviously still besotted with Gavin, and Beth hadn't the heart to tell her about the incident in Winchester. So they just talked girl talk until Hamish reminded them that, like every other dog, he had had his day.

'You still haven't told me why you wanted to come over,' Ali commented, as she reached forward to stroke his silky head.

Beth shook her head. She was too tired to go over it all again just now. 'Nothing in particular,' she said. 'I just needed company. Thanks for obliging.'

'My pleasure. I get fed up with my own shadow at times. Stay as long as you like.' Catching the infectious yawn from Beth, she glanced at the clock. 'God! Is that the time? No wonder I'm desperate to get my head down. I've had quite a day.'

'Me too,' said Beth, with feeling. 'Come on, Hamish. Beddy-byes.'

The little dog was curled in his basket at

the foot of Beth's bed before she'd finished undressing.

★   ★   ★

Beth was filling Hamish's water bowl in Ali's office kitchen next morning when Amanda Whitehorn arrived and introduced herself to Ali. The girl's voice was pleasant, with a slight north country accent. She sounded just a little nervous, which was natural, Beth thought. Don't want someone who is over-confident and might seem pushy to the clients. While she sprinkled a few biscuits into another dish, Beth listened as the girl answered Ali's questions and asked a few of her own. Age twenty-four. Not looking for a permanent job, just something to tide her over while she stayed with a friend in Southampton for a few weeks. Preferably in the city, so she wouldn't have to travel too far. What sort of clients did Quality Temps deal with? Mainly legal. That sounded interesting. Were they big firms? She had worked for some of the larger chartered accountants and insurance companies up north. Might be persuaded to stay on in Southampton a little longer if there was regular work available. It was a nice city, with lovely shops. Yes, she would be interested in working for an estate agent. How far was the Waterside? Oh. A little further than she really wanted to travel, but if there was nothing else available? That was the most urgent vacancy. Well, it might be possible. Did they handle industrial properties, or only domestic? And some lettings. Right.

Time to make an appearance, Beth thought.

The girl's back was towards Beth as she entered the office. Neat appearance, good suit, beautiful hair, no dark roots.

'This is Beth Lewis, who is in charge of the estate agency while the proprietor is on maternity leave,' Ali said.

The smile faded from Beth's face, and her extended hand dropped back to her side as Amanda Whitehorn turned around.

'How do you . . . ' The girl faltered, looked at Ali, then back to Beth, with a puzzled expression. 'Is something wrong?' she asked.

Yes, Beth thought. Something was very wrong. What was this girl doing in Ali's office? She said she was staying in Southampton but, not very long ago, she had been outside a secretarial agency in Winchester. What was going on?

'Could I have a word?' Beth nodded towards the kitchen. Now she had to tell Ali, before she said anything to this — Amanda Whitehorn.

'Sure. Excuse me a moment.' Looking as puzzled as Amanda, Ali followed Beth back to the kitchen. It wasn't much bigger than Sarah's office kitchen, but there was room for Beth to close the door behind them.

'I've seen that girl before.'

Ali listened quietly while Beth told her story, her face reflecting her inner turmoil. All she said, when Beth had finished, was, 'Why didn't you tell me before?'

'To be honest, I didn't know how to. I kept telling myself there was probably quite an innocent explanation, and I didn't want to add up two and two and get my sums wrong.'

Ali nodded. 'Do you think she has followed Gavin down here? Could she be his girlfriend — or — ?' She looked even more miserable. 'His wife? Oh, God, Beth! I couldn't bear that.'

'I don't know, Ali. But I think we should find out.'

'Yes.' Ali looked distraught. 'But what shall I say?'

'Leave it to me. I'll wheedle the truth out of her, somehow.'

When they returned to the office, Beth pulled up another chair alongside Ali's, so they were both facing Amanda Whitehorn across the desk. Beth wanted them to appear as intimidating as possible, hoping to unnerve the girl. For some moments, they sat silently staring at each other. As Beth hoped, the girl was the first to speak.

'What is it?' she asked, her voice showing her nervousness.

Beth leaned across the desk and rested her chin on her linked hands.

'Why don't you tell me?' she quietly answered.

'What is there to tell?'

'For starters, you can tell us what you were doing in Winchester last month.'

The girl's tongue moistened her lips. 'Nothing. Well — just shopping. There's nothing wrong with that, is there?'

'No. Except that you were not outside a shop, you were outside a secretarial agency.'

Her eyes flickering from one to the other, Amanda said, without conviction, 'Was I? . . . I didn't notice . . . I don't remember seeing you.'

'No. I was further along the road.'

'Oh. Well — I still don't see why there should be a problem, just because you happened to see me standing outside an agency in Winchester.'

Beth leaned back, not taking her eyes from the girl. 'The problem, Amanda, is that you were not actually outside the agency. You came out of it. That makes quite a difference, don't you agree?'

'Yes. I can see your point.' The girl cleared her throat. 'I admit I'd just popped in there to see what their rates of pay were — in case . . . '

'In case?' Beth prompted.

'In case I couldn't get any work in Southampton.'

'So why didn't you say that, just now, when I first mentioned it?'

'I don't know, really. Sorry.' The girl was obviously struggling to stay in control. 'Does it really matter?'

'On its own, perhaps not.' Beth saved the best till last. 'But what does matter is the fact that you were greeted by Gavin Moorhouse.'

The girl's gasp was significantly loud. She opened and closed her mouth a few times, but no words escaped, until she whispered, 'Does Gavin know you saw me?'

'I don't think so,' Beth said. 'But I want to know the truth — correction — we want to know the truth.' She motioned her hand to include Ali.

Now the girl's expression changed from misery to fear. 'It's really up to Gavin to tell you. Not me. I can't . . . '

For the first time, Ali spoke. Her voice was

expressionless. 'What are you to Gavin? Girlfriend? Mistress? Wife?'

Amanda's reaction was amazing. Her pale cheeks flared with red blotches of colour and her eyes widened. Even her voice changed key to a high screech. 'Is that what you think? No! My boyfriend would kill me if he thought . . . if he found out that you thought . . . Oh, God! It's nothing like that.' She babbled on, trying to find the right words. 'Please. You've got to believe me. There's nothing between Gavin and me. Only . . . ' Her blue eyes filled with tears.

'Only what?' Beth prompted, now a little concerned at the girl's hysteria.

'Only business.' The tears began to flow as Amanda lost control.

Beth and Ali glanced at each other. Then Ali said, 'What do you mean by business?'

'He's . . . he's my . . . boss.' Amanda's body was convulsed with sobs.

'Your boss!' Ali and Beth spoke almost in unison.

For some moments, the silence was broken only by the sound of weeping. Then Ali took a box of tissues from her drawer and pushed it across the desk. 'I'll put the kettle on while you pull yourself together,' she said. 'Perhaps some strong coffee will help you to tell me the truth. And don't think of doing a runner

301

while we're gone. Beth's dog will soon find you.' Right on cue, Hamish gruffly barked.

Motioning to Beth, Ali went through to the kitchen and filled the kettle.

Beth followed, closing the door behind her, and letting Hamish out into the enclosed courtyard. 'Well!' she said. 'What do you make of that?'

'Right now, I'm too gobsmacked to make anything of it.'

Thoughtfully, Beth took three mugs from the cupboard. 'Could it be anything to do with Gavin trying to persuade you to go public?' she asked.

Ali's head swivelled towards her friend. 'I hadn't thought of that,' she admitted. 'But — if so — what would the girl's connection be?'

'I don't know. But I think she'll tell us.'

After two cups of heavily sugared coffee, and half a box of tissues, Amanda Whitehorn was ready to confess all.

'It isn't really Gavin's fault,' she began.

'What isn't?' Beth felt as though she was doing a crossword with rather obscure clues.

'The whole thing. Simon thought up the idea and we went along with it.'

'Simon?'

Ali broke in, 'He's Gavin's boss.'

'Oh. Do go on, Amanda.'

'Well, he did it a few times in Cheshire, and then got greedy and decided to expand down south.'

'Did what in Cheshire?' This was going to be more difficult than Beth thought.

'Persuaded small agencies to go public, bought up most of the shares, then made a take-over bid.'

Open-mouthed, Beth and Ali stared at each other. Ali recovered first.

'So what was your involvement?'

Amanda squirmed in her chair. 'I had to suss out the agencies, get a job as a temp, find out what the rates were, who were their major clients, and so on.'

'And Gavin?' Ali's voice was ominously quiet.

'He had to try to persuade the owners to go public, then buy up as many shares as he could.'

'Did he now?' The tortured expression in Ali's eyes told Beth only too well what she was feeling inside.

'Yes.' Amanda clutched at a straw. 'He didn't really want to do it. Neither did I.'

'So why did you?'

The girl took another sip of her coffee. 'Simon had a hold on both of us.'

'What sort of hold?'

There was a long pause before Amanda

answered. 'I'd been in a bit of trouble once. To do with some grass at a rave. Nothing major, and I regretted it later, but I do have a police record. Foolishly, I told Simon about it. I thought he was a friend, but then he threatened . . . and I needed the extra money he offered to set up the flat with my boyfriend.'

Ali nodded. 'And what sort of hold did he have on Gavin?'

'Simon had loaned him some money a couple of years ago when his house was being repossessed, and was pressing for repayment quicker than Gavin could manage. So Simon said, if he helped him out with this, he'd not push for the higher interest. Gavin didn't really have much choice.'

'I see.' Ali sounded as though she didn't see at all.

'So — what are you going to do?' Amanda looked appealingly at Ali.

'I know what I'd dearly love to do,' Ali said, through gritted teeth. 'But it's probably illegal. I need time to think. Is that address correct?' She tapped her pen on the card Amanda had just filled in.

'No.' Amanda scribbled the name of a hotel on the notepad. 'But this one is.' Her voice was low.

Ali read it and nodded. 'Wait there until I

phone you. And don't contact Gavin, or Simon.'

Amanda agreed.

'Now, please go.'

With drooping shoulders, the girl opened the door. Turning back, she gazed at Ali and Beth. 'I'm sorry,' she whispered. 'So very sorry.'

'Not half as sorry as I am,' Ali replied.

When the door had closed, Beth looked at Ali in despair.

'Oh, Ali. What can I say?'

'Now I know how you felt when Bryn left.' Ali sighed deeply. 'It's the fact that you've been used — ' There was a slight break in her voice. 'It really hurts, doesn't it?'

23

Despite all attempts to immerse herself in work, Beth found her mind going back again and again to the events of the morning. Who would have thought that Gavin, of all people, could be such a conniving ratbag. She had been so sure that Ali had, at last, found her perfect man. It might have been more understandable if he had been two-timing Ali with the blonde. But to think that all this time he'd been wheedling information out of his lover, intending to use that information to take away her business — the business she had nurtured and cared about for so many years — and to destroy her dreams. Pretending to make plans for their future — buying a boat together, buying a house together. Living together, Ali and Gavin, for ever. His treachery was unspeakable, even within the seedy bounds of industrial espionage.

The shrill ring of the telephone made her jump, out of her dark reverie, into the present. It was Thora.

'Just wanted to thank you again for helping out last night.'

'That's OK. Did you enjoy the play?'

'Very much. And Edie was quite over-whelmed that she'd actually talked to someone she'd seen on the telly.'

'I'm glad it was a success.' Beth prepared for a polite ending to the conversation, but Thora had something else to say.

'Beth . . . was Vanessa all right?'

'She was a bit concerned about Tom, but nothing untoward. Why? Is she poorly this morning?' Beth wondered if their conversation had overtired Vanessa.

'Not so much poorly, as — fidgety. She's usually so calm and listless, but this strange mood bothers me.'

'Oh?' Beth waited for Thora to continue.

'It's a bit delicate — are you sure it's all right to speak to you at work? I would have come down and taken you out to lunch, but I don't really want to leave Vanessa while she's in this mood, and if you're staying with a friend, I can't slip along tonight.'

Now Beth really was curious. 'There's nobody else in the office at the moment, Jane has just popped along to the post office. What's the problem, Thora?'

'It's something that Edie said, that made me wonder . . . ' Thora paused, then blurted out, 'Has Vanessa asked you to help her end her life?'

This was the last thing Beth had anticipated. 'No. It's not been mentioned at all. Why do you think she would ask me such a thing?'

'Because she has asked Tom to help her die with dignity. He refused, and I can understand that.'

'Oh, God. Poor Tom.'

'Indeed. Then she asked me. I could, and part of me wants to put the poor girl out of her misery, but I can't. I'm trained to save life, not end it, although . . .'

'What?'

'I did agree to her request that if she was ill with something else, such as an infection, she didn't have to have medication to make her better, and could allow nature to take its course. There seemed no point in prolonging the agony, and that would be an act of God.'

'Yes, I can see that. But what did Mrs Cooper say that worried you?'

'Just that Vanessa has been sussing her out over her views on euthanasia. As a devout Catholic, Edie is obviously completely against it, but she thought I ought to know.'

'And you thought Vanessa might have broached the subject with me?'

'Yes. In fact, I wondered if that was why Tom had come back in such a state. I thought perhaps you'd told him that Vanessa had asked you . . . Anyway, I'm glad she didn't put you on the spot.'

'But she might.'

'That's a possibility, I'm afraid.'

'And you'd like to know how I would respond?'

'Please.'

Beth thought deeply before answering, 'I thought about it quite a lot when my mother was dying. She was in such pain, I used to feel we wouldn't allow an animal to suffer like that. But at the same time, I knew I couldn't be the one to make that final decision, even if it was legal.'

'But how do you feel about Vanessa?'

'I see Vanessa as a helpless woman in a wheelchair, who is going to deteriorate to unthinkable misery. If the doctors could do something it would be a merciful release, but I know I couldn't bring myself to do it. Perhaps I'm just too much of a coward.'

'Or perhaps, like me, you're too fond of Vanessa to have it on your conscience for the rest of your life.'

'That just about sums it up.'

'And Tom?'

'What about Tom?'

'Are you too fond of Tom to help his wife into an earlier grave, even if she begs you?'

Beth caught her breath. 'How did you

guess?' she whispered. There was no point in beating about the bush, not with Thora.

'I've seen the looks, heard the tenderness in his voice.' Thora paused for a moment, then went on, 'I like you, Beth. I like you a lot, and I sense you're terrified of being thought of as someone waiting to step into a dead woman's shoes. Am I right?'

'Yes,' Beth answered truthfully. It was something that had crossed her mind more than once.

'Thought so. And, as we're putting cards on the table, I just want you to know that if you and Tom get together later on, that's fine by me.'

'Thank you, Thora.' Beth couldn't tell Tom's mother that there was little likelihood of a happy ending, not after that fiasco last night. 'But we haven't said anything, made plans, or anything like that.'

'Some things are obvious without words.'

'Also, there are the girls to consider.'

'Ah, the girls.' Thora sighed. 'Cassie adores you, but Nadine might take just a little longer to come round.'

'She certainly seems to see me as a threat just now. That's one of the reasons I feel it would be better if I back off for a bit.'

'Don't do that, please. Vanessa needs you, now more than ever. And she loves having

Hamish. It would really upset her if you stopped calling.'

Beth was silent for a moment, then reluctantly agreed. 'When I come back, I'll bring him down again. But I think it would be best if Tom and I don't spend so much time together. Nadine has enough to worry about as it is, and you need to be very much a united family.'

'You're right, of course.' Thora sighed, then went on, 'Well, I'd better go downstairs and see if I can find out what has made Vanessa so restless. I'm so worried about her that I keep checking her room, making sure there's nothing within her reach.'

'Surely she wouldn't be able to do anything on her own? She can barely move.'

'I know, but I wouldn't put it past her to store up some of her medication. Or even to have a go at cutting her wrist, if she could lay her good hand on a sharp knife.'

'I honestly don't think she'd have the strength.'

'No. And I don't think she'd want any of us to find her like that. It's just that I keep asking myself what I would do if I were in her shoes. It's such a bloody awful disease. Especially for someone like Vanessa. I wish you'd known her when she was known as the Golden Girl by the media.'

'I should imagine she was rather like Cassie.'

'Oh, yes. So full of life. It breaks my heart to see her disintegrating like this.'

'She's lucky to have someone like you to care for her.'

'Well, there wasn't anybody in the States who gave a damn. Anyway, this won't get the potatoes on. Thanks again for helping out.'

'Before you go, Thora . . . '

'What is it?'

'Did Tom say anything? When he came back last night.'

'I didn't see him. God knows what time he came in. And this morning he was off early before I had a chance to speak to him. No explanation, and no apology.'

'Perhaps he forgot.'

'Perhaps.' Thora's voice was dry. 'But that's no excuse for his disgraceful behaviour, and I shall tell him so as soon as I can pin him down.'

★   ★   ★

Before Beth had time to assimilate the ongoing effect of her conversation with Thora, Ali phoned. She had been trying to track down Gavin without success. The receptionist in the Cheshire office was vague, thought he was away at a conference somewhere, and Simon would be in a meeting all day.

'What about the girl, Amanda whats-her-name?'

'I phoned her at the hotel and told her to go home and phone in sick, and not to dare contact Gavin or Simon until I said she could, or I would give her name immediately to the police as being part of a conspiracy.'

'Would you do that?'

'I'm mad enough to . . . I don't know. But she thinks I will, and that's the important thing.'

'What are you going to do? About Gavin I mean.'

'I've left messages for him to phone me, but I shan't let him know that I've uncovered his rotten scam, just try and get him down here as soon as possible. He has to look in my face and see what he's done. I'm not going to let him get away with this, Beth, and I'm going to make sure that they don't try it on anyone else.'

'How will you go about it?'

'I'm not sure but, believe me, I'll think of something.' Ali paused, then went on, 'By the way, I've found you a temp. One of my older regulars called in, just back from holiday and broke. She's good. Are you coming over again tonight?'

'Please, if it's OK. But only if I can provide supper. Chinese take-away OK?'

'You're on. And I'll let you have Brenda Mason's details then.'

★　★　★

It was just as well that the office was fairly quiet that day, because Thora phoned again, just as Jane came back from the post office.

'Sorry to bother you again, my dear, but Vanessa asked me to find out when you will be home.'

'Not tonight, I'm afraid. I'm going straight over to Ali's, but I'll be home tomorrow afternoon. I get time off midweek as I work most weekends.'

'OK. I'll tell her.'

'Do you know why she's asking?'

'I think she wants to talk to you about something. Which reminds me. Would you give me your e-mail address? Vanessa finds typing easier than talking.'

'At home? Or here?'

'You'd better give me both, as you're going to be away for another night. Do you have the chat room facility?'

'Yes, on both lines.'

'Good. It saves time logging on and off.'

24

The evening with Ali was not particularly pleasant. Beth wanted to help her friend, but there was little she could do except make sympathetic sounds and pour the wine. Every half hour or so, Ali tried Gavin's mobile phone number, without success.

'He's probably disconnected it and thrown it away in a field somewhere, so I can't get hold of him, the rat.'

'He'd only do that if he found out that you know what he's up to. And there's no reason to believe that.'

'Amanda could have told him.'

'Not if she wants to keep out of trouble, she won't.'

'Maybe he's just guessed, because I've been trying to get hold of him.'

'It's all ifs and buts, Ali. And it's tearing you apart.'

'I know I've made some terrible mistakes over men in the past. But this time, I really thought it was different. I would have staked my life on Gavin's decency.' Ali's face was pale with anguish as she turned to Beth. 'How do you think that makes me feel about myself? About my judgement in people?'

Beth understood only too well. No point in trying to reassure Ali that it wasn't her fault. Nothing would convince her, any more than it had convinced Beth when Bryn had left. Better to let Ali pour it all out, rather than bottling it up inside, and if opening another bottle of wine would do the trick, then so be it.

By the time the girls went to bed, Ali was well and truly legless. Beth had been more cautious with her own drinks, knowing she had to drive to work in the morning, and remembering how she'd felt the morning after her dinner party.

As expected, Ali had a hangover to match the one Beth had suffered that morning when she had first met Tom. Only a few months ago, but it seemed like light years, and she couldn't believe how she had detested him at first sight. Who would have thought such mutual dislike could turn to warm friendship and love? And now she had antagonised him again, and couldn't put things right. Her love life was as much a mess as Ali's — and Sarah's, come to think about it. Oh, hell! Why did everything have to be so — so complicated.

She was no nearer an answer after she had dropped Ali off at her office. It hadn't taken much to persuade her to leave her car at home, rather than risk losing her licence if she was stopped. Her alcohol intake the night before would probably blow the breathalyser sky high until the end of the day at least, especially as she'd refused to eat anything at breakfast time.

Once at her own office, Beth didn't have much time to ponder on anyone's problems, as a steady stream of prospective house-buyers trickled through from the time she arrived. Damon called in as she was discussing the exchange of contracts with clients. He was very subdued, just nodded in Beth's direction, had a word with Jane and picked up the few letters Beth thought Sarah should see, although she had dealt with them. Then he left.

When the clients had gone, Beth asked Jane if there were any messages.

'Only that Sarah said she's not happy with the surveyor's report on the basement flat at Estuary House. Something to do with flooding risk. She wants you to query it with him.'

'I thought she might. How is she?'

'Apparently, she's been going through the house like a dose of salts this morning, turning out cupboards and getting under Mrs

317

Hosey's feet. So I suppose she must be feeling OK.'

Smiling, Beth sat back in her chair. 'Sounds more like she's getting near her time. I washed all the curtains the day before Katie arrived.'

'Funny. You'd think nature would make you rest, so you could be ready for the Big Push.'

'Doesn't quite work like that. More like a tremendous surge of energy. Things have to be done. Can't stop.' Beth laughed. 'Though in Sarah's case I'm surprised she can even get out of the chair, let alone turn out cupboards!'

'Well, maybe we'll get a phone call soon.'

'Hope so. Right, that's the letters signed.' Beth took her bag from the desk drawer and clipped the lead onto Hamish's collar. 'If you hear anything about Sarah, I'll be at home for the rest of the day.'

★   ★   ★

The books were still strewn across the bedroom floor. Beth had been too scared to tidy up before she left, two days ago, but now she decided to follow Sarah's example and blitz the house. For a moment she listened. Not a whisper. Nothing. Just silence. She switched on the little radio on her bedside table, and jiggled the station controls, searching for something cheerful to speed up her dusting. Ah, yes. ABBA was just the job. She even knew some of the words of 'Waterloo'. Would have jigged along as well if there had been room.

No wonder the suitcase had fallen from the top of the wardrobe. She had been foolish enough to ask the carpet fitters to lift it up for her. They must have left it precariously off balance. Well, there was no way she could get it back up there by herself. And there wasn't room for it to stay on the floor of her bedroom, not without stubbing her toe every time she got out of bed. Only one thing for it. The spare room.

It was a lengthy process, first dragging the empty suitcase across the landing, then carrying the books, four at a time. Eventually, they were neatly stacked away, every inch of suspect carpet tacked back into place, and paintwork washed. Now for the Hoover.

Beth had checked her e-mail as soon as she arrived home, but another message had come through while she was upstairs. It was from Vanessa. Would Beth please log on to chat room?

Once on line, Vanessa asked Beth if she could spare an hour to visit, with Hamish.

Thora was having a perm and Edie Cooper was helping the gardener plant spring bulbs. She was nearby to help if she heard the tinkling of the hand bell, but Vanessa really wanted some company.

Hesitating for a brief moment, Beth replied that she would come straight down. She had intended to clean the cooker, but any excuse . . . The only thing that bothered her was whether Vanessa might broach the subject of euthanasia.

As soon as Beth greeted Vanessa she understood what Thora had meant. There was a feeling of restless energy about Vanessa that had not been there before, yet it was obvious that her condition was worsening. Each word took such an effort, but her eyes were darting everywhere, and she asked Beth to lift Hamish on to her lap.

After Mrs Cooper had left them a tray of tea and biscuits, and Beth had decanted the drink into Vanessa's special drinking cup, Beth became anxious when Vanessa croaked, 'I'll talk on PC. Something to say.'

It was the weirdest conversation. Beth speaking normally, and Vanessa replying by using her right hand to manipulate the keys. Fearing the worst, and wondering how she would reply, Beth asked Vanessa what she wished to say.

It's about Eliza, Vanessa tapped out.

Now that was a surprise. 'What about her?' Beth replied.

About the curse. Your grandfather was a gypsy.

'That's right. But I don't understand . . . '

Vanessa shook her head and turned back to the keyboard. *Theory. Maybe she felt you would believe. Gypsy blood.*

Slowly, Beth said, 'I hadn't thought of that. Do you mean that I could be a kind of — medium?'

Vanessa nodded. *More than that.*

'How do you mean?'

Kindred spirits. Bastard husbands. Babies lost.

Beth glanced at her companion, who was now watching her with an expression of deep compassion. 'I think I understand,' she said, 'and her story will be in that anthology. So why is she still in the house, not at the castle?'

Guardian angel.

'You mean she's watching over me?' Beth mulled over the thought. 'But that would mean you believe the house really is cursed.'

The faintest shrug from Vanessa's shoulders.

'So what can I do? I can't afford to move again.'

You'll be safe while Eliza is there.

'Do you really think so?'

A little smile, then, *Why not?*

Why not, indeed? Beth thought about it, then said, 'So if Eliza exists, she's a friendly ghost, who will protect me.'

A nod.

'In that case — I should welcome her and not be afraid.'

Another nod.

'It's weird, but I think I can live with that notion.' Beth drained her cup. 'Let's talk about something else. It's too nice a day to dwell on spooks.'

Vanessa smiled, then typed, *Will you take me for a walk?*

'Of course — if you feel up to it.'

Yes please.

'OK. I'll just tell Mrs Cooper. And you must promise to let me know when you want me to turn back.'

Hamish trotted beside them as they walked along the road towards the Castle. After a while, Vanessa touched Beth's arm and motioned her to stop. Her beautiful blue eyes shone as she focused on the view across the sea, the Isle of Wight forming a picturesque backdrop to the yachts skimming off shore.

'It's lovely.' Her voice was little more than a hoarse whisper.

'Yes. It's one of my favourite views.' A

breeze played with their hair, and Beth tucked the rug more securely around Vanessa's knees. 'I'd better take you back. Don't want you catching cold.'

'Not yet. I'm fine.'

The silence was companionable as Vanessa seemed to drink in the view, smiling at Hamish as he pawed a tiny crab. Then she turned her gaze towards the castle. 'Poor Eliza,' she murmured, then looked enquiringly at Beth.

'Oh, no. Much too far.'

Vanessa shook her head.

'Too far for me, I meant.' Beth laughed. 'And definitely too far for Hamish. Look at him.'

Tiring of the crab, he'd flopped beside the wheelchair, panting.

Vanessa pulled a face, then said, 'Your home then.'

'My home? Whatever for?'

'I'd like to see it.'

'Not much to see, I'm afraid. It's very tiny.'

'You can show me your story. About Eliza.'

The effort of talking caused Vanessa to gasp for breath. Beth became anxious.

'I really ought to take you back to your house. You will be more comfortable. And Mrs Cooper will worry if we're not back . . . '

The fragile hand gripped Beth's with a

surprising strength. 'Phone her,' she said. 'I want to see your house. Your things. Please.'

Beth knew she should refuse. Take Vanessa home. But she couldn't resist the pleading in those eyes. Reluctantly, she agreed. 'But only for a little while. Nadine will be home soon, and she's very concerned about you.'

'I'll explain. Thank you.'

All the way through the development, Vanessa's head turned from side to side, studying the houses and gardens. She smiled at the antics of Ginger Tom and Hamish, and signalled Beth to turn the wheelchair around and pull it over the threshold backwards. It was a tight squeeze, but eventually they were in the living room.

'Nice.' Vanessa acknowledged the pictures and lustre vase.

'Thank you. I bought them recently in Winchester.'

'Your story?' Vanessa reminded.

'Ah, yes. It's quite short.' Beth took the copy from the bookcase and placed it on the table so Vanessa could reach it. 'I'll just refill the water bowl for Hamish, and phone Mrs Cooper.'

When Vanessa had finished reading, she looked up. 'Good,' she said, simply, then nodded towards the computer. 'Can I use it?'

'Will you be able to? Without your gadget.'

Vanessa looked around the room. 'Cushion,' she said, and Beth was able to make her reasonably comfortable in front of the PC.

That's better, Vanessa typed. *Doesn't hurt throat.* She thought for a moment, then went on, *Do you have photos? Family? Your baby?*

'I've an album in the sideboard. Do you really want to see them?'

Yes. You are my only friend. I want to know more about you.

For the next few minutes, Beth turned the pages of the photo album, pointing out her mother, father, school-friends, colleagues at an office party. Then she took an envelope from the back of the album and pulled out the snapshot of Katie. It was the first time she had shown it to anyone. Not even Ali had seen it.

Vanessa held it for a long moment, then passed it back to Beth. *I'm so sorry,* she typed. *But one day you will have another baby.*

Beth's laugh was bitter. 'I don't think so.' She stood up. 'But I do think I should take you home. You're looking rather tired.'

Not just yet. I want to ask you something. It's important.

It was just as well that Beth had sat down again when the next message appeared on the screen.

You love Tom, don't you? Please be honest.

Beth stared at the words on the screen, her hand over her mouth, unshed tears behind her eyes. Then she looked at Vanessa, and knew she must answer with the honesty that was expected.

'Yes. I'm sorry.'

Don't apologise. It's time someone really loved him.

'You loved him once.'

Not enough. He deserves better. I've been a bitch. And he's repaid me by taking care of me. He's a good man, Beth.

'I know.'

He deserves someone like you. The girls deserve someone like you. Promise me you'll take care of them.

'I'll do anything I can, of course. But they have Thora. She loves them dearly.'

They need a mother as well as a grandmother. And Tom needs a proper wife.

Despite the closeness of the tears, Beth couldn't help laughing. 'He may have his own views on that.'

I think he loves you. He will need time. Just give him time and don't let other things get in the way. It would make me happy to know that . . .

The telephone rang. Beth hadn't taken it

off the Ansafone since they returned. If it was someone trying to sell something, she would leave it. It wasn't. It was Damon.

'Beth! For Christ's sake answer the phone if you're there. Sarah is in labour. We need you.'

She glanced at Vanessa. 'I'd better talk to him,' she said. 'Not that I can do anything from here. Excuse me a moment.'

Vanessa smiled, but as Beth passed her chair, she put out her arm. 'Promise?' she croaked.

'Of course.' She patted Vanessa's hand. 'I won't be a minute.'

Now Damon sounded desperate. 'Beth! Jane said you'd be at home. Please answer the phone.'

Pulling a wry face at Vanessa, Beth closed the door behind her and grabbed the phone. 'For goodness sake, Damon. What's the panic? Sarah has given birth before. You both know what to do.'

'Her waters have broken, Beth, and she's in agony.'

'Then get her to the hospital.'

'I've had a few drinks, and I don't think I should drive.'

'Oh, Damon! You're bloody hopeless. You know your wife is going to need you at any moment, but you still . . . ' Words failed Beth.

'I'm sorry. Beth, please come and drive us to the hospital.'

'Vanessa's here and I can't leave her.'

'Can't you find someone to stay with her? I need you, Beth.'

'So does Vanessa. Get a taxi, or . . . ' The conversation was interrupted by a long howl from Hamish. 'Phone for an ambulance.' She hung up.

As she opened the door, she almost fell over the little dog, who shot upstairs.

'Whatever happened to . . . ' she began, then noticed that Vanessa was slumped to one side of the wheelchair, her head lolling on her shoulder. Her eyes were closed and her face as pale as . . .

'Oh, no.' Beth placed her fingers against the pulse point in Vanessa's throat. There was nothing. Vanessa was dead.

25

Standing at the graveside on a humid Indian summer day, Beth went over the events of the last ten days in her mind. Everything seemed so unreal, as though she had dreamed the whole thing, or it was happening to someone else.

Just after Beth had dialled 999, Thora rang the bell, having decided to call on Beth on her way home from the hairdresser. She didn't seem shocked that Vanessa was dead.

'That's why she was behaving so strangely,' she sighed, gently kissing her daughter-in-law's cheek and smoothing back the golden hair. 'I think she knew the end was near.' Thora looked at Beth. 'You're shaking like a leaf. I don't suppose you have any brandy? We'll make do with a strong cup of coffee. Perhaps the caffeine will help.'

It didn't, but it gave them something to do while they waited for the doctor. Anything to take their minds off that frail figure in the wheelchair. The only other thing they could think of was to watch out for Nadine, walking home from the school bus stop.

At first, she had knelt by her mother for some minutes, rocking her in her arms in silent grief. Then she raised her head. 'What killed her?' she asked Thora.

'I don't know, dear, but I imagine it was a heart attack, from what Beth has told me.'

The expression on Nadine's face, when she turned towards Beth, changed from grief to suspicion. 'What happened?' she asked, her voice hostile.

Beth could hardly speak. 'I went into the hall to answer the telephone, and when I came back, Vanessa was . . . ' She gestured helplessly towards the body.

As Nadine stared at Beth her expression changed again, to accusation. 'You must have said something that frightened her to death. What did you say to her? Tell me!'

'Nadine.' Thora put a comforting arm around her granddaughter. 'It's natural that you're upset, but you can't blame Beth because Vanessa had a heart attack. These things happen, I'm afraid.'

'She had motor neurone disease, not heart disease. The doctors would have known if her heart was weak.'

'Not necessarily. Sometimes people just have a massive coronary for no reason at all.'

Nadine shrugged off her grandmother's arm. 'My mother was an international athlete. One of the fittest people in the world. There was no way she could have run like she did, for all those years, if her heart wasn't functioning one hundred per cent.'

Gently, Thora reminded Nadine of another athlete's tragic death. I'm afraid it can happen, even to perfectly fit athletes. Remember that beautiful American runner, Flo-Jo?'

Nadine shook her head. It was obvious she didn't want to believe her mother's death was from natural causes. 'What was mother doing here in the first place? She was hardly in a fit state to go visiting.'

Beth tried to soothe the girl. 'Your mother asked me to bring her down here,' she quietly said. 'I can't tell you how sorry I am.'

'Why should she want to come here?'

'She asked to see photographs of my family.' Beth motioned towards the album lying on the table. 'I think she just wanted some company. To talk to someone.'

'Don't be ridiculous. She could barely say two words without gasping for breath.'

'Nadine,' Thora interrupted. 'Vanessa could communicate with people through the computer. You've seen her do it at home.'

All eyes went to the computer screen, and

Beth was thankful that the screensaver was scrolling. The one thing she didn't want was anyone reading Vanessa's last words.

'That's exactly what we were doing before the phone call,' she said, moving quickly to the computer and pressing the necessary buttons to log off.

Still stroking her mother's hair, Nadine was silently thoughtful. Then she bit her lip and nodded, as though reluctantly agreeing. But her suspicions weren't quite over. 'What were you talking about?' she wanted to know.

Beth shrugged her shoulders. 'Just chit-chat. You know — girl talk.'

Again Nadine accused Beth. 'You must have seen she was ill. Why didn't you phone for a doctor? She might still be alive if it wasn't for you.'

'It was all over in seconds. There was nothing anyone could have . . . ' Beth's voice faltered, before she went on, 'Believe me, if I could have got help to her in time, I would have done it.'

'Would you?' Nadine's tone was supercilious.

'Nadine?' Thora sounded unbelieving. 'What are you suggesting?'

'I'm suggesting that Beth might have had her own reasons for wanting my mother out of the way.'

For a moment there was a shocked silence, then Thora said, 'I can't believe you just said that, Nadine.' She looked sternly at her granddaughter. 'Beth has been a good friend to our family. You have no grounds to make such a dreadful accusation.'

Nadine still had questions to hurl at Beth. 'I find it a bit odd that you should be on the telephone at the exact moment that my mother died,' she said. 'How are we to know you were out of the room at all?'

Without answering, Beth went out into the hall and touched the message replay button on the Ansafone. Fortunately, the only call was the one from Damon, and the whole conversation had been recorded, including Hamish's howl.

Beth felt like saying 'Satisfied?', but reminded herself that Nadine was young and extremely distraught over her mother's death. At least the girl had the grace to look a little sheepish, before she turned to her grand-mother.

'What will happen now?' she asked.

'As soon as the doctor has certified the time of death, he'll phone the funeral directors.'

Nadine looked down at her mother. 'I suppose they'll take her to a chapel of rest, or something like that.'

'You don't need to know all the details, dear.'

'Yes I do.' Nadine's voice was stubborn. 'She's my mother — and I want to know everything that's going to happen to her.'

'You won't like it.'

'I still want to know.'

'Very well.' Thora sighed in resignation. 'They'll take her to the hospital. There will have to be a post-mortem.'

'No!' the girl cried. 'Her doctor knows about her disease. Surely he can tell if she has had a heart attack without cutting her about? Please, Thora. Don't let them do that.'

'We've no choice, I'm afraid, dear.'

It was just as Thora had said. First the doctor, then the funeral directors with a private ambulance. By that time, the curious neighbour had also put in an appearance, watering her hanging baskets until they were overflowing.

Now for the really difficult part. Tom.

Thora decided not to phone him on his mobile. He would be on his way home by now. Cassie had gone to a friend's house for tea, so they would wait until she came home. She would need someone to hug and comfort her, and you couldn't do that on the telephone.

Nadine sat slumped in an armchair, staring bleakly at the empty wheelchair, refusing all offers of tea, coffee, water.

Thora, looking troubled, watched from the window. Eventually, she broke the uncomfortable silence. 'Nadine,' she quietly advised, 'I really think you should apologise to Beth. You have said some terrible things about her. Practically accused her of wanting Vanessa to die.'

'Oh, I know you and Cassie and father think she's wonderful, but she'll never be able to step into my mother's shoes. I'll leave home rather than live in the same house with her.' She glared at Beth. 'And I don't see that I have anything to apologise for.'

'Then I'll apologise on your behalf,' Thora said. 'Beth, you have brought friendship and warmth into our family, when we needed it most. Your visits to Vanessa were the highlight of her day, and I thank you from the bottom of my heart for helping my son to retain his sanity.' She sighed, deeply. 'I'm sorry to have to say this, Nadine, but your mother would be ashamed to hear you say such hurtful things about her friend — her only friend. And I'm going outside to wait for Tom. Just at this moment I can't bear to be in the same room with you.'

Nadine gasped, and stared at her grandmother, open-mouthed. The words had obviously struck deeply.

★ ★ ★

His face pale with shock, Tom came into the living room. First he held Nadine close, then his mother. 'Were you here when it happened?' he asked.

'No. I'd gone to the hairdressers. Beth brought her down.'

Tom nodded. 'Vanessa said last night she wanted to get out a bit more, while she was still able. But who would have thought she'd have a heart attack?' He turned to Beth. 'It must have been a dreadful shock for you.' He began to fold up the wheelchair, then went on, 'Does Mrs Cooper know?'

'No.' Beth put a hand to her mouth. 'Oh, dear — we ought to warn her what has happened.'

'I'll tell her — and Cassie,' Tom said, frowning thoughtfully. 'Then I must contact the funeral directors. Probably have forms to sign, things like that.'

Nadine looked hopeful. 'They won't be able to do a post-mortem without your consent, will they, Dad? Don't agree to it — please.'

He took her hand. 'I don't know the legal situation on this, and I don't like the idea any more than you do, but Nadine, dear . . . ' He seemed to be choosing his words carefully. 'The doctors in America told me that Vanessa would probably die of pneumonia eventually, because the lungs wouldn't be able to cope with infection.' Again he paused. 'I hadn't expected anything quite so sudden as this. So — I would like to know whether there was any connection with the disease.'

Stony-faced, Nadine stared back at her father, then withdrew her hand from his clasp.

Tom looked at Thora, as though for some guidance, but she just shook her head, in a way that suggested it was best to leave the matter alone.

Murmuring, 'I'll just put this in the car, then take you home,' Tom picked up the wheelchair. At the door, he paused and looked back at Beth. His expression was sympathetic. 'Are you all right?' he asked.

'I think so, but I just can't believe it has happened.'

★   ★   ★

Even standing at the graveside, knowing that the coroner's verdict had been natural causes, a heart attack, Beth still couldn't believe that Vanessa had died so suddenly. And in her house, of all places. Some people said it was a merciful release, and she knew it was. But an awful thought persisted in niggling away at the back of her mind. What if the house really was cursed? And Eliza hadn't been able to help.

26

It was another two weeks before Bradley and Hannah Martin were strong enough to leave the baby unit and go home to 'Hawthorns'. Big brother Jamie immediately decided that they needed him all the time, so Sarah and Lorraine had their hands full on Tuesday and Thursday mornings persuading him that the babies would still be there, waiting for his attention, when he came home from nursery school. He wasn't the only one to be quite besotted with the twins. Lorraine almost vied with Sarah to be the first to comfort a crying infant, and Mrs Hosey found every excuse possible to help out — including nappy changing. Said it was a pleasure, as with these disposable types, she didn't have buckets of terry towelling to soak and wash. As for Damon, he would hold first one, then the other, with the smuggest of smiles on his face, as though he couldn't quite believe that he was half responsible for the two little beings.

Beth watched him carefully place Bradley into Jamie's arms and hoped that, this time, fatherhood would tame his roving eye. With Sarah and Damon flanking Jamie, Sarah holding Hannah, they made the perfect family group for Beth to capture on her camera.

Three snaps later, Sarah stood up and held out her daughter towards Beth.

'Sit in that armchair by the window, Beth, and I'll take one of you — with your god-daughter.'

Beth's eyes misted. 'Do you really mean it?' she asked.

'No, I'm just making it up.' Sarah laughed. 'Of course I mean it. That is, of course, if you want to. I should have asked you properly.'

'Want to? I'd be delighted. Oh, Sarah, thank you so much.' Before she took the baby, Beth kissed her friend's cheek.

'We both wanted you to be one of the godparents, didn't we, Damon?' Sarah beamed at her husband.

Damon looked so happy, Beth couldn't be churlish, so she leaned over and kissed his cheek also. 'Thank you,' she murmured.

There was a strange expression in his eyes. Was it gratitude that she hadn't told Sarah about that day in the office, Beth wondered?

'Couldn't wish for anyone nicer,' he quietly said, then busied himself making Bradley more comfortable in Jamie's arms.

As Sarah focused the camera, she added, 'And we're going to ask Ali if she will be

Bradley's godmother.'

'I'm sure she'll be thrilled,' Beth said, wiping away a stray tear.

'My two best mates as godmothers. It doesn't get better than that.' Sarah grinned as the camera clicked. 'One more for luck,' she went on, then, 'Do you think Gavin would like to be godfather? Or is that jumping the gun a bit?'

Beth knew that Ali was still trying to get in touch with Gavin, and felt there was little chance that their romance could be resurrected, but Ali obviously hadn't mentioned the split to Sarah.

'Maybe you'd better not mention it to Ali just yet. I have a feeling that things might be cooling off between them, and it could be embarrassing.'

'Oh,' Sarah's face expressed her disappointment. 'That's a shame. I thought they were really good together.'

'I could be wrong, of course. It's just that he hasn't been down for a while. But do ask Ali to be a godmother. She was wonderful with Katie.' Trying hurriedly to get away from the subject of Ali and Gavin, Beth went on, 'Who else are you having as godparents?'

'Well, as my brother and sister are Jamie's godparents, we thought we'd ask my cousin, Louise, and her husband, to be the other godparents with you for Hannah.'

'I remember Louise. She used to come and stay with you in the holidays. Loved riding.'

'Still does. And Damon's brother, Howard, has agreed to be one of the godfathers for Bradley.'

'Isn't he working in Kuwait?'

'Yes. That's why he couldn't be here for Jamie's christening. But he's due some leave at Christmas, so we're arranging the christening for early in the New Year.' Sarah looked thoughtful. 'We'll have to think of someone else for the other godfather if Gavin isn't around.' She sighed. 'Poor Ali. She doesn't have much luck with her guys, does she?'

Driving home across the forest, Beth's thoughts wandered to the fact that Damon didn't seem to have any friends. He'd always been a loner at school, and it seemed as though even now, all these years later, there was no one close enough to consider being a godparent. They'd had the same problem when Katie was born. Bryn's family wouldn't travel for the christening, and Beth had lost touch with most of her friends, partly because they didn't like Bryn and he didn't like them. But Ali, bless her, had remained a true friend and adored her little god-daughter, for the short time she'd lived. They'd eventually decided to have just two godparents, and

Bryn had asked one of his colleagues at work to share the honours with Ali but, like Bryn, he didn't respond to Beth's letter telling him that Katie had died. She had been hurt at the time, but now she felt that they were the sad people, more so than her.

Beth glanced over her shoulder at Hamish, snoozing on his blanket in the back, secured by his harness. He had caused her considerable worry after Vanessa died, hardly touching his food, and he wouldn't go back into the living room. At night, he would only settle if he was close to Beth, so she allowed him back on to her bed for a while. Eventually, she took him to the vet, who assured her he was a healthy young animal and would return to his normal self in his own good time, given plenty of TLC. After another week, Beth still wasn't satisfied, so tried a homeopathic remedy that one of her clients recommended. Whether it was the remedy, or just time, that did the trick, she didn't know, but within a few days he was as bright-eyed and bushy-tailed as ever.

Today, his behaviour had been impeccable. Beth had watched him closely for a reaction to the babies, but he showed no signs of jealousy, and was much more interested in scampering around with Jamie.

She hadn't seen Tom since the funeral.

Thora had telephoned twice to see if she was all right, and Cassie had hugged Beth tightly at the churchyard, but Nadine had not even glanced in her direction. Beth wasn't surprised, but it made her promise to Vanessa increasingly difficult to keep. Better give them time to grieve first, time to cling together as a family. Perhaps later there would be some way she could help, with Thora and Cassie, if not Nadine.

As she turned the corner, Beth saw the Range Rover, parked outside her house. Tom had been waiting for her, and followed her as she carried Hamish into the house and refilled his water bowl.

Finally, she turned and faced him. Trying to keep her voice calmer than she felt, she asked, 'Can I offer you something? Coffee? Or a drink?'

'Beth!' The anguish in his voice was apparent. 'We have to talk.'

She closed her eyes. When those words were said in a play or film, it usually heralded trouble. Eventually, she managed to speak.

'I think it was all said last time we were here alone, don't you?'

He fidgeted with the mouse on the computer table, then turned back with a frown. 'I realise now that I was too hot-headed.' His smile was wry. 'Put it down to lust overriding good manners, if you like.' He glanced away again, as though trying to collect his thoughts. 'Something was troubling you and I should have tried to find out what, instead of going off half-cocked . . . '

For a moment, they stared at each other, then the implication of what he had just said hit them both and they found themselves laughing, out loud and almost hysterical.

Sinking on to the settee, Tom gasped, 'I think I will take you up on that drink, Beth.'

After he had recovered, Tom placed his glass on the coffee table and leaned towards Beth. 'Am I forgiven?' he asked, seriously.

'Of course.'

He held out his arms and she moved to his side. They didn't kiss, just hugged. Then he held her at arms length, looking closely into her face.

'I've missed you,' he said.

She nodded. 'Me too.'

He took her hands in his. 'Don't get me wrong. I know it's too soon, for both of us, but do you think we can . . . I don't know quite how to say it . . . '

Beth placed a finger over his lips. 'Then don't,' she said softly. 'I'll just say that, yes — I think we can. But you're right. It *is* too soon.'

He smiled, then was serious again. 'It must

have been awful for you, that afternoon when Vanessa . . . ' Again words failed him.

'It was awful for everyone.'

'Did you know she wanted me to help her die?'

'Yes. Thora told me.'

'Part of me wanted to do what she asked. She so dreaded what was ahead. But I couldn't bring myself to do it.'

'I know. Thora felt the same.'

'It's strange, but she changed during those last few days. Became — contented, in a funny sort of way.'

'I'm glad.' Beth was not sure what to say.

'I know she had been quite — selfish in the past, but she began leaving messages for us on her computer, kind messages, thanking us for all our help, completely out of character. She even told the girls how much she loved them, and she'd never done that.' He sighed. 'It was as though she knew . . . '

'Perhaps she did,' Beth murmured.

'I think she was trying to find her true self, before it was too late. For the first time, I began to like her. I'd loved her once, but never really liked her.'

Beth was silent, sensing that he needed to talk about Vanessa. 'And she told Thora that she liked you,' he went on, 'and hoped we would all stay in touch, whatever happened.

346

Do you think she guessed that there was something between us?'

'Perhaps. I don't know.' Beth found herself perilously close to tears.

'I keep wondering if she was — giving her consent — wanting us to be happy?'

'Please don't, Tom.' Now the tears were spilling over.

He bent his head and kissed her hands. 'I'm sorry. The last thing I want is to upset you. You've been through enough. But . . . ' He looked around the room. 'I'm glad she was with you. She felt you were the first real friend she'd ever had, and that's a comfort to all of us.'

'Not to Nadine, I'm afraid.'

'Ah, yes. Nadine.' He sighed, deeply. 'Just give her time, and she'll accept the situation.'

'I wish I shared your optimism.'

'Between them, Cassie and Thora will bring her round, I'm sure.'

'Oh, Tom, I do hope so. But we mustn't rush things. Nadine has so much grief bottled up inside her.'

'You're right, of course. But will you drop in sometimes, when you're out with Hamish? Cassie misses you both.'

Beth nodded. 'Let's just take one day at a time and see what happens, shall we?'

'And may I also drop in sometimes? I still

need a friend, you know.'

Beth sniffed back the tears. 'What about Mrs Walker? Aren't you afraid my nosy neighbour might ruin both our reputations?'

His laugh was just a little bitter. 'As the man said — frankly my dear, I don't give a damn.' He stood up. 'I'd better go, or my supper will be inedible.'

Beth glanced at her watch. No wonder she was hungry. 'I've just been over to see Sarah's new babies,' she said. 'That's why I'm so late.'

'Ah, yes. The twins. One of each, I think Thora said.'

Beth nodded. 'And she's asked me to be godmother to the little girl. Isn't that lovely?'

'I'm glad for you.' Tom cupped her face in his hands and kissed her. It was a nice kiss. Not passionate, but warm and loving.

'Goodbye, Beth.' He smiled down at her. 'Don't forget what I said, will you?'

As she closed the front door behind him, Beth fervently hoped that 'too soon' would not linger 'too long'.

27

Many people consider autumn to be the best time of the year to see the full beauty of the New Forest. Beth was one of them. On a crisp, bright day, with the sun touching the trees to highlight every hue of red and gold, there was no need to travel to New Jersey to see nature at its best during 'the fall'. She also considered that Caprice's steady canter through the glades and clearings was the best form of transport to see such beauty, particularly when your companion was the man you dearly loved.

As if reading her thoughts, Tom looked back and slowed Maverick just a little, to allow Beth to ride alongside him. His smile was the same sweet smile that had trans-formed his face all those months ago, making her reassess her opinion of him. How could I ever have thought of Tom as anything but warm and kind, she wondered.

They both reined in their horses to a gentle walk as they approached another thickly wooded area.

'Penny for them,' Tom said, noting her little smile.

Beth shook her head. 'They're worth much more than that.'

Grasping her reins, he pulled both horses to a halt, leaned across and kissed Beth full on the lips. It was a long, lingering kiss that left her gasping.

'Now will you tell me what you were thinking?' he said, his eyes teasing.

'I was just thinking how wrong I had been about you when we first met.'

'Oh.' He lightly tapped his feet against the horse's flanks and clicked his tongue. As they moved forward again, he asked, 'Was I really such an ogre?'

'Yes. You were quite horrible.' Beth's mischievous smile belied her words.

Smiling back, Tom said, 'But I'm not an ogre now, am I?'

Pursing her lips, she considered his words, then shook his head. 'No, I don't think so.'

'Is that the best you can do, woman?'

'All right. If you must know, I think you're absolutely gorgeous.'

He threw back his head and laughed. 'That's more like it. I'll have to tell them about that at work. They still think I'm an ogre.'

For a while, they walked on, the only sound being the crunch of leaves beneath the horses' hooves, or the occasional flutter of wings as a disturbed bird moved to a watchful distance. Tom broke the silence. 'What made you change your mind, Beth?' he asked.

Thoughtfully, she said, 'I suppose it was when I fell on the beach . . . '

'You mean when Cassie knocked you flying.'

She grinned at the memory. 'Poor girl. She was so apologetic. And you . . . '

'What about me?' he prompted.

'You were so considerate and helpful. I suppose that was when I began to realise you weren't such a stuffed shirt, after all.' She paused for a moment, reflecting. 'After that, it was just all sorts of little things. Then when I realised what you were doing for Vanessa, I knew that you were a very special kind of man.'

Looking slightly embarrassed, he shrugged his shoulders. 'Nonsense. Any man worth his salt would have done the same. Or any woman.' He gazed at her for a moment. 'I bet you would have done the same for Bryn if the need arose.'

It was a thought that had never occurred to her, and she didn't like having to confront it. 'I don't know,' she said. 'How does anyone know what they would do until the situation arises?'

'True,' he agreed. 'If you had asked me a

year ago whether I would take Vanessa back, whatever the circumstances, I would probably have said 'no'. And if it hadn't been for her illness, I certainly wouldn't have done, even though I still had feelings for her.'

Gently, Beth said, 'I'm glad you lost the bitterness towards each other, at the end.'

He nodded. 'One thing I did learn from Vanessa was that there is no benefit to be had from bitterness. It took time, but I learned it.' He looked at Beth. 'What about you?'

'I don't feel bitter towards Vanessa. Far from it.'

'No — I didn't mean that. I meant — do you still feel bitterness towards Bryn?'

Truthfully, she answered, 'No. But I feel nothing for Bryn any more. In fact, I don't give him a thought if I can help it. I'd much rather think about you.'

Again he laughed loudly, startling the horses, so that Maverick reared a little in protest.

'Whoa, boy. Good boy.' Tom lightly touched Beth's shoulder with his crop. 'I've half a mind to throw you down under that tree and take you here and now.'

Beth looked at the ground under the tree. 'Don't even think about it,' she grimaced. 'Unless you want to stink to high heaven for at least a week.'

His gaze followed hers. 'I'll wait,' he said, wrinkling his nose. 'Rolling in the hay is one thing, but rolling in *that* . . . '

For a while they walked on, each with their own thoughts. Then Tom said, 'I'd give anything to ask you to move in with us, you know.'

'It's a lovely idea, but it wouldn't work.'

'I know. Nadine would leave straight away. I do realise that she's a pain in the butt, but she's still a child.'

'And she is your daughter. I do understand.'

'Do you? Really?'

'Of course. You have a responsibility to her, and Cassie and Thora.'

'Cassie and Thora aren't a problem. But Nadine . . . ' He sighed. 'I hate having to meet you secretly like this.'

'I don't,' she reassured him. 'There's an element of excitement about clandestine meetings that I hadn't realised before.'

'Cobblers!'

Now it was Beth's turn to laugh aloud. 'Language, Tom, please. Not in front of the animals.'

'I'd still rather tell the world that we're . . . ' he hesitated.

'An item?' she prompted.

'I hate that expression. But I suppose it will

have to do, for want of something better. So — I'd rather tell the world that we're an item than have the clandestine meetings, however exciting you may find them.'

Beth's expression was serious as she turned to him. 'Listen to me, Tom. We both know we have to be sensible, whatever we might feel inside. Nadine has been hurt enough, without us making it worse.' She chose her words carefully. 'I want to be with you every minute, every hour, every day. But I know it isn't possible, not yet. So . . . ' She drew a deep breath. 'I am going to make the most of what we have, and enjoy feeling like a girl who is being courted.' Her smile was broad, but her lashes glistened with tears, as she went on, 'And just think how marvellous it will be when we both know the right moment has come and no one need be hurt.'

He gazed at her for a moment, then held out his hand. 'I don't deserve you,' he said.

Taking his hand, she laughed. 'Oh yes, you do. You're a good man, Dr — Tom! Look out!' she warned.

Just in time, he ducked under a low branch.

Back at the riding stables, he escorted her to her car. 'Same time next week?' he asked, before he drove home in the Range Rover.

Later, when Beth was relaxing in the bath,

she contemplated her non-consummated romance. At first they had just met on the beach from time to time, when she was exercising Hamish, always at the far end, away from Tom's house. Then, when they met Nadine and a young student from her computer class, the reaction had been so frosty they had decided that it would be better if Beth found another route to walk — alone. Once or twice they had met for a drink, but there was always the risk that someone would see them, and gossip. Neither of them was particularly worried about the gossip, only the effect it might have on Nadine. So Beth had suggested they take up riding again.

Cassie had been more distressed by her mother's death than they had imagined, probably because it had been so sudden, and sooner than she had anticipated.

'I didn't have a chance to say goodbye to her, not properly,' she had sobbed. She was still fairly subdued, but beginning to surface again with her school activities and social life. She had telephoned Beth to ask when she was bringing Hamish to visit, but there had only been one opportunity since the funeral, when Nadine stayed on for her computer studies.

Thora and Tom had converted Vanessa's room into a study area for the girls, but it seemed strange without the wheelchair, and Beth felt uncomfortable, as though Vanessa's shadow still lingered in the house. Thora invited Beth to Sunday lunch the following weekend, but she declined. Nadine wasn't ready yet to accept her at her mother's house, and the last thing Beth wanted was to spoil her relationship with Tom by rushing things, even though she loved him more than she would have thought possible.

She probably wouldn't have heard the doorbell if it hadn't been for Hamish, barking outside the bathroom door. Pausing from briskly towelling her hair, Beth listened. She wasn't expecting anyone. If it was someone selling something, they would go away. But the doorbell rang persistently.

Wrapping her hair in a towel and her body in a bathrobe, she padded downstairs. The bell was still ringing.

'Who is it?' she called through the door.

'It's Tom. Hurry up and let me in, I feel a right prat, standing here with my finger on the bell.'

He practically fell into the hall. 'You said you enjoyed being courted, so I thought I would do the job properly,' he grinned, thrusting an enormous bouquet of flowers into her arms and holding aloft a bottle of wine.

'Oh, Tom! Thank you. They're lovely,' she cried.

'So are you.'

Suddenly, the atmosphere between them was charged with electricity. For a moment, they just stared at each other, then the flowers and wine were placed carefully on the telephone table. Silently, Beth held out her hand and led him upstairs, to her bedroom.

They allowed themselves time to explore each other's body slowly, tenderly and passionately. Beth had often wondered what Tom would be like as a lover. He excelled her wildest expectations, rousing her to a peak she had never experienced with Bryn.

Afterwards, she lay back on her pillow, fulfilled and contented. 'Oh, Tom,' she whispered. 'I never knew anything could be . . . '

'Shush.' He placed his finger on her lips. 'Don't talk. This is too magical for words.'

Later, they made love again, this time with even more intensity. Then they dressed and went downstairs, drowsy from their after-love emotions. While he opened the wine and found the glasses, she put the flowers in water and placed the vase on the coffee table. They filled the room with their fragrance.

'My hair's a right mess,' she commented, as

she caught sight of her reflection in the mirror.

'I love your hair like that,' Tom said. 'It makes you look wild, like a gypsy.'

For a brief moment, she thought of Eliza. Then she pushed the thought into the furthest recesses of her mind. Nothing was going to spoil the magic. 'I am a gypsy,' she told him, laughing. 'At least, my grandfather was.'

'Is that a fact?' Tom swung around. 'Yes, you remind me of the beautiful gypsies in old movies, dancing seductively around the camp fire. Flashing dark eyes, heaving bosoms and wildly swinging hair. Your hair's too short to swing wildly, of course.' He topped up her glass. 'Do you have mystical powers, my little gypsy Beth?'

'None that I know about . . . '

'Well, you've certainly cast a spell over me. Come here, you adorable little witch.'

Eventually, he had to go home. They both knew that, although their relationship had changed, the circumstances hadn't. There was no way they could take it any further, until Nadine had come to terms with her mother's death and would accept Beth as a friend of the family. But they also both knew, without discussing it, that Tom would visit Beth at home, and they would continue to make love.

As long as they were discreet, no one need know, no one need be hurt.

Beth was quite happy to allow this to go on for now, and only one thing niggled at her new-found happiness. Although she loved him to bits, she had no wish to be a permanent mistress; tucked safely out of sight in a little love nest.

There was also a second little niggle. Tom couldn't have been more tender and loving, but not once had he actually said he loved her.

28

The city car parks would probably be full to queuing, and Beth was tempted to use the park and ride facility, but she needed discs and cartridges for her PC, and a bulky box of paper for the printer, so decided to go straight down to West Quay Road. For once, luck was with her and someone was preparing to move out of a bay right in front of one of the stationery suppliers as she arrived. Waiting for the parking space, Beth felt sympathy for the woman who was struggling to hang on to the slippery bags being tugged from her grasp by the wind, strap a crying toddler into the car seat and fold up a cumbersome buggy. Not an easy feat in a force seven wind. At one point, Beth wound down her window and called out to the woman, asking if she could help.

'I'm OK, thanks,' the woman shouted back, shoving the buggy into the boot of her car, then advised, 'Don't bother with an umbrella. Look at that one over there.'

Beth followed her gaze to where another woman was unsuccessfully trying to control an umbrella that had blown inside out.

Eventually, in frustration, the woman threw the disabled brolly into the back of her car, bleeped the central locking with her remote control and took her chances with the weather. Beth followed suit, with a quick dash in and out of the store. Now for the really tricky part.

Bracing herself, she fought her way through the elements to the huge West Quay Shopping Mall, then continued fighting, this time through hordes of shoppers, tripping over small children gawping at the sparkling decorations above their heads. No matter how organised she was, there was always at least one last-minute present to be searched for. This year there were three, and time was running out. The twins weren't too much of a problem, even on the day before Christmas Eve. Numerous baby gifts vied for her custom, and she finally settled on two furry elephants, one pink, one blue. If only Tom's present was that easy. Fleetingly, she toyed with the idea of buying him the huge teddy bear on display.

What do you buy a man who has everything, well almost everything, she wondered? Eventually, she bought a double album CD of his favourite composers, remembering how they had listened to the Dvorak *New World Symphony* in her house one evening, after a particularly satisfying encounter of a sexual kind. Not even Nadine could find something to sneer at in a classical CD, although she might if she knew what sensual memories it held. But she would have her father's company at Christmas, which was worth more than all the gifts in the world.

Beth's heart sank at the prospect of Tom being so far away, but she understood the reason. None of his family felt they could face the first Christmas in their new house without Vanessa. There had been plans to make it the best ever, knowing it might be her last, but that had been cruelly snatched from them. So Tom decided to take them to America on Christmas Eve, anticipating a white Christmas. He hoped some skating and skiing might revive the girls' spirits, and when they came back . . . but she would not allow herself to dwell on the future. It was too uncertain.

Outside in the Bargate, it seemed as though the wind was dropping a little. Good. White Christmases were unlikely in southern England, but nobody really wanted a 'batten down the hatches' festive season, particularly with so many telephone wires down.

She glanced at her watch. Yes, there was time for a quick dash into Boots before she met Ali for lunch. Thank God for Ali, or Beth would have been sharing a lonely Christmas bone with Hamish. Sarah and Damon were having a real family gathering at the home of Sarah's parents, with every relative who was prepared to make the journey and risk being wakened at the crack of dawn by an excited Jamie and two hungry babies. Ali's first idea had been to go to a hotel, but most of them wanted a minimum stay of five days, which didn't fit in with their businesses, not to mention the expense. So Ali suggested that they stay at her flat.

'We can get disgustingly drunk and maudlin together,' she said. 'Watch *Sound of Music* for the umpteenth time, and I'll try and get tickets for the panto on Boxing Day. Let's turn back the clock and be kids again, hissing and booing the villain. Like we used to when we were at school.'

'Sounds good to me. We could go over to the Biddlecombes the day after, if you like. Take the presents.'

'Why not? I haven't bought a christening present for Bradley yet. Any ideas?'

'Not really, apart from an engraved tankard. Boys aren't quite so easy as girls.'

'What are you buying Hannah? Jewellery?'

'No.' Beth had laughed a little self-consciously. 'Actually, I've embroidered a picture, with her name and the date and everything.'

'Wow! I seem to remember you weren't much good at needlework at school. When did all this come about?'

'I'm still hopeless, but I do like cross-stitch, and this one was quite simple. It's being framed at the moment.'

Hurrying along the High Street, Beth made a mental note to call in at the framing shop on her way home, to see if her picture was ready.

They had arranged to meet in a pub near Ali's office. Brushing the rain from her eyes, Beth searched for her friend among the throng at the bar. Then she saw her, sitting at a table in the non-smoking mezzanine area, sipping a glass of wine and talking to a man, who had his back to Beth. Ali waved and beckoned, but Beth pointed to the bar, and managed to get her own glass of wine after five minutes. It wasn't until she had pushed her way through to the mezzanine, that the man turned and looked at Beth.

Good God! It was Gavin.

Almost frozen to the spot, Beth looked first at Ali, who shrugged her shoulders, then at Gavin, who stood up and pulled out another chair from the table.

'Hallo, Beth,' he said, his eyes searching her

face. She could only register shock.

'Gavin,' she murmured, sitting down and taking a good swig at her drink.

Ali smiled ruefully. 'Now you know how I felt,' she said.

Beth stared at Gavin, this time noting the discoloration around his eye. 'You're the last person I expected to see,' she commented.

'That's what Ali said. I'm not sure whether it was before, during or after she threw her desk diary at me.'

'If it had been me, I think I would have thrown the desk as well.'

'She tried the chair. Thankfully, it only landed on my foot.' He grimaced. 'I expect you'll be glad to know it hurt.'

'Good.'

'No more than I deserve. Look, why don't I go and order our food while Ali explains everything to you. What would you like, Beth?'

She glanced at Ali, who nodded agreement. 'Oh — fish and chips if they have it. If not, anything.'

'Same again?' He nodded towards her almost empty glass. For a moment, Beth was tempted to order brandy and take a taxi home, but she shook her head and asked for orange juice.

'He'll be lucky if he's served this side of

Christmas,' Ali observed, as Gavin joined the horde, three deep around the counter.

Beth sat back and drained her glass. 'Are you going to tell me what's going on?' she asked.

'He just turned up in my office, two hours ago.'

'And . . . ?'

'After I'd thrown at him everything I could lay my hands on, he told me why I hadn't been able to contact him.'

'Busy working another scam, I suppose.'

'Actually, he was busy trying to reverse a scam.'

'Ha! A likely story.'

'Beth! If you're going to contradict everything I say, I might as well give up.'

'Sorry. You were saying.'

'He'd worked one scam up north. I was his second — and he couldn't go through with it.'

'Did Amanda tell him his cover was blown?'

'No. She told Simon she had ME and resigned. Gavin didn't know we'd met.'

'So why didn't he return your calls?'

'I'm coming to that. He wanted to get everything straight first, and the only way he could do that was to acquire enough money to repay the loan, and buy enough shares to restore the first firm to independence from Simon. And that's exactly what he's done.'

'How? Did he win the lottery or something?'

Ali smiled. 'He sold his house.'

'Really? But I thought that was the reason . . . '

'It was, but not at any price. So he told Simon to stuff his job.'

'What was the reaction?'

'Nasty. Vicious. Said he'd make sure he never worked in Cheshire again. But Gavin turned the tables on him by threatening to talk to the police.'

Beth turned it all over in her mind. 'Where's he living?' she asked.

'He had booked into a cheap guest house, but . . . ' Again Ali shrugged her shoulders.

'You haven't . . . ?'

'Don't look at me like that, Beth. I didn't just fall into his arms. There's more.'

'Tell me.'

'He's asked me to marry him.'

Open-mouthed, Beth stared at her friend. 'Ali, he's jobless, homeless and penniless. What can he possibly offer you?'

'His love,' Ali said, simply.

'Could you trust him, after what's happened?'

'Yes, because he loved me enough to stop

before it happened to me. And because he has made restitution to the other company. And because — ' She hesitated. 'If you truly love someone, you have to trust them. Otherwise your life is full of suspicions and quite meaningless.'

Beth didn't answer. Her thoughts went to Sarah, and how she had learned to forgive Damon, because she loved him and their children too much to throw it all away. Then she asked herself if she could have been as forgiving with Bryn. No. She hadn't loved him enough to ever want him back. Tom, though, was different. Even if he never asked her to marry him, she couldn't contemplate life without him.

She put her hand over Ali's. 'So when's the big day?' she asked.

'We haven't got that far yet. He's sold his classic car for a decent price, and the coin collection he inherited from his father, and wants to invest that money into my business — so I won't need to go public.'

'I'm impressed. He loved that car.'

'I know. But it's more than just the money. His management consultancy knowledge from Simon's firm will be very useful, and we'll be partners. It won't be easy, but I think it will work, Beth.'

'Are you happy about it?'

'Yes. I wasn't sure at first, but the more I think about it, the more I'm positive I've made the right decision.'

'Then that's all that matters, and you certainly didn't let him off lightly. Look at his face.'

Looking decidedly the worse for wear, Gavin rejoined them.

'Has Ali told you everything?' he asked.

Beth nodded.

'I hope you understand, Beth. We both value your friendship.'

'I still can't understand why you agreed to do something like that in the first place. Why the hell didn't you tell him to take a running jump?'

Eventually, Gavin said, 'In retrospect, that's just what I should have done. I can see that now. But, at the time, I was desperate not to lose the house, and Simon was so helpful — it seemed the perfect way out.'

'But all that buying shares and forcing people out of their business. You're an intelligent man, Gavin. Surely you must have realised that what you were doing was 'iffy', to say the least.'

'At first, the way Simon explained it, it just seemed like business practice. Maybe a bit dodgy, but not illegal. And there was another reason why I wasn't thinking straight.'

Beth glanced at Ali, who was staring into her drink.

'After my divorce, I met someone else and we lived together for a while. I didn't know she had a drugs problem until it was too late.' Gavin paused. 'She had been forging my signature to steal from my bank account to feed her habit. When she walked out, I was stuck with a house I couldn't sell, a mortgage repayment I couldn't pay, and I felt as though I was at the bottom of the pit. So, when Simon offered to bail me out if I helped him with a business deal, I . . . ' Gavin spread his hands eloquently.

Understanding a little better, Beth nodded.

'It wasn't till I realised what would happen to Ali's business, that I knew I couldn't allow it to happen. I cared too much for her. That was when I began to think about the other people.'

'Were you very sure that Ali would forgive you?'

'No. And I wouldn't have blamed her if she'd shown me the door.'

'What would you have done?'

'I don't know. Looked for another job. Started over, I suppose.' He looked anguished. 'Even now I feel sick at the thought of being without her.'

'Well,' Beth smiled. 'This must be the best

Christmas present either of you expected to receive.' Then realisation dawned. 'Christmas — yes, of course. It changes everything.'

Not understanding, Gavin looked at Ali.

'Beth's coming to me for Christmas,' Ali explained.

'Oh right. I see.' Now he looked at Beth. 'I hope you don't mind my sharing your Christmas as well.'

'Don't be silly. I wouldn't dream of coming now.'

Both Gavin and Ali protested that, of course Beth must still come for Christmas, but she was adamant.

'Listen, you two,' she said. 'This will be your first Christmas together — almost like a honeymoon. The last thing you need is someone else helping you to stuff the turkey. I'll be fine, honestly.'

It took the whole of the mealtime to convince them that she really would be fine, and Beth wasn't too sure about it herself, but there was no way she would play gooseberry, so eventually they compromised by agreeing to have dinner together on New Year's Eve.

Forgetting to collect the embroidery, or look at tankards, Beth drove straight to the cemetery and put a tiny holly wreath on Katie's grave. She didn't linger too long. Although the wind was still abating, it brought a chill from the north-east.

Hamish's greeting was warm, though.

'Looks like it's you and me, kid,' she told him as he licked her face. 'Let's see what's in Mother Hubbard's cupboard.'

Not a lot, was her conclusion, so it would have to be a quick dash to Tescos first thing in the morning, along with all the others stocking up for Christmases past, present and future, if last year was anything to go by.

The phone was still silent, and she used her mobile to check that Jane was OK on her own. Not many people were interested in looking at houses two days before Christmas, but there were a few appointments for next week. Beth flicked through the post. Credit card bill — bigger than usual, but what else did she expect? A few Christmas cards, including one from her father. His letters were always depressing, so she just skimmed through it in case there might be any lighter observations. None. A card from the paper boy, thanking her for the tip she had left with the newsagent, and a slim package, containing a book. *New Forest Tales*, she read on the cover. Inside was a covering letter from Ken and Margaret Beamish, thanking her for her contribution. She turned to Eliza's story. It was exactly as she had written it.

Impulsively, she held it high. 'There you

are, Eliza,' she cried. 'You're in print. Now perhaps you can rest in peace.' What a stupid thing to be doing, she thought, talking to a non-existent ghost. Perhaps she really had been a figment of an over-active imagination. There'd been not a sound from her since the near-miss with the suitcase. But Beth couldn't resist a final crazy statement. 'And I think I've exorcised Aunt Bazill's curse. Just by falling in love.'

With a contented giggle, she picked up the last envelope. Typed, with a London postmark. It was from a firm of solicitors, informing her that the decree nisi was now absolute. She hadn't contested the divorce. The grounds given had been irreconcilable differences. In other words, incompatibility. They had been compatible enough when she was working and supporting him for all those years it took him to qualify. The only reason he had left was because he couldn't cope with the fact that Beth had given birth to a handicapped child and would not agree to locking Katie away in a home. Yes. That was an irreconcilable difference.

Even though she no longer loved Bryn, Beth felt a slight pang at the realisation that a door had finally closed on ten years of her life. She must have had poor judgement, to marry him in the first place. Still, mustn't dwell on the past. Once again, she was a free lady.

Should she revert to her maiden name? Beth wondered, as she put the kettle on and turned the heating up a notch. It really was quite cold. Sitting with her hands cupped around the mug of tea, Hamish at her feet, she picked up the book that Vanessa had given her. At first, she hadn't been able to bring herself to read it, but a few days ago had decided that she should.

Some of the anecdotes about unexplained happenings were quite incredible, and it was well researched and written. The author had not only investigated ghosts and poltergeists, but also some of the cult beliefs, and curses. He had a theory that nothing supernatural could survive fire.

Shuddering at the thought, Beth slipped a bookmark inside to mark the page. 'A little too macabre for me just now,' she murmured, gently moving Hamish from across her feet.

Feeling restless, she decided to boot up her computer, see if there were any e-mails for her. There might be something from Tom. He had gone to Brussels yesterday for a business meeting, but should be back today. Then she remembered her dash into Boots. Might as well sort it out now.

As she had suspected, the test strip showed

positive. She was pregnant.

Sitting on the edge of the bath, she knew when it had happened. Tom had decided he would take responsibility for protection, but that first time, that very first time, neither of them was prepared.

Her emotions were so mixed, she didn't know whether to laugh or cry. She really wanted another child. Especially Tom's child. But she didn't want him to feel pressurised into marrying her. Better to keep it to herself for now, she thought. Wait and see how things were when he returned from America. Even if he decided he couldn't marry her, she knew she wouldn't consider an abortion. This minute particle of humanity inside her was their baby, conceived in love. If the worst came to the worst, she would move away and bring it up alone. Anything rather than destroy this precious gift.

29

The lights flickered a warning. Beth knew she must put some candles around the house — just in case. Soon it would be dark. Wow! What a Christmas it was going to be. No lover, no friends, no phone and, if the electricity went up the spout, no heating. 'Thanks a bunch,' she muttered, looking upwards. And she was pregnant. Still, at least she would have someone special next Christmas.

A cold nose nudged against her leg. 'Oh, Hamish. Of course I have someone special this year.' He woofed and licked her hand. 'Hungry? At least your side of the larder is well stocked.'

Beth was melting wax to secure candles to saucers when she noticed her computer screen telling her a message was waiting. It might be Tom.

It wasn't. The message was from his daughter.

Beth. Please contact. Urgent. Nadine.

Her stomach turned. Had something happened to Tom? *Is something wrong?* she tapped.

I need to talk to you.

The lights flickered again.

Do you have a mobile?

Yes.

Give me your number. The power is dodgy.

When Nadine answered, she sounded close to tears. 'I'm so sorry, Beth,' she cried, 'I didn't know. It was such a shock.'

Beth tried to calm the girl. 'Just take a deep breath, Nadine,' she said, 'and tell me what has happened.'

'Sorry. I'm not thinking straight.' The girl breathed heavily for a moment, then went on, 'Dad said I could use Mother's computer for my school project, so I decided to sort out her discs while they were out. See if there were any I could use.'

'Go on,' prompted Beth.

'One of them was marked *My Journal.* At first I was going to clear it. It seemed too personal. Then I'm afraid — my curiosity got the better of me, and I scanned it. I'm so glad I did, for your sake.'

Now Beth was just as curious. 'Why? What did she say about me.'

'It was all there, Beth. I thought she died of a broken heart, because of you and Dad, but I couldn't have been more wrong. She wanted him to be happy again after . . . '

Nadine's voice cracked, then she went on, 'Mother wrote how much she liked you and that she thought you would make him a better wife. I thought she meant she couldn't be a proper wife because she was an invalid, but she seemed troubled about something that had happened in her past and wanted Dad to know she was sorry. What did she mean?'

If Vanessa hadn't given details, there was no need for her daughters and Thora to know the truth. But Nadine was waiting for an answer. Thinking carefully, Beth said, 'It was probably some row they had at some time or other, when things might have been said. You know what it's like. I shouldn't worry about it.'

'Perhaps you're right. Dad will know what she meant.'

'Do you know what time he'll be home?'

'Thora and Cassie have gone to pick him up from Southampton airport, but they're expecting flight delays because of the weather.'

'It's pretty grim. Are you all right on your own?'

'Yes. I just want to read it all through again, and think about it. But can I come up and see you later on? I feel bad about the things I said.'

'Don't feel bad, and do come up, but be careful. There are trees down all over the place.'

'Thanks. And Beth . . . '

'Yes?'

'I think Mother sensed she hadn't got long, and intended to let us know about the journal, but . . . '

Beth completed the sentence. 'Didn't have the time. None of us expected her to have a heart attack, least of all, Vanessa.'

'Yes. I think it's what she would have wanted.'

'I'm sure of it. Thanks for telling me this, Nadine. You didn't have to.'

'Yes, I did. Goodbye, Beth.'

For some time, Beth sat thinking deeply. Vanessa had wanted Tom to love Beth, Thora had given her blessing, Cassie had never been a problem and now Nadine seemed to accept the situation. There was nothing to stand in their way, except — Tom. He'd never hinted that he might want to marry again at some future date. Perhaps he would be wary, after Vanessa's unfaithfulness, and that was under-standable. But now there was a child to consider. Beth wondered about the reaction of the whole family when they knew, as eventually they must. Sighing, she continued to place candles around the room.

Fed and watered, Hamish trotted into the room and watched, his head on one side, as the lights on the little Christmas tree in the corner twinkled on and off. Wondering whether Tom would be home soon, Beth logged on to the airport's information website, but before the information came through, the screen went blank and the tree lights popped. Time to light the candles. If it became too cold she would light the gas oven and stay in the kitchen.

Glancing through the window, she noticed the huge conifer outside swaying at an alarming angle. Everyone said they had safe roots, but she wasn't so sure. Then she remembered the even bigger elm near Tom's house. Better warn the girl and make sure she had enough candles. Perhaps she would prefer to come up to Beth now, for company at least, until the others came back.

As she picked up the mobile phone, she heard an almighty crack. From outside. The conifer had split down the middle, as though attacked by a giant axe. Startled, Hamish nudged the coffee table and the candle toppled over, flaring as it found a loose sheet of giftwrap. Beth rushed to grab it, but the flames swiftly ran through the loose pile of cards and envelopes, towards the Christmas tree. Grabbing one of her new cushions, she tried to stifle the flames, but once they were fuelled by the dry pine leaves, there was no stopping them.

Rushing into the kitchen and shouting to Hamish to get out of the way, Beth filled a bucket with water and ran back to dowse the fire, which was now greedily devouring the curtains. Then she froze. Almost in slow motion, the nearest half of the top split of the conifer crashed down on to her house, one of the branches thrusting through the window, trapping Beth's legs and, encouraged by the wind, bursting into flames.

Horrified, Beth watched the fire creeping along the branch towards her. She tried to lift it from her legs, but the weight was too great and she fell back.

Hamish was barking frantically, rushing towards her, then backing away in fear.

'Go away!' she shouted, wanting to get him out of danger. 'Go out in the garden. Good boy.' Perhaps someone might see him and come to the rescue. But he wouldn't leave her. And her mobile was out of reach.

Then she remembered a game they sometimes played on the beach. It was her only chance.

'Hamish,' she cried. 'Get Cassie. She wants to play. Go on. Fetch Cassie.'

He knew the way to Tom's house and,

although Cassie wasn't there, Nadine was. She might bring him back.

'Please,' she pleaded. 'Get Cassie.'

As though recognising the desperate tone of her voice, Hamish barked, and ran out into the kitchen. Beth heard the rattle of his door flap, but realised that there wasn't much hope.

The room was filling with thick, choking smoke. Once the fire reached the TV and computer, there would be terrible, poisonous fumes. She tried screaming for help, but her throat was sore already and she could only gasp for air. Perhaps it would be better if she breathed in the smoke more quickly, rather than burn to death.

One more. 'Help,' she cried. 'Someone, please help me.'

It was no use, she was too weak. Weeping for her unborn child, and the love that was not to be, Beth raised her head and began to gulp.

'Beth!' It was Eliza's voice. 'Don't give up. I'm here. I'll help you.'

'You can't,' Beth gasped. 'It's too late.'

'But you don't want to die.'

'No! Of course I don't want to die. But I can't move.'

'Keep your head down. Really low. You'll breathe better.'

It was true. But Beth was beginning to feel the lethal heat searing her legs. She screamed.

'Keep calm, Beth. Cover your mouth. Your scarf will do.'

Like a puppet, Beth did as she was told. But the effort was almost too much. It would be so easy to just close her eyes and let fate . . .

'Beth! Stay awake. I'm here.'

'Where? I can't see you,' she whispered. 'I've never seen you.'

'Keep your eyes open, and I'll show you.'

Trying to focus her aching eyes through the smoke, Beth saw a shimmering shape, not much more than a shadow. Like a figure appearing out of a fog, the shape became a girl, wearing a long, shabby dress. A girl with dark, tangled hair hanging around her shoulders. Her face must have been pretty once, but now it was pock-marked, and pustules marred her hands and forearms.

'Now you knows why I don't appear,' Eliza said. 'Are you frightened?'

'No,' Beth whispered. 'I'm just so sorry. Is it over now? Am I dead?'

'You're not dead, Beth. But it's over.'

'What do you mean?'

'You believed me, and told the truth. I can go now.'

'Where will you go?'

'I don't know. But it will be better. Thank you for setting me free.'

'And the curse?'

'That's gone as well. The fire got rid of it, once and for all.'

Beth felt tired. So terribly tired. Then she heard another voice calling, 'Beth!' It was Nadine's voice. 'Where are you, Beth?' Nadine shouted. 'I can't see you.'

But Beth couldn't answer. She was too exhausted.

Eliza answered for her. 'She's in here. Cover your face and follow my voice. Get down on the floor. She's by the window.'

The shape began to waver. 'Goodbye, Beth.' Eliza smiled. 'You'll be safe now.'

Nadine crawled through the door from the kitchen, a wet towel over her head. Beth couldn't feel anything, nor could she speak. She could only watch the girl lift the burning branch, and drag her clear. It was as though it was happening to someone else.

'Don't die, Beth,' Nadine cried. 'Please don't die.'

The fire reached the computer, which seemed to explode.

'We've got to get out of here,' Nadine said, pulling Beth out through the kitchen and into the garden.

The neighbours had already fled from their

homes and helped Nadine carry Beth out into the road. As the roof of Beth's house caved in around the tree, a gasp swept through the small crowd, like a Mexican wave.

The neighbour from across the road pushed her way through. 'I've phoned for the fire brigade,' she said.

'Thank you.' Nadine looked up briefly. 'Could you make sure they send an ambulance, please. Beth needs help.'

At that moment, Tom arrived, racing ahead of Thora and Cassie. Gathering Beth into his arms, he held her close. 'Oh, my love,' he murmured. 'When I saw . . . I thought . . . '

'If it hadn't been for Nadine . . . ' Beth began to cough, the most painful cough she had ever known. She held out her hand towards Nadine.

Suddenly, the girl began to cry, unleashing all the grief that had been locked away inside her. Sinking to her knees beside Beth, and still holding her hand, she buried her head in her father's shoulder and sobbed her heart out.

When Cassie arrived, she threw herself at Beth, almost knocking her from Tom's arms.

'Careful, child,' warned Thora. 'Remember what happened last time.'

'Sorry, Beth, but I'm just so glad you're

safe. I couldn't bear it if I lost you, too.' Then she noticed her sister. 'Nadine! Were you in the fire, too? You're almost as black as Beth.'

'Well, she was in the fire much longer than me,' Nadine reached for a tissue and tried to wipe the tears and grime from her face. 'It must have been such an effort for her to talk, but I'd never have found her, with all that smoke. To tell the truth, I thought she was dead. She was unconscious by the time I found her.'

No, I wasn't, Beth thought. Then wondered — or was I? But another thought worried her even more.

'Where's Hamish?' she croaked. It would be too dreadful if he had come back with Nadine, and . . .

'He tried to come back with me, but I saw the red sky, so shut him indoors.'

'Excuse me.' The paramedic edged Mrs Walker out of the way, and Beth gratefully took the oxygen mask.

Tom's arm was still around Beth. 'I'll come with you in the ambulance,' he said.

'Do I have to?' she appealed to the paramedic. 'I'm feeling much better now.'

'I can put dressings on your legs, but you really should have an X-ray, to be sure there are no broken bones. And there's the shock.'

'I'll take her to the hospital first thing

tomorrow,' Tom said, responding to the pleading in Beth's face. 'I think a good night's sleep will be more beneficial than hanging around A & E for hours while all the Christmas drunks are treated, don't you?'

The paramedic looked doubtful, until Thora said, 'I'm a nurse. I'll keep an eye on her and phone the doctor if necessary.'

'Well — I'll have to put it in my report that you've refused hospital treatment.'

Beth nodded, wincing slightly as he began to clean the area around the burns.

'Reckon this has just about ruined your Christmas, miss,' he commented.

'Not at all,' Tom answered. 'I think we'll have an even better Christmas together.' He began to smile a rather secretive smile, but waited until the paramedic had moved away to speak to the fire chief before he said, 'I bought your Christmas present in Brussels. Give it to you later. Hope it's what you want.' He opened his coat pocket just enough for her to see the small, square, jeweller's box.

Surely it could only mean . . . ?

It was as though he was holding his breath when he asked, 'Will you?'

Beth loosened the mask. 'Oh, yes. And as soon as possible, please.' She reached up and whispered in his ear.

The biggest grin imaginable spread across

his face as he said, 'That's the best Christmas present I've ever had.' His gaze embraced his family. 'I know it doesn't have quite the same ring to it, but would you be terribly disappointed if we had Christmas in Calshot, instead of New Jersey?'

Their grins matching his, they looked at each other, then chorused, 'No!'

Thora added, drily, 'But I hope there are still some turkeys in the shops or it could be sausage and mash for Christmas dinner. I've emptied the freezer.'

'Even a cheese sandwich will be a feast,' Tom said, 'as long as it's washed down with champagne.'

Leaving the fire brigade to do what they could with an impossible task, the ambulance crew took Beth to her new home. As they waited for Thora to unlock the front door, Beth glanced at the outline of Calshot Castle, silhouetted against the night sky, far along the beach.

Well, I found out why they died, she thought. But not many people would believe me. She wasn't sure she believed it herself, any more than she could believe that she was alive, and not . . . What on earth had really happened before Nadine rescued her? Perhaps it was best not to question, but to just be thankful.

Tom tightened his hold on Beth as a shower of sparks shot upwards through the red glow around Beth's house, a few streets away.

'Oh, Beth,' Cassie cried, tears running down her cheeks. 'You've lost everything.'

'No,' Tom gently corrected his daughter. 'We've *found* everything. Now I know how Scrooge felt, when he danced around wishing everyone a happy Christmas.'

Hamish dashed through the front door, tail wagging furiously, and barking excitedly as Tom carried Beth over the threshold, as though she were a bride.

THE END

We do hope that you have enjoyed reading this large print book.

Did you know that all of our titles are available for purchase?

We publish a wide range of high quality large print books including:
Romances, Mysteries, Classics
General Fiction
Non Fiction and Westerns

Special interest titles available in large print are:
The Little Oxford Dictionary
Music Book
Song Book
Hymn Book
Service Book

Also available from us courtesy of Oxford University Press:
Young Readers' Dictionary
(large print edition)
Young Readers' Thesaurus
(large print edition)

For further information or a free brochure, please contact us at:
Ulverscroft Large Print Books Ltd.,
The Green, Bradgate Road, Anstey,
Leicester, LE7 7FU, England.
Tel: (00 44) **0116 236 4325**
Fax: (00 44) **0116 234 0205**

Other titles in the
Ulverscroft Large Print Series:

STRANGER IN THE PLACE

Anne Doughty

Elizabeth Stewart, a Belfast student and only daughter of hardline Protestant parents, sets out on a study visit to the remote west coast of Ireland. Delighted as she is by the beauty of her new surroundings and the small community which welcomes her, she soon discovers she has more to learn than the details of the old country way of life. She comes to reappraise so much that is slighted and dismissed by her family — not least in regard to herself. But it is her relationship with a much older, Catholic man, Patrick Delargy, which compels her to decide what kind of life she really wants.

IF HE LIVED

Jon Stephen Fink

Lillian is a woman who feels too much. As a psychiatric nurse, she empathizes with her patients; as a mother, she mourns for her lost, runaway daughter. Now suddenly she has a new feeling, that her house, one of the oldest in the small Massachusetts town where she lives with her husband Freddy, has been invaded, violated by some past evil. And then Lillian sees the boy . . .

THE SANCTUARY SEEKER

Bernard Knight

1194 AD: Appointed by Richard the Lionheart as the first coroner for the county of Devon, Sir John de Wolfe, an ex-crusader, rides out to the moorland village of Widecombe to hold an inquest on an unidentified body. But on his return to Exeter, the Coroner is incensed to find that his own brother-in-law, Sheriff Richard de Revelle, is intent on thwarting the murder investigation. But Crowner John is ready to fight for the truth. Even faced with the combined mights of the all-powerful Church and nobility . . .

SLAUGHTER HORSE

Michael Maguire

The Turf Security Division is surprised and suspicious when playboy Wesley Falloway's second-rate horses develop overnight into winners. Simon Drake investigates, but suddenly there is a new twist — someone is out to steal General O'Hara, the star of British bloodstock, owned by Wesley Falloway's mother. With a few million pounds at stake, lives are cheap; Drake finds himself both hunter and quarry in a murderous chase where even his closest associates may be playing a double game.

MERMAID'S GROUND

Alice Marlow

It's been five years since Kate Williams' beloved husband died, leaving her with two young children to raise. Now she's built a good life in one of Wiltshire's prettiest villages, and she has her dream job, as gardener at Moxham Court. For the last year, Kate has had a lover, roguishly attractive Justin Spencer, but he won't commit to more than a night here and there. When she takes in a male lodger, Jem, Kate's secretly hoping his presence will provoke a jealous reaction in Justin. What she hasn't reckoned on is exactly how attractive Jem will turn out to be.

HOT POPPIES

Reggie Nadelson

A murder in New York's diamond district. A dead Chinese girl with a photograph in her pocket. A plastic bag of irradiated heroin in an empty apartment. A fire in a Chinatown sweatshop. The worst blizzard in New York's history. These events conspire to bring ex-cop Artie Cohen out of retirement and back into the obsessive world of murder and politics that nearly killed him. The terrifying plot uncoils first in New York — in Artie's own back yard — then in Hong Kong, where everything — and everyone — is for sale.